CW01426172

Murder in the Library

Steve Demaree

Steve Demaree

Copyright © 2008
Steve Demaree
All Rights Reserved

2

This book is dedicated to the two people I love the most and whose love I deserve the least, my wife Nell and my daughter Kelly. May God continue to bless me with their presence in my life.

This book is also dedicated to Connie McBrayer and Wanda Cornish, both who have told me that they cannot wait to get another Lt. Dekker-Sgt. Murdock mystery.

May each of them and each of you enjoy this book.

Books by Steve Demaree

Dekker Cozy Mystery Series

52 Steps to Murder
Murder in the Winter
Murder in the Library
Murder at Breakfast?
Murder at the High School Reunion
Murder at the Art & Craft Fair
Murder in Gatlinburg
Murder at the Book Fair
Murder on a Blind Date
A Body on the Porch
Two Bodies in the Backyard
A Body under the Christmas Tree
Murder on Halloween
A Valentine Murder
A Body on April Fool's Day
A Body in the Woods
A Puzzling Murder

Off the Beaten Path Mysteries

Murder in the Dark
Murder Among Friends
A Bridge to Murder
A Smoky Mountain Mystery

Other Mysteries

A Body in the Trunk

Aylesford Place Series

Pink Flamingoed
Neighborhood Hi Jinx
Croquet Anyone?
Scavenger Hunt

Other Fiction

Stories from the Heart

Non-Fiction

Lexington & Me
Reflecting Upon God's Word

Steve Demaree

1

Just in case this is the first time you have wandered into our neighborhood, let me introduce ourselves. I am Lt. Cy Dekker, a longtime member of the Hilldale Police Department, and one-half of the homicide department. The other half is my childhood friend and police force partner for over twenty years, Sgt. Lou Murdock. A few months ago Lou and I worked out an agreement with the department where we could work during any homicide investigation, but ease into retirement during the other times. Neither Lou nor I have a propensity for any other form of police work, and since both of us had put in over thirty years with the department and were eligible for retirement, we decided to opt for the best of both worlds.

+++

Seldom does anyone other than Lou call my home, and few others know my number, so one day when the phone rang I answered by saying, "Don't tell me that you've decided to quit eating at the Blue Moon?"

"I've never been there, but I understand you, Cy, are mainly responsible for keeping that establishment in business."

"Colonel, is that you?"

"I'm surprised you still remember me since it's been so long since you and Lou stopped by to visit."

"I'm sorry, Colonel. It seems like Lou and I stay so busy these days."

"Really, I'd heard the department finally got rid of the two of you."

"So, you heard we've turned over a new leaf?"

"You mean you've quit eating between meals? Or have you reverted back to kindergarten and have nap time each day?"

"Sometimes we take naps, but we do other things, too. Lou and I've started reading."

"Well, I'm glad. I remember you never read for any classes you took in school. Anyway, Cy, it's good to talk to you again. I was wondering if you and Lou might be able to take some time out of your busy schedule this afternoon to stop by and see me. I would invite you to lunch, but I know how much that diner means to you. Plus, I don't think Martha could fix enough food on such short notice."

"We'd love to stop by. How does somewhere around 2:00 sound?"

"Sounds fine. Whenever you feel you've eaten enough and gotten enough rest to drive the few blocks to my house, come on over."

"Looking forward to it, Colonel. See you this afternoon."

I hung up the phone. Even with the Colonel's jovial demeanor, I couldn't help but think that something was bothering him.

Lou and I had known the Colonel since we were boys. One day the two of us were out walking, bored to death because we had nothing to do. Neither Lou nor I were ever into sports, and building or fixing anything never appealed to us. Our dads worked. Our moms stayed home, and both of us left our houses for only two reasons. We liked being around each other, and at least one of us had to leave home to make that happen, and our moms kept after us to get out and get some exercise. How were two boys who didn't like sports supposed to exercise?

One day we decided to walk through the neighborhood looking for an idea of something to do. We were walking around, downcast, when we heard someone say, "Say, fellas, what's wrong?"

Both of us turned, looked up, and saw this man, somewhere around our dads' ages, standing in front of a house bigger than any I had seen in our neighborhood.

"Ain't got nothin' to do," I said.

"What about playing catch?"

"We're not much into sports."

"Do either of you have a fort or a treehouse?"

"Nope. Wouldn't know how to make one, either."

"Well, have you got a good, big tree in your backyard?"

"Nope. Our trees are all on the puny side."

"Well, I've got a big one. Want to see it?"

Our parents had cautioned us about going somewhere with strangers, but this guy seemed okay, lived the next street over, and it wasn't like we were going anywhere. He wasn't inviting us to go for a ride, or even inside his house. And he couldn't catch both of us at once. Well, more than likely he could have, as slow as the two of us ran, but we decided to check out his backyard. Besides, the people across the street were sitting on their front porch. I couldn't imagine that this man would try to kidnap us with witnesses around.

I turned to Lou and he gave me the look.

"Okay, we'll look at your tree."

Lou and I followed the man around the house to his backyard, and sure enough, there was a tree that was bigger than any tree I'd ever seen. It certainly looked big enough to hold the two of us, if we were foolish enough to climb it.

After we stared at the tree and looked at each other a few times, the man asked, "Well, what do you think? Do you think this tree would make a good treehouse?"

"I'd say you'd know more about that than we would, Mister."

He laughed, then offered us a proposition.

"If you boys are interested, I'd be glad to talk to your parents and see if it's okay with them for you to build a treehouse in my tree."

"It sounds like fun, but I don't think I'd want to climb up into anything I built."

He laughed again.

"Oh, I'd build it. You can be my helpers."

And thus began our friendship with the Colonel. The Colonel and his wife became friends with our parents and a mentor to Lou and me. Oh, we both had good relationships with our parents, but as we soon found out, the Colonel was a professor at the university and had summers off, which allowed him time to help us build a treehouse. And what a treehouse it became. And what fun we had. The Colonel had two daughters, neither of whom was interested in a treehouse, so he gave us free rein over when we could use the treehouse.

+++

The Colonel's phone call so distressed me that before I left the house, I meticulously unwrapped a Hershey Almond bar and took a bite, rewrapped it, and put it where I could get at it again. If it wasn't for the Colonel, and picking Lou up so we could enjoy lunch at the Blue Moon Diner, I would have started to think about whether or not I should get a computer. People have told me that encyclopedias have been replaced by something called Google. I'm not sure what that is, but some people seem to think it's an improvement. Supposedly, if I had a computer, I could find out all I'd want to know about Hershey bars without having to lift a heavy book.

Wonder where Hershey is, anyway? Is it closer to Pittsburgh, or Philly? It sounds more like something God put in the Garden of Eden. I'm not sure how I would have reacted if God had told me that I could eat from any tree except the chocolate bar tree. I bet there is no exercise equipment in Hershey, PA.

I picked Lou up and drove to the Blue Moon. On the way, I informed him of the Colonel's phone call. He too sensed that the Colonel was in some kind of trouble, but he didn't pull out his bag of M&Ms. I wondered if that was because he had turned over a new leaf.

No sooner had we arrived at the Blue Moon and plopped down on our stools until Rosie, the daytime waitress, accosted us.

"Okay, Frick and Frack. What's wrong today? Someone steal your feeding shovels?"

"No, it's just that we're afraid a friend of ours might be in trouble."

"Well, there's one way to find out. Go see him."

"That's what we plan to do, as soon as we leave here."

"Well, in the meantime, get those glum looks off your faces, and act like you usually do when you come in."

"So, it's okay to have a food fight?"

"Neither of you would ever throw a speck of food because both of you know that each bite thrown means one less bite in your stomach. So, what can I get you today?"

2

I drove up Cherry Hill Lane and parked in front of the Colonel's house. The two-story, white brick house, spread out over two lots, hadn't changed that much. One tree stood over to the side, away from the driveway. Everything else was a wide, flat front yard.

Up until then, life had been good for the Colonel. As a young man, he had inherited a great deal of money from his grandmother. This allowed him to do what he always wanted to do, teach school, and help young people find their way. Lou and I were just two of many the Colonel had helped over the years, but since we didn't go on to college, we never had him as a professor. Well, Lou went to college for one year, but he didn't have the Colonel for any of his classes.

Eager to find out why the Colonel had summoned us, Lou and I lifted ourselves from the car, walked as quickly as two recently well-fed men could walk. Lou seemed to walk quicker than me, even though I had been better fed.

I reached out, rang the bell, waited for someone to answer.

"Well, Cy, Lou, what brings you here?" asked Martha, the Colonel's wife, as she opened the door, admitted us to the house. Although now in her mid-seventies, the woman still looked elegant, and her white, well-coiffed hair looked like she had just returned from the beauty parlor.

"Just checking in with the Colonel. It's been a while since we've seen him."

"I'll say it has. What's been keeping you away?"

"Work and poor planning."

"Buck's in the library. Don't let me keep you from him."

Buck was the Colonel. James Buckham Hardesty, and as far as we know, his students are the only ones to have ever called him Colonel. To everyone else, he was Buck or Mr. Hardesty.

I knocked on the library door. A few seconds later the Colonel opened the door. He removed the frown he was wearing, but not quickly enough. I noticed and turned to Lou to see that he noticed too.

"Cy, Lou," the Colonel said as he stood between us and wrapped his arms around our shoulders, "so good to see you again. It looks like life is treating you well."

The Colonel offered us seats, seats he had already arranged in front of his massive desk. It was the Colonel's meeting, so we let him direct it. We spent a few minutes reminiscing about our treehouse and school before the Colonel got down to business.

"Cy, Lou, I really respect you boys, and what you've done for this community. You've made me proud to be a friend. The Hilldale Police Department has never had two finer officers. I don't care what the others say."

On that note, he laughed, and we did, too.

"Boys, you've had a good record, and we've had some good times together. Up to now, I've never asked anything of you boys, but I've got a problem, and I can't think of anyone better to turn to for help."

I wanted to ask if it was money- or health-related, but I knew the Colonel would soon share his troubles with us.

"I'm not sure if you boys have been in this library before, but let me tell you about it. This library is my haven, my sanctuary. It's where I spent all those years preparing lessons for my classes, where I got my ideas for my inventions, wrote my books, and many years ago, it's where I did some work for the government. Then, as now, the government expected secrecy and silence. I couldn't then, nor can I now share anything about the work I did for them, but that has nothing to do with why you're here. I only share that because the government insisted that I include a safe room below, a surveillance camera at the door, and another entrance or exit that no one other than I can use. You may have noticed the camera just before you stepped into this room. It sets idle until someone comes to the door. Then, it takes a picture of anyone who crosses its path. A trapdoor lies under the large rug in the middle of the room, a door that leads to a room under this one, but a room that has no other exit. The far end of the bookcase over there," the Colonel said as he motioned toward the bookcases on the other end of the room diagonal from the door we entered, "is a hidden exit, and on the other side is a secret entrance that can be used only by me because it takes my thumb and fingerprints for it to work. In other words, the room we're in is safe, and yet it's not. Sometime yesterday, when all of us were away from the house, someone left this piece of paper in the middle of the floor, right between where your chairs are now placed."

The Colonel handed us a wadded up piece of paper. I opened it and held it so Lou could read it, too.

SOON YOU WILL DIE IN YOUR SANCTUARY

"I checked the camera. I checked the secret entrance. No one has entered this room, and yet, it was here that I found this note, right where you're sitting."

"Is it possible that the note has been here for a while?"

"No, I noticed it as soon as I came in the room, but it doesn't matter, Cy. No one else has a key. I've run the video back and forth. Since the camera is one of my inventions, I feel certain no one has tampered with it. No one else has been in this room for the past three days until the two of you came in just now. Naturally, I'm worried. I'm acting as if whoever wrote this means what he or she typed. And I want the two of you to look into this for me."

"Naturally we're willing to help, but we'll have to ask you some questions. We need for you to answer them as truthfully as possible."

"Of course. I'm willing to cooperate in any way I can. Otherwise, I wouldn't have called you. I've anticipated some of your questions and have been thinking about who might have done this."

I studied the library as I gathered my thoughts. True, it was a library. Thousands of books gave evidence to that. But what a room. I'd seen a few homes not much larger than the room we were in. I guessed the ceiling to be around twelve feet, possibly higher. Bookcases climbed from the floor to the ceiling and covered two walls, the one behind the desk straight in front of the door and the long wall down the side opposite the door.

Two movable ladders, one on each wall, were connected to the bookcases and slid along when someone needed to reach a book on a higher shelf. A cordovan leather couch faced away from us toward a fireplace at the other end of the room. Polished brass studs accented the couch and held it together. My guess is that the matching chairs on which Lou and I sat normally bracketed the couch and faced the fireplace. There were tables with brass lamps, floor lamps, and track lighting housed in the opposite wall, but not a window in the room. Nothing gave evidence of where the note had come from, but I didn't expect to learn anything, because the Colonel knew the room much better than I.

The Colonel gave us time to get our bearings, waited for me to take over.

"Of course, Colonel, the important thing is to find out who could've put this note in this room, and how they could've done it. I'd think you would have a better idea than we would how someone could've done this, so let's start with who. I want a list of people who've been in the house in the last six months. Why don't you begin by telling me who lives here now?"

"I'm only going to say this once, Cy, because it's your investigation, but I don't think any of my family is in any way involved, but I will answer any question you ask of me. Of course, there's Martha and me. We share the master bedroom which is located directly above this library and the living room you passed on the left when you came in the door. All the other bedrooms are on the other end of the house. I'm sure that you remember that we have two daughters. Our oldest, Darlene, died when a drunken driver hit her when she was a senior in high school. The youngest, Jill, and her husband, Frank, are missionaries in Africa. They had two daughters, both of whom are currently living with us. Jennifer, the oldest, is married and a senior at the university. Her husband, Scott, is a graduate student. Our other granddaughter, Trish, has been with us for a year and is about to complete her freshman year at the university. We also have a young man staying with us. Tom Brockman is new to the area, and a teacher's assistant at the university."

"Even though two of those living with you are family, I imagine you've spent little time with them as they grew up. How well do you know your granddaughters, your grandson-in-law, and the young man who's living here?"

"While it's true that the girls were born in Africa, Jill and Frank returned to the states one month out of the year, and they always spent two weeks of that month with us. We spent time with the girls then. Also, once every five years, they were required to spend the year in the states, so that gave us time to get caught up with them then. I feel that we got to know our granddaughters as well as most grandparents get to know their grandchildren who live at a distance. Besides, Jennifer has been with us for over four years. She is on schedule to graduate in five years. She met

Scott at the university, so we got to know him while they were dating, and they have been married and living here almost two years now."

"And what about Tom Brockman? How well do you know him, and did you check him out before you offered him a room?"

"You know me, Cy. I thoroughly checked Tom out. He comes from a fine family. His father is a doctor, his mother a teacher. He has given us no problems. One thing that has helped us become a family to Scott and to Tom is that most evenings we eat together as a family. Everyone is expected at dinner unless they let us know they have other plans. We don't mind if someone has plans. We just want to know so we won't hold dinner."

"You hold dinner?"

"Well, not really, but Martha still wants to know that everything's okay and everyone's accounted for."

"None of them have nine-to-five jobs. How many of these people are in and out of the house during the day?"

"During the week they are usually gone all day. Scott and Jennifer drive to school together. When Scott's not in class, he spends a lot of his time in the library, writing. Most days their schedules allow them to eat together. Trish has classes every day. Some days she gets out of class early, but most of the time she doesn't come home until 3:30 or 4:00. But she does get out at 2:00 on Tuesday and Thursday. Tom doesn't want to be a bother, so he spends most of his free time in his office if that's what you want to call it. I've been there a couple of times. It looks more like a closet."

"But any one of them could find the time sometime during the day to come home if he or she so chose?"

"I suppose so, but none of them have made a habit of doing so."

"No one has made a habit of leaving you notes until now."

17

"That's true, Cy. By the way, Cy, Lou, I've got an idea. I don't know whether this will help or not, why don't I show you around, have Martha fix a little something to snack on, and then we can come back and pick up where we left off?"

3

I was tired by the time we got through with the tour of the house. Remind me never to go to the Biltmore. I could never handle the tour. As we toured the master bedroom, Lou whispered to me, "Cy, this bedroom is larger than my apartment." I whispered back, "Yeah, and get a load of that sunken tub. It even has steps on one side to help you get out." The right-wing of the second floor was nothing but bedrooms, six large ones. A trip down the steps revealed a finished basement, which included a game room that most men would kill for. I wondered if either of the men who lived in the Colonel's house would kill him to have it. I decided to curtail such thoughts until after I'd met these men and focused my attention on the tour. The main floor included a room for anything a person could think of to do that the basement and second floor missed out on. After we finished our tour, we understood why everyone was so eager to live with the Colonel. If Lou and I hadn't liked our privacy so much, we might've checked the upstairs rooms for "Vacancy" signs.

We ended our twelve-mile hike in the kitchen, where Martha had just finished making sandwiches and hors d'oeuvres.

"Buck, you haven't talked the boys to death, have you?"

"No, dear, we're just getting caught up. And since we have more catching up to do, do you mind if the boys and I take our food into the library and finish up our talk in there?"

Instead of answering her husband, Martha turned to Lou, whom she considered the quietest of the three.

"Lou, send me some kind of sign if they end up talking you to death and you need to be rescued."

We all laughed. Between the four of us, we managed to carry enough food and drink to the library to last us until we could reach into our pockets and pull out a candy bar. If things got desperate, I promised myself I'd share my candy with the Colonel. I brought extras. I always do.

As I helped carry our replenishments, I looked at Martha to see if she looked like someone who was returning to the scene of the crime. I saw no guilt. I doubted if she knew why we were there.

After devouring a few sandwiches, I turned to the Colonel and resumed our conversation.

"Well, Colonel, if we may, I'd like to discuss two other groups of people. First, think hard and tell me who's been in your house in the last six months."

"I've been thinking about that. We had a party at Christmas, but most of those people haven't been in the house since then. No one comes regularly, except for Joe Guilfoyle, my best friend. Joe and I have a standing date every Monday afternoon at 3:00."

"Has Joe ever been in the library?"

"Sure. Most of the time, at least in the winter, that's where Joe and I hang out. When the weather breaks, Joe and I head to the closed-in back porch, but it has only ceiling fans, so when the summer heat hits us, we head back inside to the air conditioning, which usually means the library."

"What do you talk about?"

"Oh, usually, what happened in the world of sports over the weekend. Plus, Joe and I are avid mystery readers.

We both love a good whodunit, so we talk about the ones we've read, how we would have done it if we were the murderer, and we recommend other good mysteries or authors to each other."

When the Colonel mentioned a good whodunit, I thought about our newest hobby, and I began to smile.

"What's so amusing, Cy?"

"Oh, when you said whodunit, I got to thinking about our new hobby." I pointed at Lou, then to myself to let the Colonel know who "our" was. "Have you ever been to Scene of the Crime bookstore?"

"Oh, course. Everyone knows that's the best place to find a good mystery."

I thought of Scene of the Crime and all their good books, which took me to the people we'd met there, and then for some reason, my thoughts migrated to computers, Hershey, Pennsylvania, and the candy bar burning a hole in my pocket.

"Colonel, do you mind if I eat a treat I brought with me?"

"If you boys are still hungry, I can have Martha fix us something else."

"Oh, no. It's just that I have a craving for Hershey Almond bars, and Lou loves M&Ms."

"Go ahead. If you make a mess the maid will clean it up."

"Do you really have a maid, or are you speaking of Martha?"

"No, really, we have a couple who comes once a week, on Thursday. She cleans and her husband does yard work, carries out the trash, and fixes anything that might need it."

"Is either of them ever in the library?"

"Oh, yes, but never without me present."

"Tell me something about them."

"Their names are Earl and Myra Hoskins. I'd say they're in their early sixties. They work together, have five clients. They work at a different house one day each week. Our day is always Thursday. I say always. All the families know each other, so if anyone wants a different day they check with one of the other families to see if someone is willing to trade. You know, like if someone has a party planned or something like that. In case you're wondering, Earl and Myra came to us highly recommended and have been with us for seven or eight years. Not the kind of people I'd think would leave a note. Besides, they weren't here today."

"How do you know?"

"Well, neither of them has a key. One of us is always here to let them in. Besides, they were cleaning someone else's house today."

"Speaking of keys, tell me everyone who has a key to the house."

"Everyone who lives here has a key. No one who doesn't."

"Back to the Hoskins for a moment, are they the kind of people who might talk about you or your house to others?"

"I don't think so. They don't talk to us about anyone else. They just come in and do a good job. That's the reason they stay as booked as they want. I don't think either of them would have anything to do with the note."

"It looks like you have a long list of people who wouldn't do this. Any idea who might?"

As soon as I asked the question, I was sorry that I did. I knew the Colonel was more anxious than I was to cooperate. I raised my hand to let him know he didn't need to answer.

"I'm sorry, Colonel. It just seems like your world is filled with all these nearly perfect people."

"Probably so, but I've got a list of not-so-perfect people, too, only it's a shortlist."

"We'll talk about them in a minute, Colonel, unless your not-so-perfect person falls into this next category.

What about people who come to your house occasionally, people you don't think about? Like the mailman, repairmen, people like that? People you wouldn't normally think of as being in your house."

"Let me see."

The Colonel reached into his desk and pulled out a calendar. This allowed me to reach into my pocket and pull out my candy bar. Most of it remained. I'd eaten one bite before I took off to pick up Lou, and then a second bite a few minutes ago. I looked for a luscious almond surrounded by chocolate. I didn't want to eat two nuts in one bite, nor take out my knife to slice off a piece. I took a bite, looked over at Lou. He was all smiles, having just shaken a few M&Ms from his package to his mouth. Lou isn't a one M&M at a time kind of guy. Besides, he rips his package open with his teeth. I can't blame him. I had a wife for a few years to refine me. Lou's never had anyone but me. Well, now he has a girlfriend, but she got in too late to refine Lou. Lou and I looked around and spotted the Colonel looking at us. He shook his head and smiled.

"Still boys, aren't you?"

"You got that right. So, what did you find, Colonel?"

"This calendar includes anything that has happened this year that isn't a part of our normal routine. I was right about events at the house, nothing since Christmas, but we had a plumber in, and the pest control was by three times to spray for ants. The first time we've ever had ants in the house. And I can't believe we had a problem with them before summer. Anyway, they're gone now. And you mentioned the mailman. He has stopped in a couple of times with a package that's too large to fit through the slot in the front door, but I don't think he's ever come any farther than just inside the front door."

"I assume the pest control guy was in the library."

"No, Martha told him that we'd never spotted any ants in the library. He said he'd do better if he could spray the whole house. We said we'd try it our way first, and if that didn't work we'd let him in the library."

"Did he seem anxious to get in the library?"

"Not any more so than any other room."

"Did you ever see him?"

"No, Martha always helped him, tried to follow him as much as possible."

"Are those all the people you can think of?"

"Well, we bought some new furniture last month. That was delivered."

"Were the men in here?"

"No. I doubt if they know I have a library. The only special things about this place are that it is where I spend a lot of time, and that I have the only keys to the place."

"If it's not someone who lives here who's doing this, he or she is doing their best to make it look like it. It would be so much easier to slip a note through the mail slot in the front door."

"Yeah, but I must say, Cy, that wouldn't scare me nearly as much as what was done. To think that someone has access to my library, and I have the only keys."

"Any possibility that the note has been in here for a while, and when you opened the door, it blew to the floor?"

"This desk is the only place close enough for it to blow from, and, as you can see, I don't keep a lot of things on my desk. I would have noticed it for sure."

"Well, let's move on. Tell me about your neighbors. Are you on good terms with all of them? Any of them ever come over?"

"I get along with all my neighbors. Sometimes we socialize with some of them, but no one's been over this year."

"Are there any you've had any problems with?"

"No, we've been lucky. We speak to everyone. Everyone speaks to us."

"Any possibility that someone's jealous because you have the largest house on the street?"

"If so, I'm not aware of it."

"Do you have any new neighbors?"

"The newest one is Bob Downey, next door, but he has been there for a couple of years or so."

"What can you tell me about him?"

"Speaks when I see him, but mostly keeps to himself. He's retired. A businessman I think."

"Is he married?"

"No, he lives there alone."

"I know his house isn't nearly as large as yours, but why would he buy such a large house at his age."

"Well, I said he's retired, but I don't think he is much older than the two of you. Maybe even younger than you."

"So, who else can you think of? What about anyone who's threatened you?"

"I can only think of a couple of people. Three actually. All of them were when I was at the university before I retired. But that was a few years back. I would think if anyone wanted to do anything to me, he would have done it back then."

"Some retaliate right away. Others wait until the person has forgotten about the incident, in order to increase their chances of getting away with it. Tell me about these people."

"Well, one was a colleague, Michael Belding. He blames me for not getting tenure at the university. He's still in town, teaches at the high school. I've run into him a couple of times over the years. I can tell by the look on his face that he still blames me. The only others I can think of were students. Both blamed me for not getting into the graduate program. One was a male, Daniel Terloff. The other was a female, Carla Bauerman. I always figured Terloff might have been the one who drove by and threw an open bucket of paint against the house one night, but I never was able to prove it. Both of these cases happened in my last year of teaching, but that was several years ago."

"Sometimes people carry hatred a long time, Colonel."

4

In my years on the police force, I've never been very good at preventing murder. Solving, yes. Preventing, no. Never did I want to prevent a murder as much as I did that day. My good friend, my mentor, had been threatened. Lou and I had to think quickly. What could we do to help the Colonel?

We sat, talked, and wondered. It seemed like we'd toured the whole house, except for the room where we spent the most time. The Colonel rose to give us a tour of his sanctuary. He lifted the oriental rug and unlocked the trapdoor. The Colonel descended, followed by his lemmings. The room below resembled a small trailer. There we found a couch, a chair, a double bed, a refrigerator, a sink and commode, and some canned goods. Not much else. But a little more than most people take on a camping trip. At least, I guess it was. The closest I've ever come to a camping trip was overnight surveillance with Lou. It wasn't the worst of times, but surely it wasn't the best of times. The Colonel pointed out that there was no way in or out, except the stairs we walked down.

Satisfied, we climbed back up, a wheeze at a time. Well, one of us wheezed. Lou seemed to have gotten over his wheezing. The Colonel didn't seem to have any problem, even though he was a quarter of a century older than we were. The Colonel marched us to his secret entrance and exit. He pointed to his Hardy Boy collection, kept from his childhood. He reached behind a couple of books, *The House on the Cliff*, and *The Secret of the Old Mill*, and pulled forward, pulling both spines down to the shelf. When he did, the last bookcase slid aside. The Colonel motioned for us to take a step out into the corridor. He flipped a switch, and all we saw was a corridor twenty feet long and four feet wide, and a concrete floor. The Colonel hit another switch and the wall slid back into place, only we were still in the corridor. Our mentor took a remote from his pocket, hit a button, and a panel slid away, leaving some numbers and a place to put your fingertips.

"Hit, numbers two, four, six, and eight, and rest your fingers in the grooves."

I did. Nothing happened. Then, Lou tried. Still, nothing.

"Now, I will do it."

The Colonel hit the numbers in the same sequence Lou and I had done, rested his fingers where we'd placed ours. The wall slid back, allowing us reentry to the library.

"See, boys. The place is a fortress, and yet it isn't. Any ideas?"

I looked at Lou. He looked at me. It reminded me of high school. The test looked vaguely familiar, yet it didn't.

I had no ideas, but a couple of questions.

"So, Colonel, I assume the maid knows of the passageway."

"No. No one else knows about it. Not even Martha."

"So, does it lead anywhere? Can you get out that way?"

"In and out. At the back of the living room closet is a hook, like you hang your coat on. If you turn the hook clockwise, then pull it down, the wall slides away, and I can enter the passageway. From this side, it's very easy. There's just a button you push to exit, but there's also a mirror that lets me know if anyone is in the living room. You cannot see the mirror from the other side."

27

"Are you certain that no one has seen you use the passageway?"

"No, but I'm certain no one else can gain entrance to the library from there, and I've never seen any footprints when I've run the vacuum out there, which I did yesterday. Oh, and by the way, both the passageway and the library are soundproof, for whatever that's worth."

"Colonel, would you like for me to get an expert from the department to come out to see if he can come up with anything?"

"For the time being, boys, I'd like for it to be just us. Besides, I doubt if anyone else can help. I designed this room. Still, I'm flabbergasted. Here's what I want to do. Tomorrow night, I'd like for you boys to come to dinner, meet the family, see what kind of reaction you have. Tomorrow, during the day, if you have time, talk to some of the neighbors, but don't mention me or my house. Say you've gotten a report of suspicious activity somewhere in this area. Tell them you're checking out an area of a few blocks. Ask them if they've seen any strangers on the street, cutting through to the next street. Let's see where this goes. Then, decide if we have to go further. I mean, it could be a prank, but whether it is or not, I'm still dumbfounded as to how someone could've put a note in this room."

"Would you like for us to stay here for a while? You still have that room above the garage, don't you?"

"We do, but I don't want to alarm anyone unnecessarily. Later, I'll tell Martha that the reason you boys stopped by was to let us know that someone has been breaking into homes in this area, in the daytime, but houses where no one was home. I want to ask her to stay home tomorrow since I will spend a lot of my time in the library and won't be able to hear an intruder. Thursday the Hoskinses will be here, so they'll be a deterrent."

"Unless they're the ones we're looking for."

"I'll watch my back. Oh, I've two keys to the library, both on my person. I want to give you one, in case something does happen to me and you need to get into the library. And if I do figure out anything, but don't live to tell about it, I'll do my best to leave you a clue. I want you boys to promise me a couple of things. One, if something happens to me, I want you to find out who did it and protect my family from violence. And two, whatever happens to me, don't let it change you. I'd be awfully disappointed if I knew that the two of you were moping around because of me. I know how much the two of you like having fun. Don't stop. You'll catch up with me someday."

The Colonel paused to look at his watch.

"Look at the time. Everyone's probably home by now, and I'm sure Martha is wondering when we're going to come out. Let's call it a day."

The Colonel opened the door, and the two of us stepped out into the hall, near the kitchen. Martha looked up as we did.

"Well, it's about time! Did you talk them to death, Buck? Dinner will be ready in fifteen minutes. Why don't you boys stay and eat with us?"

"I've already invited them for tomorrow night, dear."

"Well, good. Then, they can eat with us two nights in a row. I planned to have them stay as soon as they walked in the door. I know how the three of you can talk."

"Well, boys, what do you say? Can you stand us two nights in a row? Or do you have plans for the evening?"

"I don't have. You, Lou?"

"Just to eat."

"Then, it's settled. Since no one else is down yet, while the missus is getting things ready, why don't the three of us check out your treehouse? It's been a while since you've used it. We'll even let you camp out there tonight, won't we dear?" the Colonel said, as he smiled at us and gave his wife a wink.

+++

No matter how hard the Colonel tried, neither Lou nor I were willing to take the express to the treehouse. The express was another of the Colonel's inventions. The Colonel keyed in the bodyweight of whoever was ascending to the treehouse, and an equal amount of weight would descend, getting the party there in record time. Lou said he would do it, as long as I went first. I'm not sure if he wondered if I would shoot off into space and he'd get an opportunity to break in a new partner, or if he'd smirk when the Colonel removed twenty pounds or so before it was Lou's turn. Either way, I wasn't game.

Until Martha called us to dinner, the three of us stood and talked over the good times Lou and I spent in the treehouse.

Lou and I had a couple of moments alone while we washed for dinner. If dinner wasn't up to our expectations, we'd make up some excuse not to return the next night. We'd eaten at the Hardesty home before, but that was long ago before our taste buds had matured.

It didn't take us long before we knew we planned a return trip. The Swiss steak was plentiful, and there were enough mashed potatoes, gravy, corn on the cob, green beans, and rolls with butter to get us through. My only disappointment was the lemon meringue pie. I got only one piece. It had been a while since I quit after one piece. Anyway, I had a solution. Lou and I would stop at Every Loving Spoonful and order a banana split before we went home.

+++

The next day was uneventful. We sandwiched meeting the Colonel's neighbors in between lunch at the Blue Moon and dinner at the Colonel's house. We found a few of the neighbors at home, but none of them had seen a stranger in the neighborhood. No one answered the door at the newest neighbor's house. Either Bob Downey wasn't at home, or wasn't receiving guests. We'd round him up later if we needed to.

+++

I called the Colonel on Friday to make sure that the maid and handyman didn't do away with him on Thursday. He had received no new notes or unexpected visitors with a key to the library. Satisfied, I spent a lot of my weekend reclining with a good book. I was beginning to read enough to note that, if I was undisturbed, I could finish a good book in two Hershey Almond bars. Although when I came to the end of the book and the author divulged the name of the murderer before I guessed it, I ate more candy to help my thought process.

+++

Since nothing had happened, Lou and I made plans for Saturday night with Betty McElroy and Thelma Lou Spencer. Betty was merely a friend, a companion for our double-dates. Betty was still in love with her deceased husband Hugh, and I still loved my Eunice. We were friends that expected nothing but companionship from our dinners out with Lou and Thelma Lou. Those two, on the other hand, were smitten with one another. Not quite smitten enough to get married, but smitten enough that neither dated anyone else. Saturday night, we enjoyed a good meal together while we sat and conversed with each other. Lou and I tried to listen when we were around the girls and tried to learn as much etiquette and manners as was possible for two old dogs. The four of us were very comfortable together. We always referred to them as the girls, and they referred to us as the Colonel always had, as the boys. The four of us enjoyed our evening immensely, and Lou and I took the girls home at a reasonable hour because all of us had a church service to attend the next morning. While I always drive when it is just Lou and me, he drives when we take the girls out. While Lou doesn't like to drive, everyone likes to ride in his red '57 Chevy.

5

Hilldale is a quaint little town, a good place to raise two-and-one-half children. Such might be the comment of someone who dissects our little community on the way to somewhere else. It might even be said by most people who grow up in our hamlet, at least those who don't live next door to the most recent murder victim or are called out of bed to track down each murderer. If I had chosen to work at the corner grocery with hopes of someday buying the place, I might have said it myself. But when I graduated from high school and looked at my limited possibilities, I chose to do my best to help our little corner of the world. Thirty years later, I have no regrets.

Lou and I had wrapped up our latest murder investigation in late January, and while neither of us puts a notch on his belt each time we bring another criminal to justice, I'd say that we are closing in on solving one hundred murders since we offered to take over the homicide department of the Hilldale Police Department twenty-two years ago when Lt. Dolan and Sgt. Eversole retired. Retirement. Lou and I made that same decision just a few months ago. Sort of. Both of us had long since grown tired of all police work except murder investigations. We also knew that no one was knocking on

33

the door to take our jobs. So, we sat down with the Chief one day and formed an agreement. Technically, Lou and I retired, but we agreed to come out of retirement each time another murder was committed within our jurisdiction until the department found someone to replace us. We knew the chief wasn't in any hurry to send us on our way. Both of us recently celebrated our fiftieth birthday, so we're not over the hill yet, merely striding it, and we've solved every murder we've investigated. And not too many people migrate to Hilldale, police officer or not, so it wasn't like the line forming to snatch our jobs resembled that of the masses that descend upon those well-known stores during the pre-dawn hours on the day after Thanksgiving. Lou and I knew we could stay as long as we were an asset.

I can still remember that day, when Chief Collins, now retired, called Tom Morgan, George Michaelson, Lou, and me into his office to let us know that Dolan and Eversole would soon be retiring. He told us they would need two men to replace them, and he felt the four of us were the most qualified to handle the job. Tom Morgan had talked for some time of moving on, which he did less than a year later, to a larger city, and a bigger department. Two years later, he came back to tell us he regretted the move but planned to stick it out a while longer. When Tom passed on the promotion, that left George, Lou, and me, and all three of us are still with the department over two decades later. Lou and I've been buddies since before we started elementary school, and George wasn't about to break us up. Besides, George told me then, and many times since, that Lou and I were more suited to homicide than he was. Lou has always liked solving things, and while small-town murders are a lot different than figuring out the latest crossword puzzle, or even identifying the murderer before Perry Mason catches him or her. By the grace of God, and the six months training we received from Dolan and Eversole, we were able to step in without missing a beat. Oh, we've stumbled around a few times, but we've learned a lot in our stumbling, and always managed to arrive at the right conclusion.

When we solved our latest murder at the end of January, we had no inkling of what was to come in April, but other than hoping for warmer weather, we never thought of April at the end of January. April was over two months away. We still had the slushy snows of February, the howling winds of March, and the spring rains of early April to deal with first.

Snow. Hilldale is far north of sunny Florida, so each year we know there is a good possibility of snow through February, and into March. Still, retired or not, we have refrained from taking up any new hobbies, such as ice fishing or snowmobiling. We don't get enough snow in Hilldale, Kentucky to do either of them. Besides, both activities require more exertion than Lou and I've been used to, and there is an element of danger in each, and neither provides enough warmth to heat our bodies to the temperature we prefer. We toyed with the idea of going shopping for snowshoes, if we lost our senses, but decided to strap tennis rackets to our shoes if the silly notion became more than a notion. Besides, snowshoes means walking. Walking means exercise. And exercise is something I don't plan to do unless it involves catching a murderer, or a good meal. The only way I will take up any winter sport would be if my next-door neighbor promises to try out for hockey goalie without any protective equipment. Lou and I adhere to the same exercise program; recliner to the bathroom, bathroom to the recliner, recliner to Lightning, Lightning to Blue Moon Diner, Blue Moon Diner to Lightning, Lightning to the recliner.

Neither of us had a reason to retire. Lou is a bachelor, and I've been a widower longer than I've been anything else. My wife Eunice succumbed to cancer just a few years after we married. Both Lou and I felt we needed some kind of hobby if we retired because no one can eat twenty-four hours a day, although the idea seems mighty tempting. Both of us were adamant that we didn't need any hobby that caused our weight to yo-yo because we knew that was unhealthy. So, we decided to read about the literary world's version of people gifted in the same way Lou and I are. Nero Wolfe became my hero. Anyone who loves food and staying at home as much as he does is all right in my book. True, the man has issues. No man should fool around with orchids. And I never developed the love of beer that he has. It is probably his twice-a-day trip up the elevator to see those blasted orchids that keeps his weight from ballooning above three hundred pounds.

If I hadn't chosen to take semi-retirement, I might never have learned about Wolfe, Sam Spade, Hercule Poirot, Charlie Chan, Sherlock Holmes, and some of the other sleuths of days gone by. Even though I was gifted, I wasn't so much so that I couldn't learn something from the literary giants of sleuthdom. Maybe someday what I learn in those books might help me solve a case one day sooner. While these mysteries help enlighten people as to the mighty acumen of the police force, I must say that even though these men I mentioned measure up to my accomplishments, I cannot say the same about those who have sidekicks. Sgt. Murdock is much more helpful to me than Dr. Watson ever was to Holmes.

If you read rather than skimmed an earlier paragraph, you might have noticed references to Lightning and the Blue Moon Diner. Lightning is my mode of transportation. No gas-guzzling black tank for me. Lightning is a canary yellow VW beetle. The Blue Moon is the diner responsible for making us into the men we have become. No place serves stick-to-your-ribs food like the Blue Moon and has two better women to serve it to us than Rosie and Thelma. Both treat us better than any wife or mother ever could.

I don't want you to get the wrong idea about Lou and me. True, we are retired, in a way, and neither of us cooks his own meals or mows his own lawn. Lou lives in an apartment building, and I hire someone to do mine. It might sound like all we do is sleep. In truth, Lou and I lead active lives. Even though we seldom cook, we make frequent trips to the grocery. I have to stock up on Hershey Almond candy bars, and Lou loads up on M&Ms. Plus, both of us have to have enough easy-to-fix food on hand to satisfy an unexpected, late-night craving. The Blue Moon isn't an all-night establishment, and there are times when the severity of the weather wins out over eating the food God meant for us to eat. Sometimes we have to eat junk. Well, junk and candy. While I do plow into the latest plate of food at the Blue Moon, I take my time when eating my candy. I meticulously extricate one almond at a time from my candy bar. I savor each morsel of chocolate as it melts in my mouth. The feeling is so heaven-like that if I ever decide to take a vacation or to relocate, Hershey, Pennsylvania is the only place I would consider. I wonder if every store in that town sells Hershey bars. And are the streetlights shaped like Hershey Kisses? Don't they have some kind of festival up there? I must check with one of my friends who has a computer. Hershey might be worth a visit.

Yeah, that's another thing about Lou and me. Neither of us owns a computer, cell phone, or any other up-to-date electronic device except a DVD player. My phone is black, heavy, and has a rotary dial. So what if I don't have Caller I.D. or Call Waiting. I've made it this far without all that stuff.

One change Lou and I made since retirement is that we recently agreed to socialize with the outside world. I mentioned earlier some of the literary detective heroes. While I'd heard of many of them since I was a child, it was only after retirement that I began to read and study them. Lou suggested we frequent Scene of the Crime Mystery Bookstore, and since it didn't require rigorous activity or missing any meals to do so, I agreed to accompany him to check it out. We checked it out all right. Or should I say we left our checks. Our first visit cost each of us $148.23. Both of us bought the same books and had the same agenda. Read the books in a certain order and discuss them afterward. I learned something from that first visit. On our second visit, when we escaped we had spent less than $100 each. I've learned that I need to buy fewer books or buy paperbacks. At least that's my thinking until our next visit to Scene of the Crime.

In a weak moment, Lou and I agreed to attend a monthly get-together of mystery readers. So far, we have attended only once, but a couple of other readers recommended some contemporary authors to us. I made a "to buy" list for our next visit. I planned to try a book from the Death on Demand series and one from the Henri O series by Carolyn Hart, the Alpine series by Mary Daheim, a selection from the Claire Malloy series by Joan Hess, a whodunit from one of Tim Myers's series, and a book from the Puzzle Lady series by Parnell Hall. I will try those, but I've sworn Lou to secrecy. No one at the department is to know that Lou and I are reading a series with a character known as the Puzzle Lady. Who knows how much guys like George Michaelson and Frank Harris would kid us?

6

As I thought about the Colonel's dilemma, I thought back over the last couple of months and what we had been through. Much of my thoughts had to do with the change in Lou.

Evidently, the winter weather was worse on Lou than I thought. I had no forewarning of how bad he had become until he slid into the car one morning, buckled up, looked over at me and smiled.

"What's wrong with you, Cheshire cat?"

"I got a Wii."

"Excuse me," I replied.

"I said I got a Wii."

"I thought that's what you said. Why didn't you go before you came out of your apartment? It isn't like I was going to drive off and leave you."

"No, no, no. A Wii. W I I. I got a Wii Fit, too."

"Well, what's a Wii without a Wii Fit."

I assumed Lou was learning some foreign language.

"You have no idea what I'm talking about, do you, Cy?"

"I'd say that makes two of us. If we'd been on a case, I'd say that you've been working too hard, but obviously, that's not the case."

"Cy, a Wii is a video game system. Wii Fit is an exercise program you use with the Wii in order to get in better shape and lose weight if you need to."

"Well, you don't need to."

"But Doc says I need to get in better shape."

"Then change doctors."

"I don't want to. I Wiied for over thirty minutes this morning and I feel great. It's a wonderful workout. I understand there are over forty exercises altogether."

"Do they have anything for exercising your brain? I think yours has taken a hiatus."

It was then I got a dissertation on what a Wii and Wii Fit were. It was almost enough to make me lose my appetite. Almost, but not quite.

+++

We arrived at the Blue Moon, stepped out of the car and into the diner. My eyes seemed to deceive me. It looked like Lou was a little sprier as he jumped up onto his stool.

After a little small talk, Rosie took our order. I ordered the usual. Then it was Lou's turn.

"I'll have a veggie omelet and a bowl of fruit. Maybe some berries, sliced banana, and a sliced apple, if you have it."

As soon as Rosie realized that Lou was serious, she turned to me. I figured I was about to find an ally, someone whose common sense hadn't left her.

"What's wrong with him today?"

I made a mistake of telling her.

"He Wiied for over thirty minutes this morning."

I wasn't prepared for her answer or the conversation that ensued.

"You got a Wii?"

"Yeah, it came in yesterday. Wii Fit, too."

"I've had mine for two weeks. I love it. I think the Super Hula Hoop has taken a half an inch off my waist."

"I haven't done that one yet. What do you think of the Basic Step?"

"Oh, I've already unlocked the Advanced Step."

I had already decided that someone had unlocked a door that should have remained locked.

"I'm just getting started. What are some of your favorite exercises?"

As both sides of the counter reverberated with names of the exercises I'd heard about all the way to the diner, I felt I was going to lose my food, until I realized that Rosie hadn't yet turned around to hang our order on the spindle. The last thing I heard was two people agreeing on what fun it was to head soccer balls. I began to wonder if two heads hadn't taken too many cannonballs.

+++

By the grace of God, I managed to get through the rest of the day. I went home and prayed for Lou, that he would come to his senses. If he continued to work out on that contraption, he'd lose weight. Surely God would spare him if I continued to pray in earnest. Otherwise, people might start calling me Jack, as in, "Here comes Jack and the Beanstalk." I couldn't imagine Lou being skinny. He had always had a healthy body, like mine.

+++

Everything was fine until the next morning when a smiling sergeant slid into my car and asked me if I thought he looked thinner.

"You know, Lou, now that you mention it, I think you have lost weight, and all the weight you've lost is above your neck and behind your eyebrows."

Lou just looked at me and smiled, as if he thought that someday he could convert me.

+++

Wasting Away Lou dominated my thoughts. Even when I got home and picked up a good mystery, I couldn't concentrate on what I read. The next morning everything had gotten to be too much for me. I did something irrational. I set the alarm for just before daylight, sneaked out of the house and over to Lou's apartment. I got to his front window just as Lou was shutting off the TV. The sweat on his body told me he had already Wiied. I slinked back to the car, went home, fell back into the bed, and pulled the covers over my head. I had missed all that sleep for nothing.

+++

The following morning I arose even earlier. I figured that Lou Wiied at the same time each day, so I missed even more sleep to see Lou in action. I parked a few doors from Lou's building and slipped down the street lurking in the shadows as much as possible. By the time I got to Lou's place, my ears were cold and red. I set up shop in front of Lou's window and watched a very overweight man twist his hips as he emulated the cartoon character he had created on the Wii, the character he was watching on the TV, a character who was spinning a hula hoop around his cartoonish body. I must have laughed loud enough to be heard through a storm window because a few seconds later Lou stepped off his Wii Fit board and hurried to the window. I wiped the slobber from my jacket and managed to get away without being seen. As I shut the car door, started the car, and turned the heater up high, I realized that I had experienced some of the most hilarious free entertainment I had seen in some time.

+++

I went to bed extremely early that night, so that I could go back for more entertainment before dawn the next day. When I arrived at Lou's place, I noticed a shrub I hadn't seen before. It was blocking Lou's window. The night before I thought of Lou doing his imitation hula hoop and trained myself not to laugh. If I was going to get up long before God intended me to arise, I wanted to get the full show.

As I neared his window, I could see Lou Wiiing while standing on one leg. The other leg was tucked up against his thigh. I didn't realize Lou was capable of such a move, but then I noticed he was using the back of a chair for support. I stepped forward to get right next to the window. I was glad that it was a cloudy night. In a few moments, I ceased to be glad it was a cloudy night. I heard a thud inside the house. From what I gathered, Lou was no longer standing on one leg. He was lying on his front, back, or one side or the other. From what I could tell, Lou keeled over just after I screamed. I screamed just after I stepped into a bear trap and it crushed my ankle. I lay in the snow writhing in pain.

It was several minutes before I failed to notice the pain. The first thing to distract me from my pain was a voice that said, "Hold it right there!" and then someone shined a light in my eyes. I recognized Officer Davis's voice before his light illuminated my face.

"Well, Lt. Dekker, what are you doing here? Did you get the call about a prowler, too? I thought you'd pretty much retired except for murder cases."

Murder. The way I felt there was about to be another murder.

"Oh, hi, Officer Davis. I just came over to watch Lou Wii."

"Excuse me, Lieutenant."

"Wii, you know that exercise thing. Lou got one. You should see him working out on it. It's hilarious."

"Oh, he's got a Wii, too. I've had mine for about a month now. I don't have the Fit yet, but I love to bowl on it. And boxing and tennis are good workouts."

I was freezing, but my brain hadn't yet been affected. I had just figured out that the whole world had gone crazy when something else distracted me. Something whisked by Officer Davis and crawled up onto my body. I knew that the tongue seemed familiar when I heard a screech nearby.

"That's it, Twinkle Toes. Let Cyrus know how much you love him. Cyrus has been hurt."

My next-door neighbor was about to lean over and caress me when I remembered the bear trap and kicked with all my might. "Oops!" I exclaimed, as my next-door neighbor cried out in pain. From the way she hobbled around for the next couple of minutes, I think I caught her in the shin. My conscience kicked in and wiped the smile from my face, so I refrained from doing the same to her bundle of fluff. Besides, my problem was with my neighbor, not her little dog.

A day or two later, my senses returned, and I engaged Officer Davis to help me extricate the bear trap from my ankle. I decided to hold on to the instrument that caused me so much pain. I was torn as to whether to leave it outside my next-door neighbor's front door, or the door of the man inside the apartment, the man who used to be my best friend before he started having mental problems.

Officer Davis drove me to the hospital to get my ankle checked. An hour later, I was home again, soaking my ankle. It gave me time to think. There were only three ways that Heloise Humphert could have known that I had been hurt. She could have followed me, which I doubted because she would have pounced on me much sooner if she had She could have purchased a police radio, which I was pretty sure she hadn't done, or she could have been alerted by an ex-friend of a sergeant. I didn't know how, but someday I was going to get even with Lou.

+++

I was concerned about Lou. I wanted him to get help, so the next morning I placed a call to the police psychiatrist. I let him know about Lou's new fetish. He let me know what the Wii Fit had done for him. I hung up and remembered that some people think psychiatrists are the looniest of all people. I had only two other recourses, Thelma Lou, Lou's girlfriend, and Internal Affairs. I decided to wait before contacting either of them. I was beginning to think like the one man whose body hadn't been taken over by the pod people in *Invasion of the Body Snatchers*. The Wii fanatics were everywhere. Soon, there would be only skinny people. I reminded myself not to buy stock in any fast food restaurant, and to eat an extra helping of dessert unless the Blue Moon Diner quit serving dessert. After all, Rosie had been affected, too. What if the cook is next?

7

Lou and I made it through March and the first half of April without too much trouble. Well, no trouble except I had to listen to Lou expostulate about the Wii every day and received a weekly report on how much weight he had lost. I was concerned about him. His pants were slipping down, and I noticed how Lou had to move his belt over a notch or two. Also, I learned that I'd lost one of my allies. Lou had had Thelma Lou over twice to Wii. He'd Wii for a half an hour and then she'd Wii for thirty minutes. Then, they repeated their workouts until both had Wiied for an hour. I wasn't convinced. If God had meant for us to Wii, He'd have put something in the Bible about it. I challenged Lou to show me where in the Bible we were instructed to Wii, and the best I could get out of him was something about the body being a temple.

Luckily, the Wii hadn't taken over Lou's entire life, just one hour a day and most of his conversation. And Rosie had convinced Lou that he didn't need to give up any of those foods he liked, just cut back on them. Well, if Lou wanted to starve himself to death eating only half of a meal at a time, so be it. Less food on his plate meant the possibility of more on mine.

Other than Lou's workout, our routine each day was the same as it had been. We checked out the weather before we left the house each day to see if sunshine or rain was forecast and what the temperature was expected to be. We'd also developed a few friends at Scene of the Crime, mostly old women, old men, stay-at-home wives, and one guy who worked the night shift. A couple of days ago, Lou and I'd finished reading John Dickson Carr's *The Three Coffins* and were about to start a book by a current mystery author. We were beginning to enjoy our new life.

I was sitting at home, lying back in my recliner, thinking about buying a computer. I couldn't get Hershey, Pennsylvania out of my mind, so a few days earlier I asked one of the elderly women in the reading group if she owned a computer. She responded by saying, "Doesn't everyone these days?" Reluctantly, I informed her that at least two residents of Hilldale didn't, although who knew what other changes Lou would make in his life. This resulted in her sharing our faux-pas with the others in the group, and immediately everyone gathered around Lou and me to encourage us to take the plunge. For a minute it seemed like Lou and I had stepped into an A.A. meeting by mistake. The last time I'd experienced such encouragement was when one of the guys at the department bet on me in a pizza-eating contest. When someone asked why we wanted a computer, I told them I understood there was a place we could go to look up information about various people and places. My new friends told me that even a novice could learn how to do that in five minutes, and immediately I wondered how much smarter a novice was than I.

+++

It was now a few days after hearing the Colonel's bad news, which was very much still on my mind unless I made myself think of something else. One of the things I never think about is setting an alarm. I make it a point to get up each morning just after I hear the rooster crow. I will not change this habit until someone in my neighborhood buys a rooster. I wouldn't put it past my next-door neighbor to buy a rooster, an ugly one, but then the term "ugly rooster" is an oxymoron, which is slightly different than my neighbor. There is nothing "oxy" about her.

Like Lou, I began my day as I usually did, doing my morning exercise, lifting myself to a sitting position. I've learned how to accomplish such a feat in only three jerky moves, with a grunt or two along the way. After sitting upright and still until I remembered where I was, I stumbled to the bathroom, splashed some water on my face, and looked in the mirror. Immediately I wanted to replace the sleep I washed from my eyes and return to bed. Only visions of sugary and fatty foods dancing in my head kept me from doing so.

My valet had failed to lay out my clothes, so I rooted around in my dresser and closet until I located something to wear in public. Then, I looked outside at the April showers that were helping to grow the May flowers that I never plant and selected something different from my wardrobe. I detest getting wet, but there is nothing manly about using an umbrella or a raincoat to protect oneself from the elements.

After taking the time to read my daily devotional and asking God to forgive me for the thoughts I had about my next-door neighbor, I called Lou to let him know that the breakfast patrol was on the clock.

I locked the door, stepped out into pouring rain. I turned and saw something that caused my stomach to turn as well. I grasped the railing to keep from falling. Standing not fifteen feet from my door was my neighbor and her bundle of fluff, both wearing pink raincoats trimmed in silver studs. I hoisted a black umbrella I had stored by the door, more to protect my eyes from this unsightly interruption than to keep myself from getting wet. My eyes had never adjusted to seeing Heloise Humphert so early in the morning. Nor had my stomach.

"Miss Humphert, what are you doing in my yard?"

"Waiting for you, Cyrus. Twinkle Toes and I wanted to wish you a good morning."

"I would prefer that you wish it to me from the top of Mt. Everest."

"Oh, Cyrus, you're so funny. Are you hinting that you think the three of us should go away together? You know how much Twinkle Toes and I like you."

"And I like you, too. I'd like you to be as far away as possible."

"I understand, Cyrus. You're shy, and you don't want other people to know about us, yet."

"I wish I didn't know about you, yet. Maybe I can get amnesia. Or better yet, maybe you can get amnesia and forget where you live."

"Oh, Cyrus, you sly devil. You want me to move in with you. We can turn your home into a love nest."

"Miss Humphert, I might have neglected to tell you about a bad habit of mine. I wake up in the middle of the night, ready to shoot my gun. As a matter of fact, I've been known to shoot at the first moving thing I see after I leave my house each morning. You might have heard the noise and thought it was a car backfiring. My latest victim was a possum. All small animals look like possums to me early in the morning. Now, if you don't mind, I've got work to do, and I hate having nightmares on an empty stomach."

"Oh, Cyrus, are you inviting Twinkle Toes and me out to eat?"

"I sure am. It's a little place in Mexico. I'll draw you a map. Be sure and wait if you get there first, and don't forget to drink plenty of water when you get there."

"Miss Humphert, I don't know how many times I've told you this. I have no interest in a relationship with you. Yet you keep hitting on me. I have nothing against your dog except that it lives with you. I like you much better when I don't have to see you, so if you are interested in a man, find another man to be interested in."

"Cyrus, I know you really love me. You just don't know how to tell me."

When I heard her latest comment, I used the umbrella to keep her from touching me and whipped by her. Okay, maybe it was more of a stumble than a whip. Still, I managed to distance myself from my neighbor and her small companion, if only for a little while. I hoped to recover my appetite before Lou and I arrived at the Blue Moon.

+++

Lou and I sauntered into the Blue Moon, hoisted ourselves up onto our stools, and perused the menu. Rosie walked over.

"Well, hello Lieutenant, Sergeant. I didn't realize that you'd learned how to read."

"We sure have," I replied. "This 'all of the above' sounds good. Why don't you bring me one of those?"

"You know that includes the Fruit Loops with chocolate milk?"

"I understand fruit's good for you, but I'll pass this time. I might reconsider at lunch. Just bring me the Bonanza Extravaganza."

"And you, Sergeant?"

"I'll have what he's having, only bring me waffles with strawberries and whipped cream instead of the pecan pancakes, and a half order of turkey bacon instead of regular bacon, and make it two eggs instead of three, and bring them over easy, instead of scrambled with cheese. Have I forgotten anything?"

"So, you've gone cold turkey on the Wii?"

"No, I'll just work out a little longer when I get home. So, as I said, have I forgotten anything?"

"Just the pie, but you never order that until you're through with everything else."

"Just make sure you have enough pie for him," Lou said as he pointed at me.

"We had two shifts work overtime, just so he'd have enough."

"Are you two lovebirds through jabbering? I'm getting hungry."

"Cy, I was just working up to proposing to Rosie. I would too if I didn't think it would ruin a beautiful relationship."

Rosie smiled, shook her head, then turned, put our order on the spindle, and spun it around to the cook.

By the way Lou looked at me I could tell that he knew something was bothering me. I'm sure he thought it was just the Colonel. He didn't know that I'd encountered the plague from next door on my way out of the house. That reminded me. I would need to pray again, and ask God's forgiveness.

Our food came and I looked down and dug in. Sparks flashed as knife met fork. I didn't look up until I heard Rosie laugh. I looked at her, then at Lou. Lou turned to me and smiled. He had a dollop of whipped cream on his nose, and a slice of turkey bacon dangled from the side of his mouth.

He opened his mouth slightly, to talk. As he did, the bacon fell out, but Quick Hands Lou tackled it before it hit the floor. Undaunted, he replaced the bacon but held on to it.

"Say the secret word, Cy, and you win fifty dollars."

I must say that Groucho Marx never looked so bad, but I admit Lou's shenanigans made me laugh. Well, the Colonel did tell us to have fun. I was thankful that we arrived late enough that we had the place to ourselves.

I reached over and ran a finger through his whipped cream. He poked his finger into the top pancake on my plate, then put his finger in his mouth and licked it.

Rosie stood, shaking her head. She saw nothing she hadn't seen before. As we continued, she spoke.

"Tell me again about how you two were the only ones to apply for a job with the police department all those many years ago."

"I beg your pardon. We were at the top of our class."

"Is that another way of saying what I said?"

My stomach growled, so I ignored Rosie and returned to my food. I savored each morsel, and then looked at my watch to see how long we had to wait until lunch. But enough about lunch. We hadn't finished breakfast. Not all of it.

"Say Rosie, what kind of pie do you have this morning?"

"So far, you can either have peanut butter or chocolate cream."

"That will be fine."

She looked at Lou and he concurred. A few seconds later she returned with a piece of peanut butter pie and a piece of chocolate cream pie for me, and a sliver of each for Lou. Poor Lou, he seemed to lose weight as I ate. I hoped his Wii broke before he wasted away to nothing. If he kept it up, someday he would turn into a one-hundred- ninety-eight-pound weakling.

+++

Once more ensconced in Lightning where Lou's seatbelt seemed to wrap around him twice, Lou and I decided to leave our door-to-door canvassing until after lunch. The experience proved that both Lou and I walked better if we had eaten two meals beforehand. Instead, we stopped by Scene of the Crime and reloaded. I wanted to see what the top sleuths of today's literature had to say. Able to walk better because our billfolds were a little lighter, Lou sauntered and I stumbled from the bookstore, and I drove him back to his apartment.

"See you at the first growl of the stomach," I said, as I delivered my parting words.

I walked into the house, dumped my stash on the table next to the recliner, kicked my shoes off, slid my slippers on, and plopped down. I looked over my selections; *Death On Demand* by Carolyn Hart, *The Alpine Advocate* by Mary Daheim, *Innkeeping With Murder* by Tim Myers, *A Clue For The Puzzle Lady* by Parnell Hall, *Wish You Were Here* by Rita Mae Brown *and The Cat Who Could Read Backwards* by Lillian Jackson Braun. Each was the first book in a mystery series. I picked up Carolyn Hart's book. Her Lt. Dekker was a woman who owned a mystery bookstore and lived on an island off the South Carolina coast. That caused me to think. What fictional detective would I really like to be? I had heard of many of them since Lou and I started hanging out at Scene of the Crime. Owning a bookstore that sells nothing but mysteries seemed cool. But then there is something to be said about Nero Wolfe's seldom leaving home. He even has a cook, and a man to run his errands. Still, I'm not sure I want anyone else living with me. And there's that Qwill guy in *The Cat Who* series. Imagine not knowing if you're a millionaire or a billionaire. I think I'd like that. And everyone would have to be nice to me, just in case I might give them some money. Yes, rank has its privileges.

I lay back and mulled over my possibilities. I mulled too long. My snoring didn't awaken me. I had grown used to it over the years. Sometime later, the growl in my stomach woke me. My new fictional friends would have to wait. It was once again time for my favorite exercise. I called Lou to let him know.

8

Our Sunday routine differs from any other day. The Blue Moon is closed on Sunday, so we begin our Sundays like any other cop begins a normal day. We feast on donuts. Our church offers the cream of the donut crop, so Lou and I voice our approval by slipping a total of one hundred dollars into the donut fund each week. Donuts filled with custard and covered with chocolate or smothered with caramel and pecans are a fine way to get everyone in the right frame of mind to receive the pastor's message. Lou and I arrive early each week in order to feed the kitty without being noticed, pluck the first of those tasty morsels, and still get our back row aisle seats before someone else plops down in them. The only difference is that lately, Lou has cut his donut intake in half. That gave me something else to pray for. Everyone knows that all of us need to eat enough of each of the basic food groups, even if we partake of one of them only on Sunday.

+++

After a restful Sunday that offered an uplifting church experience, a couple of good dining experiences at places we don't go to all week long, and plenty of time to read and take naps, I woke up Monday morning refreshed. I almost bounded from the bed. Almost, but not quite. Well, really I never considered bounding. Bounding is too fast for my taste.

I took care of all the preliminaries and scurried from the house. Okay, not only do I not bound, I never scurry either, but I didn't dilly-dally when I left. Not with that creature hovering nearby. God really blessed me on that Monday morning. The only view I had of my neighbor was in my rearview mirror. She doesn't look so bad that way, from a block away.

I pulled up in front of Lou's apartment and waited for him to join me. He opened the door and looked worried and unsure of himself. I motioned for him to come on, which seemed to get him in gear. He hurried out to Lightning, opened the door, and plopped down on the seat.

"What's wrong with you? Did my neighbor's sister rent the apartment next to yours? Or did someone break-in in the middle of the night and steal your Wii?"

"Worse than that, Cy. I got a message."

I didn't look in the rearview mirror, but I assume that all of a sudden my look resembled his. For years, any time someone was murdered, Lou got a message from God. Not a spoken word, but a thought or thoughts that had something to do with the case we were to solve. Lou never claimed that the messages were from God, but each day, Lou got a new message which provided a clue that related to whatever we would encounter that day. Because it had been only a few days since someone threatened the Colonel, both of us immediately feared for the Colonel's life.

"I think we need to go in and call the Colonel, make sure he's okay."

"I agree, Cy."

We lifted ourselves from the vehicle and hurried to Lou's apartment. Lou opened the door and motioned for me to make the call. After a couple of rings, Martha answered the phone.

"Martha, I've something I need to talk to the Colonel about."

"He just went out, Cy. He said something about discovering something and that he needed to spring a surprise on someone. Do you have any idea what he's talking about?"

"Not a clue. Did he say where he was going and when he'll be back?"

"He said he wouldn't be long and told me that today would be a good day for me to run my errands. He told me he'd get his own lunch, that he had a couple of things to do before Joe shows up at 3:00 and that he didn't want to be disturbed. I'll be leaving shortly."

"Okay, I'll check back with him later. Thanks."

I hung up and told Lou what Martha had said. Neither of us knew the Colonel's habits, but we didn't think that whatever the Colonel had planned was a part of his normal routine. We spent a few minutes trying to find him before we devoured breakfast. We cruised down the Colonel's street a couple of times and rolled down a few other streets in the neighborhood. There was no activity on the street and no sign of his car. We drove through the parking lots of a couple of shopping centers in the area, searching for his car. Thirty minutes later, we arrived at the Blue Moon, defeated. We sat in the car, discussing the Colonel because we never discuss business in public. One of us remembered that whoever threatened the Colonel seemed to suggest that whatever would happen to him would happen in his home, in his library. Could it be that it meant that the Colonel was safe while he was out? Our only recourse was to pull a few strings and put out a missing person report on the Colonel. We knew that the Colonel wouldn't approve, so we dismissed the idea.

Abiding by the Colonel's wishes, we did our best to enjoy ourselves and not bother him when he got home. We entered the Blue Moon, tried to act normal. Well, normal for us.

"We almost called the police on the police," Rosie said.

"Do what?" I replied.

"I was getting worried about you. You're never this late. We thought something had happened to you."

"It did. The good sergeant and I were involved in a battle to the death game of Clue."

"Well, we're out of food."

"I guess the sergeant and I will have to hold you hostage until the cook shows up with more food. We promise not to tie the ropes too tightly."

"Oh, tight ropes are the best."

+++

After we finished eating and I took Lou back to his place, which allowed me to finish reading *Death On Demand* before I picked Lou up. Since we read at about the same pace, he had finished the book too, so we discussed it on the way to the Blue Moon.

As Lou scampered and I waddled from the Blue Moon, I looked at my watch. It showed 3:03. The last time we ate lunch that late was when we were working on a murder case. Thoughts of murder took me back to the Colonel.

We fell into the car, strapped ourselves in, and loosened our seatbelts as much as possible.

"Say, Lou, I don't think you ever told me what today's message was."

"Didn't I?"

"No, we started worrying about the Colonel. So what is it?"

"*The Hunchback of Notre Dame.*"

I sat there for a few seconds, looking at Lou. Then my brain engaged, the part that hadn't been on proper medication. I contoured my body to get it to look like The Hunchback I had seen Charles Laughton play. "Water," I uttered, in my best imitation of Charles Laughton playing The Hunchback.

"Sanctuary," Lou replied, in his Hunchback voice.

I must have scared Lou as I hit the gas and took off. I did because he told me that I did.

"What's the matter, Cy?"

"Don't you get it? Sanctuary. The Colonel has his sanctuary. I hope we're not too late."

A glum look appeared on Lou's face. This was one of those times I wished I drove a gas-guzzler. A few seconds one way or the other might make all the difference in the world.

9

I pulled up in front of the Colonel's house. Lou and I jumped from Lightning almost before it stopped. We rushed to the door and rapped as loudly as we could. In a few seconds, a man we didn't recognize answered the door.

"We've come to see the Colonel."

"You must be Cy and Lou. I'm Buck's friend Joe. Martha has just gone to call you. We're worried. Buck and I have a standing appointment for 3:00 each Monday afternoon. Neither of us ever cancels without notifying the other. I got here right at 3:00, rang the bell. Buck didn't answer, so I walked around back, thinking he might be in the backyard or on the enclosed back porch. No Buck. So, I came back and rang again, thinking he might be in the bathroom. Still no answer. Then, I called him on the phone."

As the man progressed with his story, his face grew more downcast.

I heard a noise and looked up. Martha came running up to us.

"Did Joe tell you? We can't find Buck. He doesn't answer his office phone, his cell phone, or my knock at the library door. We're worried."

"We'll check it out. You two wait here."

"But it takes a key to get into his office. Buck has the only keys."

"He used to have the only keys. He gave one to me last week when we were here. Now, wait here until one of us comes back for you."

Like well-trained dogs, both of them stayed while Lou and I rushed to the library door to try the key. I looked up at the camera that could tell me nothing. Well, as far as I knew it couldn't tell me anything. I slid the key into the lock and turned it.

The Colonel lay on the floor in front of his desk, facing toward us, but with his head bent toward the desk. We rushed over to him and felt his pulse. For the first time since my wife died, I cried. Lou and I embraced, then wiped away our tears. As we entered the front hall, the looks on our faces told everything.

Martha came running to us, yelling, "No. No. It can't be."

I grabbed her by her arms, keeping her from entering the library.

"He's gone, but we don't know what caused it. I can't let you go in yet. I've to call the medical examiner and have him check the Colonel. Regardless, it's best that you stay out of the library."

Once again, reluctantly, the Colonel's wife and his friend abided by our wishes. Martha pointed toward a phone in the living room. I made a call I never expected to or wanted to make.

Assured that the Colonel's wife and his friend would stay put, Lou and I reentered the library to see what we could see. We were too upset the first time to notice that the Colonel clutched a Bible. Several index cards were placed in various places in the Colonel's Bible. Four others had fallen from the Bible and were lying next to the body. Were these the clues the Colonel promised to leave us? Time would tell.

The two of us returned to the grieving widow and her husband's friend. We decided to wait with them until reinforcements arrived.

Evidently, my years as a cop allowed me to operate in a proper manner, even though I wasn't thinking clearly. In addition to Frank Harris, the medical examiner, I summoned our good friend George Michelson to bring some help, and Louie Palona, the department's expert on gadgets and technology. George would bring as many officers as would be needed, and Frank would see that the lab boys and fingerprint experts were alerted.

Everyone arrived within minutes of each other. Once everyone had arrived, we left Officer Dan Davis to see to Martha and Joe's comforts, and to see that no one left the hall and living room area. As others who lived there arrived, Officer Davis was instructed to keep everyone in the area. There would be rooms to check before anyone left the immediate vicinity.

I gathered into the library all those who were there to work.

"As many of you know, the Colonel was a special friend to Lou and me. Still, we don't expect anything from you that we wouldn't expect if a stranger were murdered.

"Frank, we'd like to know as soon as possible if the Colonel was murdered. *How* can come later. *If* needs to come as soon as possible.

"Those of you dusting for prints, first, I'd like for you to dust the Bible, the desk, the door we entered, and the secret exit I will show you. I doubt if you find anything, but we want to know. Please do the Bible first, then hand it to me. It might contain clues if there was a murder.

"George, we need a team to check all the upstairs bedrooms to see if you find anything suspicious. We want to do this as soon as possible so that those who live here can get back to their lives as best they can under the circumstances. We also need someone else to stay with

Officer Davis to see that no one leaves the house or wanders through it.

"Louie, more than likely you saw a camera mounted outside the door. You might already know this, but the camera works on motion detection. I want you to look at what transpired from the time the Colonel opened that door this morning until I opened it a little after three. If you don't find anything, and I don't think you will, I want to know if anyone has tampered with the camera. Also, there is a secret passageway that was to have been known to no one but the Colonel. We'd like for you to examine it, and tell us how easy it would be for someone to tamper with it."

"Lou and I plan to question the widow and then wait for Frank's diagnosis. Any questions?"

No one spoke up or raised a hand.

"Okay, let's go to work."

I motioned for Louie to join Lou and me.

"I want you to check the camera first, but as soon as the print guys get through dusting the Bible, I want to show both of you the secret passageway. After you check out the camera, give the Colonel's apparatus in the passageway a going over."

By the time I finished giving Louie his additional instructions, the guys on the print crew were through with the Bible. There were no prints on it, other than the Colonel's, so Lou wrapped it and secured it. It wouldn't leave our person.

After seeing that everyone understood his or her job, Lou and I left to talk to Martha. I was sure she was wondering what was going on.

"Martha, we need to use a room where we can talk to you privately."

She ushered us down the hall to the family room at the other end of the house.

"Is this okay?"

"It's fine. Let's have a seat."

"Cy, why are all these policemen here? Didn't Buck die of a heart attack?"

"We don't know yet, but what we do know is that the Colonel summoned Lou and me here last week because he had received a death threat."

Martha gasped.

"A death threat. And he didn't tell me."

"Whoever threatened the Colonel's life was someone who has access to this house. Who has keys to the house?"

"But it couldn't be anyone with a key. Only those of us who live here have keys. There must be another explanation."

"First of all, remember that we're working on the assumption that the Colonel was murdered. We don't know that yet. There were no marks on his body, at least none that we saw. We just know that someone threatened his life, so we are proceeding in this manner. Of course, there could be another explanation. Do you ever leave a door unlocked?"

"No. At least not on purpose."

"What about leaving a key for a workman?"

"No, one of us was always here if someone was expected."

"Do you or your granddaughters ever leave your purses on the table by the front door, or does anyone ever leave a key there?"

"My granddaughters. I'd forgotten all about them. What will they think when they get home?"

"Someone will stay with them. They'll be okay. Now, answer my question."

"I forgot what it was."

"Is there ever a purse or a key on the table by the front door?"

"Oh, uh, no. Not that I can remember. Oh, Cy, there has to be some other explanation."

"Let me level with you, Martha. Because Lou and I were special friends of the Colonel, I don't know if we will be allowed to pursue the case or not, but if so, we'll have to ask each of you some tough questions. Remember, there's nothing personal. We're just doing our job the best we can."

"I understand."

"Okay, where were you today?"

"I went shopping at the mall."

"Did anyone go with you, or did you see anyone you know while you were there?"

"Oh, I can't remember if I saw anyone or not. I'm so confused now. But I can tell you that I went alone."

"And what time did you leave, and when did you return?"

"At Buck's request, I left shortly after I talked to you, so I got to the mall shortly after it opened, at 10:00. I shopped, ate lunch there, shopped some more, and got home a little after 3:00. Buck was out this morning. Do you think someone accosted him when he got home, followed him into the house? That would allow for someone getting into the house without a key."

"I doubt it. If so, that someone will show up on the camera following the Colonel into the library. We'll find that out in time. In the meantime, tell me about when you got home."

"As I pulled in the driveway, I saw Joe walking away from the house."

"Any way of knowing if he had been inside the house?"

"Oh, Joe wouldn't do anything. He's Buck's best friend."

"So, what you're telling me is that you can't say if Joe had been in the house, and more than likely, he can't say if you returned from the mall early."

"You don't think I killed him?"

"No, I don't, but all possibilities have to be pursued, at least until we get a lead. Now, why don't we go back and join the others? Don't say anything about what we talked about, and we may have to talk to you again later."

We returned to the living room and experienced a double reunion of sorts. All of the house's occupants had returned, and the Chief was waiting for Lou and me. Seldom has the Chief graced the scene of a murder investigation, and I thought I knew why he had chosen to do so this time.

In a matter of seconds, Lou and I had returned to the room we'd just left, this time with the Chief in tow.

"How's it going so far?"

"We're just getting started, Chief, but as you can see, everyone is already hard at work."

"Yes, I'm impressed. I think you know why I'm here. I know the deceased was a friend of yours. Frank just told me he thinks it was murder, so now I want to know if you think you can handle this like any other case, or do you want me to call in someone from the outside?"

"It'll be hard, Chief, but I think Lou and I'll be okay. If things begin to be too much for us, I'll let you know. But we'd like a chance to solve this one."

The Chief looked at Lou, who nodded in agreement.

"Okay, it's yours for the time being. I'm not putting any time limit on you, but I'll be watching. If I feel the strain is too much for you, I'm calling someone else in. Understand?"

"Of course we do, Chief."

"Now, get busy, but don't burn the midnight oil. I'm going home. If you need anything, you've got my number."

We left the room. The Chief walked toward the front door. Lou and I headed to the library. As it turned out, Frank had more information.

Frank looked up as we entered the room and motioned for us to come over. He'd found a mark on the Colonel's throat that resembled a pinprick. His guess was that the Colonel was shot with a blowgun or some such apparatus, only the poisoned dart was nowhere to be found. Louie complicated things, even more, when he reported that the camera showed that no one had entered or left the room between the time the Colonel left the room at 8:53, and when Lou and I unlocked the door at 3:23, and to the best of his knowledge no one had circumvented the Colonel's invention that kept others from entering the library through the passageway. Louie said someone could've done it, but it would've taken far longer than a murderer would've wanted to remain in the house. Because the camera was operational, and the Colonel hadn't entered the library through the customary door, that meant that when he returned from his errand that he had entered the library through the secret passageway. But why that way, instead of the way he usually entered? Could it be that someone held a weapon on the Colonel and forced his or her way into the library and didn't want to be photographed in the process? Still, that didn't compute, either. If someone had forced the Colonel into the library and shot him with a poisoned dart, how did that person get out? Only the Colonel knew how to open the passageway exit from the inside, and no one was hiding in the room below. Officers had checked that area thoroughly. I continued to look for a scenario where someone could've entered and exited the room without anyone knowing. Oh, where was John Dickson Carr, the author of the locked room mysteries, when I needed him?

While we were no closer to solving the case, a new development transpired just after we found out this information. An officer knocked on the library door and informed me that there was a man at the front door who wanted to talk to the man in charge. Curious, Lou and I followed the officer to the front door.

I opened the door and eyeballed the man who stood there. He was of medium height and weight and looked to be around my age. As far as I knew, he was no one I'd seen before.

"Are you the officer in charge?"

"I might be. And who might you be?"

"I'm Bob Downey. I live next door. Did something happen here today?"

"Why do you ask?"

"Well, there seems to be a lot of police here, many of them in uniform."

"Maybe we're having a meeting about the policeman's fund."

"Listen, I have some information you might be interested in."

"Such as?"

"Such as I saw someone enter this house this afternoon. Someone I'd never seen before, and someone who looked out of place here."

"Go on."

"See, this house sets back farther from the street than mine does, so I have a good view of this porch. Well, I was walking by my window when I saw something out of the corner of my eye. A man was almost at the front door of this house, almost where I am now. What caused me to stop and look was that not only didn't I recognize him, but he looked out of place on this street. See, he had long, unkempt hair and a beard. I thought he was a bum, and he'd come to my house next, so I was surprised when he removed a key from his pocket, unlocked the door, and entered the house. At least, that's what it looked like to me. Someone could have admitted him, but I think he used a key. Just in case something's missing, I wanted to report him. I hope I'm not getting an innocent man in trouble."

"No, you did the right thing. Would you recognize the man, if you saw him again?"

"I doubt it. He didn't turn and look at me. He just went about his business and opened the door, just like anyone else would. He didn't seem to be nervous. I wouldn't have thought another thing about it if I hadn't looked out a few minutes ago and seen some policemen heading to this house."

"Back to this man. What about his age? Hair color? Type of clothes he wore?"

"I'm sorry. I think he had light brown hair, and my guess is he was a young man, but other than that, I can't say."

"And you didn't see him leave?"

"No, I figured once he used the key that meant he belonged here. I didn't give it another thought until I saw some officers heading to this house. I debated with myself on whether or not I should report him. I'm pretty sure it wasn't any of the men who live here, so I decided to report it and let you do whatever you think is best."

"You did the right thing, Mr. Downey. I'll let you know if we have any other questions. Oh, one other thing. Did you see this man or any other stranger on the street about a week ago or at any other time since?"

"No. Normally this street has very little activity. That's one of the reasons I chose it when I moved here a couple of years ago."

Again, I thanked Downey for his information, closed the door, and wondered where this fits in. Was there a long-haired man, or was Downey our murderer and he had come forward to pass the blame on to someone else before he became a suspect. Time would tell.

The rest of the evening passed with no new developments. Nothing out of the ordinary was found in an upstairs search. I talked to each of the house's residents and found no one who acted guilty, but that didn't surprise me. No one acted guilty when Lou and I showed up for dinner, and a guilty person might've known why we were there those two nights.

When we'd finished going over the house, we allowed everyone to go to his or her room before Frank removed the body and everyone left the house. Lou and I were the last to leave. It had grown dark by the time we left.

For the third time that day, we arrived at the Blue Moon late for a meal. Thelma, like Rosie before her, was worried about us. We ate an uneventful meal and left. It was time to rest. The next day there was more work to be done.

10

I saw no reason to suppress the news, so the next morning all of Hilldale who read *The Hilldale Herald* knew of the Colonel's death. As I took a shower, I mulled over any possible actions Lou and I might take. We could go back to the house. We could canvass the neighborhood again to see if anyone other than Downey saw a stranger in the neighborhood, or Lou and I could go over the Colonel's Bible to see what clues it held for us. I could do any of those, but first I took out my notebook and called Sam Schumann, the best investigator in the business.

"This is Sam I Am, dining on green eggs and ham."

"Hasn't that stuff killed you yet?"

"I was wondering the same thing about that greasy spoon you and Lou call home. How are you this morning, Cy? I read the paper. I think I know why you're calling. It's time for me to go to work. Right?"

"That's why I've come to you, Sam. You're the best. If anyone can make our job easier, you're the man."

"Okay. Shoot. Who do you want me to check out?"

"I hope you have a lot of paper, Sam, because this may take a while."

"Ready when you're, Red Ryder."

"Start with those who lived in the house with the Colonel. That's his wife, his two granddaughters, his grandson-in-law, and Tom Brockman, the T.A. who rented a room from him. And you might as well include his friend Joe Guilfoyle in this. I don't think any of them did it, but we need to know. Find out where each of them was yesterday, and if any of them had any problems with the Colonel. Next, check out all of his neighbors, particularly Bob Downey, his newest neighbor. He's been there for two years and claims to have seen someone enter the house yesterday. Find out what you know about him. Also, there are some people we know who've been in the house this year; a plumber, an exterminator, and the mailman. Find out which plumber, and what exterminator they used. And there's a maid and handyman who come once a week, Earl and Myra Hoskins, find out what you can about them. Talk to the other people they work for. Also, last week the Colonel remembered three people he'd had problems with years ago, all of them at the university. Two were students, Daniel Terloff and Carla Bauerman. The other one was a guy who said the Colonel kept him from getting a permanent job with the university, Michael Belding. He's still in the area, a high school teacher. Just get this to me a little at a time, as soon as you can."

"Sure thing, Cy. Have you and Lou eaten breakfast yet?"

"That's next."

"Want to stop by for some green eggs and ham?"

"And forgo the best restaurant in six states. Just get to work."

I hung up the phone, picked it up again to tell Lou I was on my way and turned to leave. Just before I opened the door, the phone rang. Even Sam wasn't that quick, but I picked it up because I was curious. Very few people had my number.

Mary, the dispatcher on duty, was calling to tell me that a young man had seen someone about to enter the

Colonel's house on the previous afternoon. When I asked what the man had said, I was told that all that the caller could say is that the man had long, brown hair and a beard. I got the young man's name and address. He was a university student, and she said he would be home from class a little after 11:00. That gave Lou and me plenty of time to enjoy our breakfast if that was possible.

+++

I added a few ounces to my frame. Lou probably took off a few. Both of us smacked our lips a few times, and ambled to Lightning, redistributing our breakfasts as we went. I'd heard that there are devices you can put on your car to tell you the best way to go to get to where you want to go, but being a man of few vices or devices, I didn't have one of those, either. But if I find out that they can also tell a person where to find a parking space close by to cut down on walking, I might change my image and splurge on one of them. But in the meantime, because we were headed to an area near the university, we had to park a couple of blocks away from our destination, which allowed us an opportunity to slosh our breakfasts some more. Many huffs and puffs later, at least as far as I was concerned, we arrived at our destination to find out our witness lived on the third floor. If I'd known what he looked like, we might've waited until he left again, but since we didn't, Lou and I had to tackle the old-fashioned version of the Stairmaster. On the way up the steps, I remembered to ask Lou for our message of the day. "Something old, something new," he replied. There was no way I was going to get married, so no one had better come up with something borrowed and something blue.

A good half hour later, we arrived at the third floor a few ounces thinner. I wouldn't be a happy camper if we got up there only to find out the building had an elevator.

We found Mark Blakeman, a tall, thin, dark-haired, young man in apartment 3-A. We identified ourselves.

"So, you must really want this guy, huh?"

"Just tell us who and what you saw."

"Not much. Just some hippie dude that looked out of place."

"Did you actually see him enter the house?"

"Actually, I did. What tipped me off is that he came slinking around the side of the house like someone suspicious. He looked too old to be some doctor's son still living at home, so I figured he didn't belong. But when he took out a key, unlocked the door, and went in, I figured that maybe he did live there. When I saw this morning's headlines, I figured I'd better give you guys a call. See, I remembered the house because it's the biggest one on the street. I was hoping to get a delivery there, sometime."

"Delivery?"

"Yeah, that's the reason I was on the street. I deliver pizzas to pick up some extra money, and people in those rich neighborhoods tip a lot better than students do, so I used my seniority last fall to get that route. This is my third year delivering for Hometown Pizza."

"And can you tell me the name of the person you delivered the pizza to yesterday?"

"I believe their name is Wilson. Next to the last house in that block, on the other side of the street from the big house."

"Mark, do you by any chance know a man by the name of Bob Downey?"

"No. Is he a student?"

"No, just checking something."

"Well, if he's not a student or a professor, I wouldn't know him."

We ended our chit-chat and walked down the steps, wishing that we had gotten valet parking. At least Lightning hadn't been towed, and no one had plowed into my baby while we were gone. At least two men had seen the long-haired man. Had they also seen the one-armed man and the second gunman on the grassy knoll?

I wanted to check on Blakeman's alibi, so we swung by the scene of the crime and stopped at the next-to-last house on the right. As it turned out, their name was Wilson, and they had ordered a pizza the afternoon before. Evidently, there was a long-haired, bearded man, or someone disguised as one, and this person entered the Colonel's house the day before. More than likely, we had our murderer. We just didn't know if that is the way he normally looks, and where we might be able to find him. Or could it have been a woman wearing that getup? No one would expect someone wearing a disguise like that to be a woman, and neither of our witnesses was close enough to know for sure.

Sometimes Lou and I plan ahead. That day was one of those times. At breakfast, we informed Rosie that we had work to do and wouldn't be back for lunch. After she had dried her tears, she handed us four bowls of banana pudding. Actually, she put each bowl in a suitable box, then stacked them in a sack. That meant all we had to do was stop by Antonio's, pick up two foot-long Stromboli steak sandwiches, and two large orders of French fries with gravy. Then, we'd be set with all of the food groups God intended for us to eat. Well, counting our candy we'd have all of them.

We arrived at Antonio's, got out of Lightning, and walked inside. I ordered my usual foot-long Stromboli and a large order of fries with gravy. Then, Lou stepped up to order. He leaned over the counter and whispered, "I'll just take a small this time, and no fries for me." I had no idea if he was as embarrassed as I was, or if Lou was looking at me because I wasn't looking at him. I knew how demeaning it must have been for him to order the children's portion. We left Antonio's and were on our way to my house to eat lunch and peruse the Colonel's Bible.

Lou smiled as I drove down the street and neared my house.

"What's with you?"

Lou pointed.

"Is that your friend? Am I interrupting something, Cy?"

I slammed on the brakes and Lou and I tested our seatbelts. My neighbor stood in my yard near my driveway, and she had her pint-size bodyguard was with her. I thought about hitting the gas and gunning it. For the second time in a week, I regretted not having a more powerful vehicle. I pulled into the driveway, considered driving all the way to the end of the driveway and making a dash for the back door. I knew that I couldn't outmaneuver *that woman*. I made a mental note to call and find out how much it cost to get land mines planted in my neighbor's yard. Actually, it would do me no good. She is always in my yard.

I got out of the car and couldn't even get in the first word.

"Oh, Cyrus, you brought a friend. You didn't tell me we'd be having company for lunch."

"Miss Humphert, what are you doing in my yard?"

"Waiting for you, Cyrus. What do you think?"

"You know I already have a gun, and Posted signs are not that expensive."

"I don't know what you've got planned, Cyrus, but it sounds exciting."

"What I've planned is lunch, Miss Humphert. That is provided seeing you hasn't made me lose my appetite."

"Oh, Cyrus, you say the sweetest things. I'm willing to skip lunch if you're. And who is your cute friend? Will he be joining us? I wish you'd told me. I would have invited a friend for him."

"This, Miss Humphert, is my bodyguard. He's just been released on parole, so he hasn't had his shots yet. The last person he bit died. That's the reason he was in prison. Understand?"

"I sure do. Your friend hasn't had a date in a long time. I know just the woman for him. Will you excuse me while I go call her?"

"I'll never excuse you, Miss Humphert, but you're free to go. I hope you go far, and take Her Yippieness with you."

With that, I grabbed my food and dashed for the house. I dropped one of the Strombolis on the way. The one whose mouth was closest to the ground managed only to slobber on the plastic bag before I snatched it away. That was okay. It was the child's size sandwich.

Lou held everything in until we got inside and I shut and locked the door. Then, he let me have it in the best falsetto voice he could muster.

"Oh, Cyrus, it's so good to see you. Let me go call my friend so she can visit with your friend."

Surely things would improve.

+++

It took only a bite of Stromboli and French fries with gravy to wipe away the visions of my next-door neighbor from my mind. It was a little bit out of character, but I decided to wait on the banana pudding until the first time deciphering the message in the Colonel's Bible frustrated us. I had a feeling that the pudding wouldn't wait long.

We cleared the crumbs and such from the dining room table and washed our hands. I went to get the Bible, still wrapped from the day before.

"Okay, Lou, let's see what we have here."

Whatever it was wasn't going to be easy. I could smell the pudding already. I looked at all the cards. Most of them were blank. I would've felt better if all of them were blank, but there were three in the book of *Obadiah*. Two of them had a +2 on them and the other one a +3. What did that mean? Also, one of the ones that fell out had an arrow on it. What did that mean? This way to the buried treasure? I turned to Lou and smiled.

"Don't tell me that you've already figured it out, Cy?"

"Okay, I won't tell you."

"You mean you have?"

"Well, I've figured out one thing."

"What's that, Cy?"

"I've figured out that the Colonel thought you and I are smarter than we are if he expected us to figure this out."

Lou laughed.

"Well, he had to make it tough, so the murderer wouldn't guess."

"The murderer already knows who he or she is. The murderer won't need to guess."

"You know what I mean, Cy. Besides, we'll figure it out if we give it enough time."

"Any idea, Cy?"

"Yeah, one. You look this over while I eat four bowls of pudding."

"Cy, I've been meaning to tell you. I had already planned to give you one of my bowls of pudding."

It's so sad to see someone you care for go downhill, but Lou had turned into a shell of the man he once was. I wondered if there was some kind of antidote for the Wii thing. But how could I find out? I didn't know about that stuff, and more than likely anyone who knew had already turned into one of *them*.

As I contemplated what to do to save Lou, he broke the silence.

"Cy, I can see how touched you are that I am willing to share one of my bowls of pudding with you."

Touched was the word I was thinking of, but I wasn't the one who was touched. What if I found out that the whole world had been turned into Wii people, except for my next-door neighbor? Would I be willing to turn to her in order to save my best friend?

My head cleared and I looked at the problem before us. The longer we put off working on the Colonel's puzzle, the longer it would take us to solve it. Still, I was smart enough that I would never agree with whoever said: "beginning is half done." We looked at our written list; *Exodus, Leviticus, Ruth, 1 Samuel, 1 Kings, 1 Chronicles, Ecclesiastes, Song of Songs, Lamentations, Amos, Obadiah, Micah, 1 Corinthians, Colossians, 1 Thessalonians, 1 Timothy, 1 Peter,* and *1 John*. All of the books contained only one card, except for *Obadiah*. Some of the books listed were named for people. Some were not. There didn't seem to be anything there that identified one suspect over the others. The best idea we came up with at the time was to split up. Lou copied down the page numbers. We hoped there was some numerical code that would help us. Since we didn't know whether the Colonel meant the left- or right-hand page, he copied both numbers. I decided to tackle it from a word perspective, which made more sense.

I looked at the written list of books. There were a lot more consonants than vowels. As a matter of fact, there were so few vowels there didn't seem to be enough of them to make words. Still, I persisted. Few would believe me if I told them that Lou and I worked on the code for an hour before we tackled the first bowl of pudding. But, we did.

I devoured my first bowl in record time. Lou took a couple of bites before returning the bowl to the refrigerator, planning to take another couple of bites later. If I wasn't afraid of catching Lou's germs I would have finished his bowl. More than likely, the creature he had turned into wouldn't notice for at least a couple of days.

Thirty seconds after I wiped the last of the pudding from my mouth, we returned to the task at hand. In order to look at things from a different perspective, we traded places. In a matter of minutes, both of us realized that we were getting nowhere.

"Let's open the Bible again, Cy. Maybe it will give us a revelation."

"I was thinking about praying, instead. Both could help, and God knows that neither will hurt us."

The numbers made no sense. Neither did the letters, but I was still convinced the letters were the way to go. The afternoon was wasting away and still, we had no idea what the Colonel was trying to tell us. It was only then that we really did open the Bible and study the index cards. We turned the pages from one card to another, careful to keep any other cards from falling from the Bible.

"Lou, if all the cards that fell out were vowels, would that give us enough letters to make words?"

Lou's "It could," wasn't enough to inspire me, but his revelation did.

"Notice something, Cy. The Colonel put some of these cards at the first of each book, but not all of them. Still, the farthest into any book that any of them are is in the fourth chapter. Let's separate them and see what we come up with. We did, and I became excited until we had separated them and written them down. They still didn't make any sense, only they made no sense in four words, rather than one. Since some of them could've been in more than one word, because there were two or three chapters on some pages, we wrote down those letters for all the words they might belong to.

Our efforts gave us the following hieroglyphics.

EAMC
LSKCCTTPJ
LRECT
LESL

We didn't know where the three Os went, and we had four other letters leftover as if that would help.

"Lou, you wouldn't happen to have Vanna White's cell phone number, would you?"

"No, and I don't have Regis's either, so you can't phone a friend. It's just you and me unless you want your next-door neighbor to take a look at this."

"Bite your tongue."

We looked at the four lines. They made as much sense as the eye chart Andy Griffith looked at in *No Time For Sergeants*. Four things immediately came to mind, none of which made sense. If all the letters in the first word were there, they could spell "mace" or "came." The second word was missing a boatload of vowels, and the third word seemed to be missing at least one. The fourth word could be "sell," provided it was intact. But "mace," "came," and "sell" made no sense. My best guess was that the murderer used mace on the Colonel, but if so, the Colonel wouldn't have been able to provide this code for us, and the murderer wouldn't have been able to enter or exit the library, depending on where he or she committed the crime. I felt we were a little closer to where we needed to be but had a long way to go.

11

We worked until we needed another break. I scooped out two more bites of banana pudding for Lou and returned his bowl to the refrigerator. Then I picked up my own bowl. I smiled when I remembered I still had one bowl left. Maybe Lou's newfound lifestyle might not be so bad on me. I had taken only a couple of bites of my pudding when the phone rang. I answered it as I swallowed the glob of pudding I had in my mouth.

"You okay, Cy."

"Yeah, Frank, you just caught me in the middle of eating something."

"So, you're eating while the rest of us are hard at work."

"Lou and I are hard at work too, trying to figure out this stupid puzzle the Colonel left us. Want to change places?"

"Did you forget what I do, Cy, which, incidentally, is why I called you? I have the autopsy results. The deceased was shot with a poisonous dart. Curare. As you might know, it's native to Central and South America. Curare is harmless if swallowed, but fatal if someone is shot with it. Death was almost instantaneous."

"That means the killer had to have been in the room with him, but how was that possible? Could it have been someone he knew and trusted who had turned against him? And if so, how did he or she get out of the room?"

"And that is the reason why I don't want to trade places with you, Cy. Most of the time, I can finish my job in a few hours."

"Speaking of hours, do you have any idea what time the murder took place?"

"As best I can diagnose it, you found him not long after he died."

"You mean like minutes?"

"Well, let's leave a two-hour window to be on the safe side. He definitely died after noon, and probably closer to 2:00 or 3:00."

"He told his wife he'd fix something for lunch. Did he eat that lunch?"

"No, his stomach showed he'd eaten nothing since breakfast."

"Thanks, Frank. I appreciate all your help."

"Say, Cy, back to the food. What were you eating?"

"Still am. It's banana pudding."

"You fixed instant banana pudding, all by yourself."

"No, but the one who takes good care of Lou and me gave us four bowls when she learned that we would be working too hard to make it back for lunch."

"And who did you share the other two bowls with?"

"Lou, but since he's gone through that change, he let me have one of his bowls."

"Change? Oh, you mean his Wii Fit workout. I'm getting one of those, just as soon as you quit bringing me bodies to autopsy."

Was there time to save Frank? Evidently, he hadn't become one of them yet, but he was tempted.

"Cy, are you there?"

"Oh, sorry, Frank. I was just thinking about something."

"Well, I'll let you get back to what you were doing. Enjoy your pudding, and try to take it easy when it comes to finding dead bodies."

"I'll do my best. I wouldn't want you to become overworked like we are."

I hung up the phone, turned and shared the news with Lou. Not only did we have no idea who murdered the Colonel, but we also had no idea how he or she did it. In the old days, a murderer would leave the dart in the victim. These days, I guess people who murder others using poisonous darts are afraid of getting caught by their DNA or like to reuse their poisonous darts.

I was tempted to put a bib on Lou and feed him his two bites of pudding, but I refrained. I finished my second bowl of banana pudding and returned to work. Too bad we couldn't make quick work of our perplexing puzzle like I had the pudding.

When we hadn't gotten anywhere in a reasonable period of time we agreed to adjourn to two more comfortable chairs to discuss the case.

After a few minutes, frustrated, and remembering the Colonel's and the Chief's words, we decided to let things rest until morning. Lou, an avid worker of crossword puzzles, told me of the many times he had put a baffling puzzle down, only to solve a new part of it the next time he picked it up. We both hoped that the same would be true in this case. Also, we realized that more than likely Sam Schumann would have some information for us the next morning. Not everything, but enough for us to know what avenues to explore and which ones to ignore.

+++

Lou and I had found out that the type of mystery we preferred to read was called a cozy mystery. Cozy mystery. That sounded good. Like curling up in front of the fireplace on a cold winter's night. The years had helped me block

Eunice from my mind most of the time, but there was something about curling up in front of a fireplace that made me hunger for the wife who was taken from me much too soon. I wanted to rid my mind of sad thoughts, so I asked Lou the question I contemplated just a short time before.

"So, Lou, have you ever thought about what fictional detective you'd be if you could be anyone you've read about?"

"I think I'd like to experience a little of all of them. Then I'd be better equipped to make that decision. I'd love to walk the foggy streets of London like Sherlock Holmes, and ride in a hansom cab."

"I'd say by the time February came, you'd want to be somewhere else."

"Oh, there's nothing like a winter breeze to ignite the brain particles."

"You mean those *leetle gray cells*, as Hercule Poirot calls them?"

"Well, you can say one thing. Hercule Poirot always thought he had plenty of them. He never lacked confidence."

I couldn't say as much for myself. More than once since the Colonel died I wondered if this would be the first case that we couldn't solve.

We wanted to be refreshed for the next day, so Lou and I called it a night. I dropped him at his apartment and stampeded for home. God was with me because my next-door neighbor wasn't.

12

I woke Wednesday morning feeling refreshed. The extra hour of sleep did wonders for me. Well, not wonders. I wandered to the mirror and found out I looked like I looked the day before, but I felt better. I vowed to make it a point to get an extra hour of sleep more often. I hoped the way I felt might translate to a break in the case. I wouldn't tell Lou, but I made a decision to take a bubble bath and mull over the case. Then I realized that real men don't take bubble baths, so I settled for just a regular bath and settled myself down in the tub. My mind wandered to what I'd find out, not what I already knew, so I got nowhere, except for a few wrinkles for lounging too long in the tub. During my contemplation, I wondered what information Sam had discovered for us, and what clue God would give Lou for the day. After realizing that no one would deliver my breakfast to me, and I wouldn't want anyone to see me if someone did deliver it, I partook of my morning exercise and pulled myself from the tub. I'm not saying that it took me a while to do so, but my arms were dry before my feet stepped from the tub.

I dressed, read my morning devotional, prayed that my neighbor would find a new home far away, and called Sam.

"This is Sam I Am dining on green eggs and ham."

"So Sam You are, what have you gotten for me so far?"

"Well, Cy, let's just say that I've been unable to narrow your list of suspects."

"And that means?"

"I located someone who saw Mrs. Hardesty at the mall a little after 10:00, but that wouldn't prevent her from returning home and murdering her husband. And the oldest granddaughter, Jennifer, skipped her last class yesterday. Plus, I talked to someone in the school library who said that Jennifer's husband, Scott, wasn't in there during the afternoon, like he usually is. Now on to the youngest granddaughter, Trish. Nothing suspicious about her, but her last class ended at 1:50, so she had time to get home, do away with her grandfather, and get away before anyone discovered her. As for Hardesty's friend Joe, he left home at 1:00 and didn't return until late. You saw him before he returned home. Nothing suspicious yet about any of the neighbors. All of the ones who have jobs were at those jobs on the day of the murder. All of the ones who don't have jobs have alibis, except for one elderly woman who said she was home alone and saw nothing. All I can tell you about Bob Downey is what I found out locally. He claims that for most of his adult life he was an over-the-road trucker who hauled for many different people. He said he has had no home since his mother died when he was young, and he, his dad, and his uncle traveled all the time. That's how he became a trucker. He told someone he has saved his money all his life, finally got tired of drifting and decided to settle down. The only reason he gave for settling down in Hilldale is that this was the closest town when he decided he had had enough. The only other people I've had time to check on so far are the maid and handyman, Earl and Myra Hoskins. According to the woman they worked for that day, Myra was there all day, but Earl went out in the afternoon with the premise of getting a part so he could fix the lawnmower. He was gone a long time, and so far I've located no one who saw him while he was out. So, that's what I've so far. I went ahead and tackled the locals first because I realized that they would be the easiest, and I wanted to give you something to get you started. I will start on the others today, but it might take a while to find out about some of them."

It bothered me that none of the Colonel's family had an alibi. I didn't want the killer to be one of them.

"Oh, Sam, you forgot one. What about Tom Brockman, the man at the university who rents a room from the Hardestys?"

"Oh, sorry, Cy. I've gotten a little on him, too. He wasn't in class yesterday afternoon, nor was he in his office. I've yet to find an alibi for him, either."

"Well, keep checking, Sam. I'll see what I can find out on this end."

+++

I hung up from talking to Sam and called the funeral home to check on the time of visitation and the funeral for the Colonel. Lou and I would be at both, and in two capacities. I learned that visitation would be today at the funeral home, from 4:00-8:00. The funeral would be tomorrow morning at 11:00 at the church.

I didn't want to confront the family so soon after the murder, but I wouldn't have been as accommodating if I didn't know the Colonel, so I followed normal procedure. Besides, I wanted to get it over with, so I called Martha to tell her I needed to stop by.

"Martha. Cy. Sorry to bother you so early, but there are some early developments in the case, and I want to eliminate all family members as soon as possible. Is everyone home this morning?"

"Yes. Naturally, Jennifer and Trish are skipping classes today, and Tom didn't feel like teaching his classes, so he called and got someone to cover for him."

"Well, I'd like to stop by this morning with just a few questions. How does 10:00 sound?"

"I guess the earlier the better."

"Okay, Lou and I will see you then."

+++

Even with an extra hour of sleep, my stomach told me it was time to pick up Lou and head to the Blue Moon. I had never known my stomach to lie to me, so I followed its guidance.

My luck continued. My neighbor was nowhere to be found. Maybe she wasn't going to show her face again until she found a friend for Lou, and she hadn't made a friend yet. Who am I to spit in the face of good luck? I merely thanked God and skedaddled to Lou. I was surprised to see him waiting at the curb.

"What's the matter, Lou? A skunk get into your apartment?"

"No, I knew you'd be hungry. I wanted to save us a few precious seconds."

"Good, you can use those seconds to let me know God's message for the day."

"You will not pass 'Go.' You will not collect $200."

"So what are we doing today? Playing Monopoly or going to jail?"

"My guess is neither one."

"Then what does the message mean?"

"Maybe it means we won't get anywhere today."

"Then why are we out here?"

"I don't know about you, Cy, but I'm out here to get breakfast."

We continued to go back and forth until we arrived at the Blue Moon. We were no closer to identifying what the clue meant, but at least we managed to keep our minds off of food until we pulled up in front of our feeding troughs.

We must've gotten there early because there were still other patrons in the diner. The nerve of some people, infiltrating our private domain. At least we wouldn't have to get rough. No one was sitting on our stools.

Rosie smiled at us. We smiled back. It's always a good idea to smile at those who are mainly responsible for your paycheck, and Rosie knew which side of the bread contained her butter. Lou and I knew that we weren't to bite the hand that feeds us, but to smile upon the favor that God bestows upon us. I had a little more energy than usual, so I sort of jumped up onto the stool. I wouldn't call my mount graceful, and I received a low score from the Ukrainian judge. I hadn't yet perfected the triple Salchow, and I wouldn't try it again.

Lou, who looked like he'd wasted away a little more each day, sidled up to his stool and mounted it without using his hands. Poor guy! He no longer had enough strength in his arms to lift himself up onto his stool. I wondered how long before he'd have to check into a nursing home.

13

Martha greeted us almost as soon as we rang the bell. She seemed nervous and distraught. My emotions matched hers. I looked around, saw no one else, and again asked her where she went Monday, and if anyone saw her. She appeared not to be thinking clearly and was no help to me. I asked to borrow the same room for questioning that we had used before and asked her to send Jennifer in first.

The tall, pretty, young woman with hair the color of honey walked in. She was more composed than her grandmother.

"Please, have a seat, Jennifer. This will take only a few minutes."

Jennifer sat and Lou and I took chairs across from her.

"Jennifer, tell me where you were Monday afternoon."

"I was at school on Monday."

"But you skipped your last class. Why?"

"Actually I had the prof's permission, and Scott wanted me to go somewhere with him."

"And where did you go?"

"I'll tell you, Lieutenant, but please don't tell Gram. She might get the wrong idea. Scott wants us to start a family. I prefer to wait until we both finish school. Scott doesn't think this place is conducive to raising a family. I think Gram would love a baby in the house, especially now. I love my husband, but I think he's moving too quickly."

"You don't think your grandmother knows. What about your grandfather? Did he know?"

"I don't think so. Neither of us ever said anything to him."

"So where did the two of you go on Monday?"

"There's a little house for sale over on Mulberry. We went by and looked at it."

"So a realtor can vouch that you were there?"

"No, we just stopped by, looked in the windows, looked around out back. Lieutenant, do you think I'm wrong for dragging my feet? I want to do what's right for my marriage."

"That's something the two of you have to work out for yourselves."

I could see I wasn't getting anything else out of Jennifer, so I had Lou go get her husband. If they hadn't had time to agree on where they were on Monday, I didn't want to give them a chance to do so before I talked to each of them separately.

It didn't matter. Scott's story agreed with his wife's. The only other thing I could get out of Scott was that in some ways he was tired of living in a castle where he had only one room to call his own and someone else decided the menu and at what time they ate.

+++

After Scott left, Lou escorted Trish into the den and asked her to have a seat.

"Sorry to have to talk to you under these circumstances, Trish, but I needed to check with everyone. Where were you on Monday afternoon?"

"Well, I had class until 1:50. Then I went to the Student Center to grab some lunch. See, I have classes from 10:00 on, and 2:00 is the first chance I have to eat. It was tough at first, but I've gotten used to it."

"And what time did you leave the Student Center?"

"Probably a little after 3:30. I'm not sure."

"Why did you stay so long?"

"Well, I took my time eating and studying, and then I got to talking to a couple of people."

"Can anyone verify that you were there?"

"I'm not sure. I mean I'm sure there are people who can say they saw me, but whether or not they'll remember that it was Monday, I'm not sure."

"But you're sure it was Monday?"

"Of course, Lieutenant. Monday was the day my life turned upside down. I loved Gramps. I'll miss him. I should've told him that more often, but he seemed to be in the library all the time. I mean unless we were eating. I didn't get time alone with him the way I used to."

With that, Trish shed a few tears. They seemed genuine, but women have a way of manipulating men any time they feel the need.

+++

Tom Brockman was the only one left to question. As soon as he sat down I confronted him on where he was on Monday afternoon.

"In my office."

"We have witnesses who say you weren't."

"But I was. I was trying to get caught up on some things. I locked the door and didn't answer the phone. I received a couple of calls and someone knocked on the door, but I didn't answer either."

I let him go. I'd check with Sam to see if his witness checked the door to see if it was locked. Our questioning was over. No one had an alibi that satisfied me, but no one incriminated himself or herself.

+++

92

On the way to my place, Lou and I devised a plan. Because some of the cards were on pages where two chapters were listed, first we'd look at those that were on a page with only one chapter. We knew which word those letters went in.

I got a clean sheet of paper and wrote down only those letters.

$$E\ A\ M\ C$$
$$S\ K\ C\ T\ P\ J$$
$$R$$
$$L$$

I studied the letters and immediately formed an opinion. Evidently, the extra hour of sleep did me no good. Only the first word remained the same. All of the letters of the first time remained intact. We were down to three possibilities. Either the first word was "mace," or "came," or it contained one or more of the three "O's" or some combination of the missing four letters, none of which we could possibly identify.

We wanted to get all of our stupid ideas out of the way as soon as possible, so we wrote down all the letters of the alphabet to see how many of them were the first letter of any book of the Bible. Well, at least it was quick. That's more than can be said for any other idea we had. After only a few minutes, we were able to eliminate B, F, Q, U, V, W, X, Y, and Z. Because so many words include the letters Q, V, X, Y, and Z, we were able to eliminate one-quarter of one percent of all the words of the English language. If we continued to make breakthroughs such as this, this puzzle could have been solved within a couple of generations, or long after the murderer has died by other means. The more I thought of this, the more I wondered why the Colonel didn't write us a note that said: "The Murderer is So-And-So." If the murderer didn't find the note, Lou and I could've solved this case before dinner the first night. If the murderer did find the note, at least Lou and I wouldn't have been sitting there trying to solve some stupid cryptogram.

Deep down Lou and I believed we'd solve the puzzle, and when we did, we'd say, "Why in the world didn't we think of that earlier?"

In the meantime, my brain had melted. Lou knew I'd lost it when he saw me go to the kitchen, pick up a knife, and bring it to the table where I proceeded to cut up an entire Hershey Almond bar until I had sixteen squares. Why sixteen? Who knows? I surely didn't. It was an awful sight. There were slivers of chocolate everywhere. For the first time in my life, I'd cut almonds in half. Lou remained silent as I took my index finger and moved the squares around until I had four lines of chocolate squares, four lines of blank chocolate that offered me almost as much information as the letters on the paper in front of me.

Lou figured that it's easier to join them than lick them, so he tore open a package of M&Ms and poured them on my dining room table. He too made four lines, only his lines were color-coded.

Jealous that he was able to color code his experiment, I moved on to something he couldn't do as easily as I. I stacked my squares. Lou tried to stack his too, but they kept falling off. Frustrated, Lou took one of his M&Ms and placed it on his thumb the way he would a marble, took aim, and sent my chocolate squares flying across the table. Oh, I still had a stack, but my stack was reduced to four squares. I was amazed that Lou could generate enough power to knock over a chocolate square that was heavier than the M&M projectile, but then I was never much good in science class.

We sat there and stared at the mess, then turned and looked at each other. We laughed until we cried. True, it wasn't very mature, and certainly not dignified, but you have to admit, it's much better than taking out a gun and blasting the candy into submission. If we ever do that, I think someone will find a place for us, and it will not be the Blue Moon, either.

It seems like there comes a time in every case when Lou and I crack and begin to act crazy. Well, crazier than usual. But each time we do, it releases our frustrations, and it calms us.

I'd like to say that this fit of madness settled us enough that we were able to solve the puzzle in a matter of minutes. I'd like to say so, but it didn't. Instead, the two of us sat there silently thinking of new ways to approach the puzzle.

+++

"So, Lou, what do we know so far?"

"We know that visitation will begin before long, and we'd better start getting ready if we don't want to be late."

Neither of us liked wearing a coat and tie, so we decided we'd go comfy for visitation and dress up for the funeral. If someone said something about us not dressing up for the visitation, we'd tell them we were on surveillance and that we have designated clothing for that. None of them would have known the difference. Lou had brought a change of clothes, just in case he spotted the ones he was wearing contained something from the breakfast or lunch menu. It was a wise decision, although he did make it through breakfast unscathed.

+++

Neither of us was prepared to see our mentor in a casket. Even at seventy-five, the Colonel seemed so alive, and in the casket, he looked like someone else. Oh, he still looked like the Colonel, but it didn't seem right.

I think it helped put Martha at ease as she came up beside us and realized that even cops sometimes shed tears.

"It was nice of you boys to come."

The words, "We wouldn't have missed it for anything," didn't seem appropriate, so I merely nodded.

Lou and I planned to stay for the entire time of visitation. We planned to blend in, and see what we could learn. Besides, I couldn't see one of us hiding behind a potted plant, while the other one hunkered down, hidden by a spray of flowers. We wanted to observe everyone, make a note of who came and who didn't, and see if anyone looked guilty. We didn't expect to solve the murder that night, and we got what we expected. I hoped that four trips to the restroom each didn't seem superfluous. I didn't know about Lou, but I actually had to go once. Each time I "went," I checked the mirror before I returned, just to make sure there were no traces of chocolate on or around my mouth.

+++

After the visitation, Lou and I headed to eat. On the way to Lou's apartment, he informed me that because he had eaten more than he had been used to eating lately, that he would Wii before he went to bed. Also, he let me know that someone had stolen a bear trap that someone had left outside of his window, but that he doubted if they would fare as well if they tried to dig up the minefield that had been planted there. I knew at least one person who would stay out of the minefield, and I felt sorry for the next of kin of the next person to mow Lou's lawn. After I dropped off Lou, I wondered how powerful my binoculars were. I quickly dismissed that thought as I envisioned Officer Davis tapping me on the shoulder, wondering what I was doing in the bushes next door to Lou's apartment building.

14

I woke up Thursday morning wanting to put closure to the whole business, but I knew that closure wouldn't come until Lou and I solved the case. I'd told Sam about the funeral and promised him I would call when I got in, or Friday morning.

Our schedule would in no way resemble our normal routine. I allowed myself enough time to tie and retie whatever tie I could rummage through the closet and find. I had many ties to choose from, and some of them had probably been out of style long enough that they were back in style. With winter giving way to spring, so to speak, I selected a tan suit that I had last worn four years ago. It had been dry cleaned and was suffocating in a garment bag. I tried on the pants, then the coat. Both fit, so I wouldn't have to go to Plan B. While my size is greater than the size of most men, my weight seldom fluctuates. I chalk it up to eating the right foods. My doctor claims it is due to good metabolism.

My suit was a solid color. So was my shirt. So, I chose a tie with a pattern in it. I refrained from selecting one that looked like I had spent time in a fingerpainting class, but I wanted something that added a little color to my ensemble. While ensemble sounds like something a runway model might wear, every now and then I choose words unbefitting my lifestyle, and most words of three syllables or more are unbefitting my lifestyle.

I had two choices when it came to my neckwear. I could see if I still remembered how to tie a tie, or I could check with my next-door neighbor to see if she knew how to tie one. I wish all my choices were so easy. I pictured myself lying on Heloise Humphert's couch with her straddling me, her hot breath nauseating me, while she suggested that she could better tie my tie if she unbuttoned my shirt first. It had been years since I had had a nightmare so ghastly.

I ripped the tie from the tie rack and wrapped it around my neck. Five minutes into the proceedings, I wished I'd chosen a pre-tied tie, but I persisted until I'd formed something that resembled a tie. I've never owned a turtleneck shirt. I consider them almost as effeminate as those short socks some men wear these days, the ones that don't even cover their ankles. A day and a half later, I emerged from the bathroom, not quite ready for GQ, but with a tie tied in a manly sort of way.

+++

I had parked in the back the night before, hoping to make an undetected getaway on the morning of the funeral. On more than one morning in the past few days, I had stepped out to one of the more joyous sounds of God's creation, a robin's call. Nothing announced the coming of spring quite like a robin, and the robins had been back for at least a month.

On the morning of the funeral, however, all the robins were in hiding, keeping out of the way of a spring downpour. I reached back into the kitchen and grabbed an umbrella. I poked it out into the rain and hit the mechanism that made it useful. Once accomplished, I strutted to Lightning like I was somebody.

I was pleased with my look until I pulled up in front of Lou's building. He must've ventured over to Thelma Lou's. No man who hasn't worn a tie in years can remember how to tie one so well. No longer was I so proud of my manly look, but I wasn't about to let another man put his hands around my neck. I took some comfort in the fact that Lou had to keep pulling up his pants as he walked. I needed to get him back to where his pants fit him.

Lou sat down in the car, looking glum. I thought it was because of the Colonel.

"I know how you feel, Lou."

"I don't think you do, Cy. See, after all that feasting we did yesterday, I gained two-tenths of a pound. And I even Wiied when I got home last night. For thirty minutes."

The "praise the Lord" I uttered about Lou's good news didn't seem to pacify him. I tried to convince him that, more than likely, it was those last two bites of vegetables that did it. I don't think he bought my story. While I was disappointed that he'd gained only two-tenths of a pound, it was a start. Maybe Lou was on the road to recovery. At the same time, I had to convince Lou that two-tenths of a pound wasn't much. I didn't want him to think he needed to fast for two days, or worse yet, eat plain yogurt.

+++

Neither Lou nor I wanted Rosie to see us dressed like we were. She might have gotten ideas about changing the Blue Moon's dress code, and then where would we be. Besides, we were pressed for time. Lightning zipped into the drive-thru lane at a local fast-food restaurant. I ordered two steak and egg biscuits with two orders of hash rounds to keep them company, and a Large Diet Pepsi to wash all of it down. Lou followed suit, only he ordered one measly pork chop biscuit and no hash rounds. Whatever disease he had, he hadn't gotten over it.

Fifteen minutes later, we arrived at the church with no breakfast staining our clothes, only a few crumbs to brush away. A man motioned for us to stop and asked if we were family and if we would be going to the cemetery. I answered "yes" to both. After all, the Colonel's boys had to be family.

The rain stopped just before we arrived at the church, but I reached back into the car and grabbed my umbrella just in case it began again. I was so nervous about doing the right thing that I failed to see someone step from behind an adjacent car. In a matter of seconds, the resident paparazzi, otherwise known as our good friend Lt. George Michaelson, had snapped our picture.

"Well, what do we have here? You look like a couple of guys I know. Do you by any chance know Cy Dekker and Lou Murdock?"

"Never heard of them," I replied.

"Well, I must say you're better off. Say, Cy, stand still a minute. I need to fix your tie."

"I fixed it before I came."

"From the looks of it," Lou interjected, "I think his next-door neighbor messed it up when she kissed him goodbye."

I was so flustered that George had straightened my tie before I realized it.

"In all seriousness, guys, I know how hard this must be for the two of you. I wanted to be here for you."

George's words didn't cause me to tear up or grab him and hug him, but I felt like doing both.

We entered the front of the church and made our way down the aisle. George was in the lead. I motioned for him to go as close to the front as possible, then move to the far side. I wanted to observe the other mourners, see who came, and how they reacted.

I don't remember much of what the pastor shared that day, because each time he said something that reminded me of the Colonel, my mind wandered back to days gone by and times Lou and I spent with him. Before I knew it, Lou punched me that it was time to go. We got up, filed past the casket, and out of the church. George agreed to drive to the cemetery, but since Lightning was already in line to do so, we asked George to go with us. I wish I had a picture of George's six-foot-three-inch frame as he sat in the back of my VW.

It was fitting that the sun came out just as the pastor said his final words at the cemetery. Lou and I approached Martha and her granddaughters as she exited the tent at the gravesite, and she invited us over to the house. She said several church members, friends, and neighbors had brought enough food to feed even Lou and me, so we accepted. We dropped George off at the church, because he had to get back to work, and headed to the home we'll always think of as the Colonel's home.

Since Thursday was Earl and Myra Hoskins's day to work at the Colonel's, both were there and had agreed to serve. They were still getting things set up when Lou and I arrived, so the two of us stepped out back and relived more memories of the three of us and our treehouse. I felt like setting the pulley in motion and hoisting myself to the top to see if the Colonel awaited us. I still hadn't gotten used to the fact that the Colonel continued to live only in our memories. One day, Lou and I will catch up with him, but the day of his funeral wasn't the day.

As Lou and I stared at our childhood sanctuary, I heard a noise behind me. The footsteps were Jennifer's.

"Gram told me that Gramps built that for you. I bet you had some happy times up there. Did he ever go up with you?"

"Sometimes, but his happiness was knowing that Lou and I enjoyed it. We spent many a time up there. Sometimes in the rain, if there were no strong winds or lightning, and at least once a year we spent the night up there. And anytime something was bothering us and we wanted to get away, we knew we had somewhere to go."

"You mean, like now."

"Yes, like now, Jennifer."

The young woman stepped between Lou and me and put her arms around us.

"Gramps was so proud of both of you. Find his killer."

"I promise you we'll do that much."

After a few moments of silence, the three of us went in to join the others.

Martha wasn't kidding about the food. Not only was there enough for Lou and me, but there was also enough for the others, too. The Colonel's friend Joe was there with his wife, as were a few others who were close to the Colonel. Were any of them responsible for his death? We promised to find out, but not that day.

15

We excused ourselves a little after two, ready to get back to work.

"Say, Lou, since I had my mind on the funeral this morning, I forgot to ask you today's clue."

"And the first shall be second."

"What's that supposed to mean?"

"Cy, some of us have been given the gift of speaking in riddles. Others have been given the gift of solving those riddles."

"Well, have you by any chance brought one of the solvers with you?"

"Apparently not."

"Okay, let's look at it. First of all, I thought it was 'the last shall be first.'"

"Maybe the second is the last. There might be only two of them, whatever they are."

"Maybe they're twins, and the second born is to rule the firstborn."

"Okay, by me, Cy. You're older than I am, so I am now in charge."

"'I don't think that's what God meant. To me, it sounds like there was a race, and there's been an inquiry. The horse that won has been disqualified and placed second.

Regardless, just because the first is to become the second doesn't mean the second is to become the first. Maybe it's like there's a new girl in the class and everyone's been moved back one spot."

"Cy, did you forget to take your medication again?"

We got back to my house and shuffled our carcasses inside. It was time to go to work. I plopped down at my customary spot at the table and Lou took his.

"And the second shall be first. Do you think it means we need to put the second word before the first word, or do we discard the first letters in the second word?"

We remembered that the second word had a mishmash of letters and decided to try that first. After looking at A, I, H, O, H, I, E, and O, we realized that we'd traded too many consonants for too many vowels. Wasn't there something in between? At least we could make songs out of what we changed to. Who doesn't like singing "Hi, ho, hi, ho, it's off to work we go?" Even those who are not eager to go off to work and those that aren't sure if it is "heigh-ho" or "hi ho" love singing that song. And then for those who like to jazz their songs up a little, there's "Hi-De-Ho." And then I thought of "Old MacDonald had a farm. A I H O H", or was it "O H I E O." Maybe Old MacDonald's farm was in Ohio, only they talk funny and pronounce it Ohieo up there. I caught Lou's look and realized I was off in la-la land. I shook my head, hoping to get all my brain cells back in place, then turned to my partner with another suggestion.

"Lou, let's just take the first two words. Let's write down the books listed in each word and see what we come up with."

Lou was agreeable to anything, so we set to work on our latest idea. The first word gave us Exodus, Amos, Micah, and Colossians. I liked things better when we had to choose between "mace" and "came."

"See anything there, Lou?"

"Yeah, I see three Old Testament books and one New Testament book. One of them is a long book and the others are relatively short."

"Thank you, Sergeant Obvious. Might you also add that two of them are named for prophets, one is named for a group of people, and the other one is named for something a group of people did and the book tells about how long it took them to do it and why?"

He got my point.

"Let's try the second word, Cy."

Lou and I are a little slow at times, but if you hit us over the head hard enough, we get the point. That was true when we wrote down the names of the books in the second clue. 1 Samuel, 1 Kings, 1 Chronicles, 1 Corinthians, 1 Thessalonians, 1 Timothy, 1 Peter, and 1 John.

"What do you see this time, Lou?"

"It looks like a bunch of 'Firsts.' Like the second shall be first. Do you think maybe the Colonel wasn't giving us a mishmash of consonants, but letting us know that the second word is 'first?'"

"You think? Now, let's see if we can make some sense out of these first two words. Give me some help here. You're the one who solves all those puzzles."

"Mace first. Came first. I've got it, Cy. Which came first word three or word four? What do you think?"

"I think you retired a wee bit too late. So you don't think words three and four are 'chicken' and 'egg?' Well, at least we're making some progress. We know that the letters E, A, M, and C are all in the first word in some order. We know that there are four other letters that would've helped us more quickly if the Colonel hadn't pulled them out when he fell and pulled the Bible off the desk, and we know that we can buy an O or two if we need one. Is there anything else we know, Lou?"

Finally, we were making progress on the puzzle. I didn't want to leave it, but I did want to reward myself for identifying one word. I jumped, hurried to the kitchen, and yanked a Hershey bar from the fridge. I plucked a knife from a kitchen drawer just in case surgery would be needed before I ate. Meticulously, I slipped the candy from its outside wrapper and freed it from its white cocoon. I studied it. Did the Hershey bars of my childhood contain more almonds, or did it just seem that way because I was younger then? It didn't matter. I had more bars where I found that one, and I wasn't about to melt the candy, add some almonds, and freeze it again. I studied my favorite of all the food groups and turned it so that it would allow me to eat the most chocolate without overstepping my bounds of one almond at a time. I bit into the chocolate, slid it into my mouth, and waited for it to melt. Surely there will be Hershey Almond bars in heaven.

I closed my eyes and began to think. Had I made a mistake oh those many years ago by not leaving town and going to work for Hershey straight out of high school? Would I've been able to eat more candy if I'd chosen a different vocation? I'll never know unless I run into someone who's worked for Hershey.

I continued to fantasize until I heard the sound of snapping fingers in front of my eyes. I opened them and realized that the sound of snapping fingers was caused by a sergeant snapping his fingers.

"Excuse me, Prince Chocolate. But would you like to help me with this puzzle, or do you want me to claim all the credit?"

"Okay, Lou. One word down and three to go. Let's see where we are now. All the firsts were gone, and there were no seconds and thirds to pull us through. The other words must be harder. Okay, Lou, we know that none of those letters can be in the third or fourth word, so let's see what we have there."

EAMC
FIRST
LRE

106

LLES

The good feeling that overcame me was short-lived. I felt we were about to solve the puzzle. I felt wrong.

"Okay, Lou, any other ideas?"

"No, Cy, other than it's obvious that words three and four are missing some letters. And they're going to be missing even more."

"You mean someone's going to come in here and steal some letters?"

"Yeah, we are."

"How's that?"

"Well, look at the letters. One 'L' may go in the third word, but both 'Ls' may go in the fourth. The 'R' definitely goes in the third word. But the 'E' goes in one or the other. The 'S' is definitely in the fourth word."

"Huh?"

"Oh, never mind, Cy. We'll figure it out in time."

I looked at my watch. I couldn't believe it was almost supper time. I was still getting used to daylight-savings time. It wasn't that long ago when it was dark when Lou and I went to supper each night.

Lou and I didn't want to get frustrated, so we agreed to save the rest of the puzzle for the next day. Besides, the next morning it would be two days since I'd talked to Sam. I imagine he'd found something we might find helpful.

Lou and I stood up, stretched. We were tired from all of our running around two days in a row. I slapped him on the back and we headed out the door to the Blue Moon.

+++

"Well, if it isn't Frick and Frack. How's the world treating you?" Thelma asked, as we opened the door and gazed upon her smiling face.

"The rest of the world doesn't treat us quite as well as you and Rosie."

"I'm sorry to hear that, and I'm even sorrier to give you the bad news."

"Don't tell me this place is closing."

"In a matter of speaking, but only temporarily. A good friend of mine is very sick, and I'm going to spend a few days with her, nurse her back to health. Rosie will still be here in the daytime to see that you get a couple of good meals, but the place will be closing at 4:00 each day."

Lou and I glanced at each other and were able to read each other's minds. If the place was going to be closed for dinner for a few days, Lou and I had to make up for it by eating a little more that night. We ordered like two offensive linemen and ate accordingly. We were almost finished before Lou realized that our feast meant he would have to go home and Wii again. When we were finally able to get up from our stools, I took Lou home, then zipped home and stumbled into my house without my next-door neighbor being aware of my return.

16

I woke up tired. I rolled over and it dawned on me that it was Friday morning. Not only was it Friday morning, but it wasn't a retired Cy Dekker Friday morning, but a go-to-work Lt. Dekker Friday morning. My friend was still dead, and we hadn't found the killer. It was time to tackle the puzzle, or whatever we had to do to bring the Colonel's murderer to justice.

+++

I did all my preliminaries, then rushed to the phone, hoping to learn something that would bring the case to its conclusion.

"Good morning, Sam. Now that you've had a few days off, I assume I can expect more from you this morning."

"No and yes."

"You mean 'yes and no?'"

"No, I mean no, I haven't had a few days off, and yes, I do have more for you this morning."

"Well, then let's dispense of this chitchat and fill me in."

"Well, I let you know what I found out about the so-called 'in-crowd' the other day. Now, let's talk about those whom we know had something against your friend. First, Michael Belding. He's the one who said Col. Hardesty kept him from teaching at the university. He is still in town and still bitter. One source told me that Belding told him the other day that he, Belding, might throw a party because the old man finally died."

Sam's words made me want five minutes alone with Belding. Then I remembered the Chief's words and the scripture I'd read just a few minutes before. Sometimes it was tough being a cop, and tougher being a Christian.

"Belding teaches at the county high school. As far as I can tell, he's never gotten in any trouble there. Maybe he was biding his time until he got a shot at your friend, the Colonel.

"But he's not the only one with a reason. Remember Daniel Terloff, the student who most people feel threw the bucket of paint against the Hardesty house? He's left the area, but I've heard from two or three sources that he comes back to Hilldale on occasion, and each time he visits he cruises by the Hardesty house, and he's not trying to decide if he wants to send them flowers."

"But you haven't been able to find out where he spends most of his time?"

"One guy told me that Terloff lives like a hippie in the woods. What woods, he didn't know."

"What else do you have?"

"Well, we can eliminate one suspect, Carla Bauerman, the one who said Col. Hardesty kept her out of grad school. She had trouble dealing with that, started drinking a few months later, and one night she drove off the road and hit a tree. Not on purpose. But that doesn't matter. Her mother, Carol, had had cancer for a couple of years and died from it a couple of months later. Her dad, Carl, the drama teacher at the local high school where Carla lived, resigned at the end of the school year and moved to New York City."

"New York City? Did you try to find him there?"

"I did. Bauerman became an actor, and I located four actors who knew him. One became a good friend of his. He said that Bauerman stayed there a couple of years, developed wanderlust, and ended up in California a year or two later."

"Were you able to locate him in California?"

"Not yet. However, he was there. Yancy Trueblood, the actor I was telling you about, has gone out to see him a couple of times since he's been there. One time was last year. Trueblood said both times Bauerman lived in an apartment, but a different apartment and a different city each time. Trueblood said he talked to one of Bauerman's neighbors the last time he visited Bauerman and found out that Bauerman had just moved to that apartment a week before Trueblood arrived."

"Anything else for me, Sam?"

"Of course, Cy. I've been busy. I found out what plumber and what pest control company serviced the Hardesty's house this year. Both check out in a way. A-1 Plumbing sent Robert Collins a couple of months ago to repair a leak under the kitchen sink. Collins made only one trip, the company received no complaints. Collins has been with them for fourteen years and has had a good record with the company.

"I called Dunleavy Pest Control. They had a man, Tom Johnson, out a couple of times to rid the house of ants. Johnson worked for the company for a year but he quit a couple of weeks ago, told them he was leaving town, but he might be back in a few months. Johnson said something about receiving a call from his sick mother. I asked for any information they had about Johnson. They gave me the name of a former employer in Indiana. I called and checked. Tom Johnson worked there. I sent them a picture of our Tom Johnson to make sure it was the same guy. It was. He worked there for two-and-a-half years before coming here. They said he was a good man, but that from time to time while he worked there he had to leave to attend to his sick mother. He came back each time until he quit and came here. I have no idea why he quit the job there to come here. The man I talked to both places said he was a good worker, knew his stuff."

"I hope that's all. Sam. I'm having trouble keeping track of all of this. Let me see if I'm right. We have a plumber who seems to have no motive and an exterminator who doesn't seem to have one, either, but has disappeared. Three people who were angry with the Colonel, one of them dead, one of them still resides in Hilldale, and another one of them has disappeared. Besides that, we have the father of the deceased girl who is supposedly now somewhere in California. See what you can find on the ones who aren't in Hilldale. Lou and I will tackle the ones here."

+++

I spent so much time on the phone with Sam that I was a little late picking up Lou for breakfast, but hardships such as these are sometimes part of the job.

+++

Lou opened the car door and slid onto the seat next to me. Well, not right next to me. There was ample space between us. Not as ample as if Lou and I were malnourished, but ample, just the same, and ampler than was true a couple of months ago.

"So, God's messenger, what words of wisdom did He share with you today?"

"I can tell you're in one of your moods, Cy. But first, let me share that I neither gained nor lost weight, so I need to eat a little less than yesterday. Now, to you, are you in one of your moods?"

"No, just finally able to hear some incriminating evidence against someone who doesn't live in the Colonel's house."

"Like what?"

I filled Lou in on what Sam had shared with me. It still didn't tell us who was or wasn't guilty, but it was something. When I finished, I realized that Lou still hadn't told me what today's message was.

"The cereal that floats."

"The cereal that floats. What cereal floats?"

"I don't know. Why don't we go to the grocery and buy a box of each of them, and see which one floats? With our luck, it will be like those letters that may be in the third word of our puzzle or may be in the fourth. Who knows? Maybe most cereals float."

"I've got a better idea. Why don't we ask Rosie?"

A few minutes later, we arrived at the Blue Moon and pumped Rosie. While more than one cereal floats, both Lou and I knew which one was our clue when she mentioned Cheerios. Lou and I had forgotten about those three Os in our puzzle. And what about that arrow clue? And how hard would it be to come up with those four missing letters, none of which we knew?

I was a little more excited eating breakfast that day if it is possible for me to be more excited over one meal than another day's meal of basically the same food.

We were headed to my house afterward. Lou and I didn't linger as long as usual. Maybe we were going to learn the identity of our murderer.

+++

We plopped down at my dining room table, opened the Bible to Obadiah. There we found three cards, two with +2 written on them, the other with +3.

"Any ideas, Lou?"

113

"I'll have to remember to beat you to the punch next time. You always ask me when you don't have a clue."

"So, you want to ask me when neither of us has a clue. Well, Clueless, let's see what we can come up with. Obadiah starts with an O. Two of these cards have +2 on them. Now, it doesn't make any sense that the +2 means two books over because the Colonel could've just as easily put these cards in that book, so let's look at "O" plus two letters. That takes us to "Q." One of the few things I can remember about our travels through the Bible the other day is that no book starts with the letter "Q," so it makes sense for the Colonel to put the "Qs" in Obadiah. But since there are no "U's," unless the "U's" are among the four that fell out, and there is more than one "Q," let's say there are more "Q's" to give us "cuse," like part of "accuse." We might have "first accuse.""

"Why would it make sense to first accuse anyone, Cy?"

"How would I know? Do you know any other "cuse" words?"

"Yeah, excuse."

"Is that your way of telling me that you think we have not yet found the key to the buried treasure?"

My partner's silence sent me back to Obadiah. And the +3 card. If I was right, there wouldn't have been a +3 card, because +3 takes us to "R," and the book of Ruth starts with "R."

I studied Obadiah. I don't mean I read the book, but I flipped through it. Short book. Very short book. But long enough to have three "O's." I closed my eyes to think. Why would the letters in one book have +2 and +3 written on them, while none of the other letters had anything written on them, except one that fell out? One of them was the card with the arrow.

It was almost lunchtime when it hit me.

"Lou, I think I've got it."

I could tell from my partner's reaction that he didn't believe me.

114

"No, really, Lou. Look at this. Have you asked yourself why the Colonel put the 'O's' in the book of Obadiah? It's the only "O" book in the Bible. But, it has only one chapter. So what if the 'O's' in the clue have to do with the second, third, or fourth word? The Colonel had no choice but to put +2 and +3 on the card. Let's try this, and see what we come up with."

I constructed our four words again. This time with O's included.

EAMC
FIRST
LREOO
LLESO

I sat with my mouth agape. I had never known such a brilliant discovery to lead nowhere. Lou was amazed.

"I have to hand it to you, Cy. You've really cleared it up. Do you want me to put out an APB on Lreoo Lleso?"

I looked at my partner and stuck out my tongue. His laughter caused me to laugh, too.

We needed a break from the puzzle, but it was too early to venture to the Blue Moon. If I were to go to the Blue Moon and see someone sitting on my stool, I'm not sure I could handle it.

"Okay, Lou, forget the puzzle. Let's look at what else we have. We have our good friend, the Colonel, dead. Sometime Monday afternoon, someone got into the library some way and shot the Colonel with a poisoned dart. At least that's the way it seems at this point. Our murderer may be a long-haired hippie seen by the next-door neighbor and a student delivering pizza. The only hippie on our list of suspects is Daniel Terloff, one of the Colonel's former students. We have family and friends with no alibis for the time of the murder. We have workmen who were in the house at some point and could've stolen a key. We have neighbors, one who is fairly new to the neighborhood. And we have others with grudges against the Colonel. So, Lou, what do you say?"

"Let's take another look at that puzzle. I want to try something to see if it works."

I wasn't ready to tackle that puzzle again, but I abided by my friend's wishes.

"Okay, Lou. What is it you want to try?"

"Let's include only the letters we know that go in each word."

"We did that before, Lou."

"Yes, but that was before we placed the 'O's.'"

"You've got a point. What can it hurt?"

EAMC
FIRST
ROO
SLO

"This time I think I've it, Lou. It says, "Mace the first room slowly. Now, who can you remember who maced the first room? Quick, now. We might be able to make an arrest."

This time my partner stuck out his tongue.

"Now, Cy, let's add a letter or two to the third and fourth words. We know that those two words contain an 'L' and an 'E.' If we add the 'L' to the third word as we now know it, we could have "rool" or "loor. If we add the 'E' too, that doesn't make it any better."

"If we move the letters around and add a 'C,' we could have 'color,' for whatever that is worth."

"I'd think 'color' would be a wasted word. It doesn't give us anything, Cy. The Colonel didn't write in complete sentences, so if he wanted to direct us to a certain color, I think he'd use that color as one of the words."

"I think I agree with that. So, let's go on to the fourth word. We could have 'sloe,' which is a word, but not one the Colonel would use here, or 'lols.'"

"The first one could also be spelled 'lose or 'sole,' but I don't think either of those is our word, either."

"What else do we have?"

"Well, there's always the arrow. Any idea what that stands for?"

"I'd say it's trying to point us in the right direction, and right now I think the right direction is lunch. What say we grab something to eat and tackle this later?"

"I make a motion that nominations cease."

"I second the motion. Meeting adjourned."

17

We left the Blue Moon. As I drove we discussed what to do next. Eating supper wasn't an option. Should we confront our local suspects, or should we hightail it to my house and solve the puzzle. The fact we could solve the puzzle while seated and interrogating suspects meant lots of steps and standing on our feet didn't weigh on our decision. I felt good about our decision until we neared my house. A vulture loomed ready to strike her prey. She even had a white bundle of fluff to fetch her catch.

Lightning veered into the driveway, rather than strike a pedestrian. I stopped the car, stared straight ahead. With my hands shaking or appearing to shake, I slid my Hershey bar from my pocket, only to find that I needed my knife to slide between two touching almonds. I wondered if I should roll down my window, in case the knife slipped. I sliced a morsel and plopped it into my mouth. I continued to stare straight ahead.

"Cy, there's a nose pressed against your window."

"What can I do about it? The windshield wipers only remove scum from the front. Do you want to roll your window down and see if she wants to lie across the hood?"

"I doubt if she'd get close enough to the wipers that they would swipe her."

"No, but I could hit the gas and then hit the brakes really quick."

"But then you'd have to clean all the mess up out of the driveway."

"No, remember, I pay a boy to do that."

"Wouldn't he report it?"

"Remember, Lou, we're cops. I'll tell him that she had a gun, but the impact knocked the gun so far we'll never find it."

The two of us shared a laugh. Some cops think of things they would never do. I couldn't help thinking that God would give me indigestion or something because of my thoughts.

"Well, Lou, let's get this over with. Should I send the Welcome Wagon home with a copy of the puzzle so we can keep her out of our hair?"

"Just give her a copy of an eye chart, and tell her not to come back until she's solved the code. We can let her know that she's helping her country."

"I thought what we have is an eye chart."

"It seems that way."

"Well, let's get this over with."

I opened the door quickly.

"Oh, I'm sorry, Miss Humphert. Was that your knee? I thought you were farther away. You know what they say. 'Objects in the mirror are closer than they seem.'"

"Oh, that's okay, Cyrus. I read about how policemen are supposed to help ladies in distress. Maybe you and your friend can come over and nurse me back to health. Maybe you can do therapy on my knee."

"I'd love to Miss Humphert, but in all my busyness, I haven't had my leprosy shots yet."

"Oh, Cyrus, you're so funny. Isn't he funny, Twinkle Toes?"

"Miss Humphert, you might refer to him as Twinkle Toes, but his name is Sgt. Lou Murdock."

"I meant my dog, but of course I could call *him* Twinkle Toes, too."

"I must be sure to let the guys on the force know that from now on Sgt. Murdock is to be known as Twinkle Toes II. If I know the guys, they'll be delighted to know that. Well, we'd like to stay and chat, but we've been cautioned against spending time with rabid women with dogs. Maybe another time?"

"Absolutely, Cyrus. Maybe you can come over tonight after your friend leaves. You know, check on my knee and see if it's okay."

"I'm afraid I can't, but I might send Twinkle Toes II over before he leaves. And I would do something about that knee if I were you. I read where it helps if you embed your body in concrete. I cannot remember if you immerse your body in concrete from the neck down or the neck up. Try either or both. I'm sure you'll see a difference."

I rushed off so quickly that Lou was left with Heloise Humphert. He felt her hot breath on his face, looked up to see that he alone faced her. He barely escaped her clutches as she grabbed for his shirt.

He was my friend. He hadn't done anything bad to me that day, so I refrained from locking the door. He yanked open the door and lunged inside.

"What were you trying to do to me, Cy?"

"Just wanted to make sure that Thelma Lou is the one for you. I wanted to give you some options."

"Don't ever give me that kind of option again."

Lou's body shook until he'd used his teeth to rip open a bag of M&Ms and downed the whole package. Still unsure that he'd survived his scare, he plopped down on the couch until he'd digested his candy.

After Lou recovered from his brush with death, he struggled to his feet and tiptoed through the quicksand to the dining room table, where he plopped down in a chair.

"Well, Lou, if you're sure you'd be more comfortable here, rather than next door, shall we get started?"

"Sure, Cy, but where do we start? I was twenty-one when we first started to work on this puzzle, and now I'm retired."

After some back and forth discussion, we looked at what we had.

EAMC
FIRST
ROO
SLO

"Just as I remember it, Cy."

"Yeah, me, too, Lou. I was hoping the puzzle fairy had stopped by and filled in the blanks."

"And we've already used our clue for the day. Does that mean we should stop until tomorrow?"

"No, Lou, let's press on. Surely we can come up with another word before supper. Let's look at it with the other letters added."

EAMC
FIRST
LREOO
LLESO

"Lou, I think it helps to look at both of these together."

"You do?"

"Well, not really, but they say it helps if your teammates think you have confidence in your abilities and theirs. It can't be too tough. We know that two 'L's' and an 'E' go in these two words. One may go in each one, or both go in the same word. Maybe we can get enough to go on so we can come up with another word, and then all we have to do is place those other four letters."

"None of which we know what they are."

"Thanks, Lou. I appreciate your contribution. Let's try them one letter at a time, and see what we get."

Something was telling me that both "L's" were not in the same word, so I suggested we try an "L" in the third word.

"Well, which do you like, Lou? 'Loor,' 'Loro,' 'Rolo,' or 'Rool?'"

"Well, whichever one it is, Cy, it takes at least one more letter. Let's try a letter with each."

We began with "Loor," and it wasn't long before we came up with "Floor." Then we realized that there wasn't a book of the Bible that began with "F." We agreed to tackle the other letters to see if any of them led us anywhere. Fifteen minutes later, we slumped. Defeated again.

There was only one thing to do. I stumbled to my fridge and selected the Hershey Almond bar that I felt would best increase my brainpower. I carefully unwrapped my treat, studied it. Each Hershey has a different configuration of almonds. I wasn't sure that the almonds in that bar were aligned right, so I rewrapped it, returned it to its cold environment, and selected another. Again, I unwrapped a bar, studied it. This time the almonds gave me a different message. The message said, "Pick me up, turn me sideways, and eat the almond in the middle." Just in case you're ready to send me to the funny farm, I don't think the candy spoke to me, but I did feel the urge to turn the candy sideways, instead of eating it the way most people devour a hot dog. Because I gingerly held the candy, I was able to rip a large bite from the side without breaking the bar in two. I had accomplished my mission. I rewrapped my candy. As I savored my delicious treat, I looked up at Lou, who was busy playing Chinese checkers with his M&Ms. Each time he jumped one, he plopped that colorful treat into his mouth.

I sucked on my chocolate until I was afraid that continuing to do so might cause me to swallow the almond and choke on it. Then, I quit and waited for Lou to jump the rest of his M&Ms.

Something must've worked, because shortly after Lou and I finished our eyes wandered from the paper where we'd written down our clues to the slips of paper than had fallen out of the Colonel's Bible. We saw the paper with the arrow, and almost immediately we knew. There wasn't a book that started with "F," but there were plenty that started with "E," and an arrow inserted there would eventually point two dumb policemen to the next letter of the alphabet.

I remember what I had said earlier about discovering another word before supper, looked at my watch. 3:34. We weren't used to eating supper that early, but whatever. We came to our senses, realized that it was too early to eat supper. Reluctantly, but at least we realized it.

"Well, Lou, whatever it is we're looking for is on the first floor of the Colonel's home. Now, all we have to do is figure out what it is and what it has to do with finding out the murderer's identity. Since no one has a room on the first floor of that house, I doubt if the other two words give us the murderer's identity. Maybe they will tell us how he or she got into the library. What's the matter, Lou? You look down."

"Oh, nothing, Cy. I was just thinking, what if we solve this only to find that it leads us to another puzzle?"

"If so, I'll crawl to my next-door neighbor's and die."

It took a few minutes for it to sink in, but we'd learned something else, other than the third word. We'd learned that the letters "LSEO" were in the fourth word, in some order or another. "Lose" is a word, and so is "Sole." But "First Floor Lose and "First Floor Sole" didn't make sense. Besides, we had four more letters that went in either the first or fourth words. More than likely some of them went in each.

We fiddled with letters for the next two hours, got nowhere. Frustrated again, it was time to leave our puzzle to the next day. We lay around for a while, then got up to go somewhere to eat. The Blue Moon was no longer an option for supper, so we chose The Feed Bucket. We took our time eating, and it was getting dark by the time we left.

+++

I dropped off Lou at his apartment and drove home. Just before turning onto my street, I stopped, donned my night-vision goggles, turned my headlights off, and coasted for home. Just before I got to my house, oncoming headlights blinded me, and almost caused me to hit a tree. I ripped off the goggles, turned on my headlights, and realized that my assailant was my next-door neighbor leaving. The cuddly companion was in her lap, looking out the driver's-side window. Even when that woman leaves the neighborhood, she creates havoc. I veered into my driveway, pulled to the back, and ran for the back door before the leech could finish her U-turn and catch up with me.

18

Saturday morning arrived a little too soon. Unlike some people, Saturday is no different than any other day to a homicide detective in Hilldale. If Lou and I are in the middle of an investigation, we usually work, even on Saturday. Sometimes we sleep a little later on Saturday, because others do, and some of those others frequent the Blue Moon at a later hour than usual. Neither Lou nor I wanted to start our day by throwing someone from our stools. I made a note to ask Rosie if we could put a cage around our stools, a cage where Lou and I had the only keys. Then, I scratched my mental note. I was sure Rosie would have quite a comment about that.

I seldom bothered Sam on Saturday. Besides, Lou and I had enough to keep us busy solving the puzzle. I hoped we'd solve the puzzle by Monday, then, if we still didn't know the murderer's identity, we'd begin to question our suspects on Monday.

I stepped into the shower and began to think about our normal Saturday morning routine, the routine we'd miss that day. It felt funny to call it normal since it had only been our routine for a couple of months. But, for the first three-plus months of the year, after we left the Blue Moon full and ready for another day, Lou and I stopped at Scene of the Crime Bookstore to visit with our new friends and select another title or two to devour during the coming week. We'd learned which of the Crime's customers have the same reading tastes as we do, got suggestions on new titles to read, and discussed books all of us had read. I continued to daydream until I felt the cold water permeating my body. I shivered, then stepped out of the shower and dried my ample body.

+++

I looked up as Lou opened Lightning's passenger side door. I noticed the look on his face and felt like driving away before he could climb inside. Was it possible my next-door neighbor had sneaked over to his apartment, clawed her way inside, and bitten him? Almost as soon as I thought of that, I dismissed the thought, because if my neighbor had done that, Lou's mouth would be wearing a scowl and have milky-green saliva dripping from it, rather than be upturned into a smile as it was.

"What happened to you, Lou? Did someone we put behind bars have a change of heart before he died and leave all of his money to you?"

Lou continued to smile but said nothing.

"You set some new Wii records?"

Again he remained silent.

"You've been bitten by the Cheshire cat?"

"It's a smile, Cy, not a grin."

"So, you can talk. How about telling me why you're so happy this morning?"

"Today's clue, Cy."

"Okay, out with it, and then maybe both of us can smile."

"How'd you get to be a lieutenant, anyway?"

"Watch your mouth, lowly Sergeant."

"Cy, today's clue is 'smile.'"

"That's it. Does it mean we solve the case today? Or possibly when I go home today there's a 'For Sale' sign in my next-door neighbor's yard? I know, Lou. You only get the messages. You don't interpret them. Well, smile, you're on Candid Camera."

"I loved that show. You, too, Cy?"

"Well, it was funny at times. A lot funnier than this puzzle we're trying to solve."

I realized that all our chitchat was keeping us from breakfast, so I unleashed Lightning and lurched forward to the Blue Moon.

No sooner had Lou and I ordered than I realized the significance of that day's clue. I turned to Lou and smiled. He smiled back. I continued to smile, but Lou's face returned to normal. I knew he didn't know, and he didn't know that I knew.

I was still smiling when Rosie returned with our drinks.

She sat them down and then turned to the good sergeant.

"What's wrong with him?"

"Well, Rosie, it's like this. Tomorrow is Sunday. I told them at the home that it's not a good idea to give Cy a double shot on Saturday, but they wouldn't listen. Now, look at him."

"A double shot of what?"

"They won't tell me. It's just something special for overworked lieutenants."

"Well, if you find out, let me know. Some days after work I could use a double shot of something."

Rosie walked away, and Lou turned to me.

"What's wrong with you, Cy?"

I merely smiled at him, reached my right forefinger into the air, and pushed it down, like I was clicking a camera. Lou still didn't get it. He thought I'd lost it. I hadn't. I'd found it.

+++

As soon as Lou and I were perfectly ensconced in the car, Lou turned to me and asked, "What's wrong with you, Cy?"

I smiled at him. Seeing that my smile didn't turn on any lights in his head, I enlightened him.

"Remember the clue this morning?"

"Yeah."

"Remember the letters in the first word on our puzzle, 'mace' or 'came.' I almost didn't get it, because of the way we pronounce, "came," but I think our first word is "camera." That uses two of the other letters, and there are books of the Bible that start with 'R' and 'A.' So, could it be that our first three words are 'Camera First Floor?'"

"I think you've got it, Cy. And it sounds like the last word should be a place in the house, but we've named all the rooms."

"And I don't think the camera the Colonel referred to is the one outside the library. Anyway, we've already checked that camera. There must be another one no one knows about. Let's try again. Let's visualize the Colonel's house. We enter the house and there's the hall. We didn't even mention the hall before, because we don't think of the hall as a room. Like cabinets, the staircase leading upstairs, the hall closet."

"That's it, Cy. Closet. 'Lose' with a "C" before it and a "T" after. Lose and closet don't sound alike, either. That's one reason we had trouble coming up with this one. I think we've solved the Colonel's puzzle. There's a camera in the first-floor closet. Now, how many first floor closets does the house have?"

"If I remember correctly, two. One in the living room and one in the hall. My guess is it's the one in the living room because that's one way the Colonel entered the library. Maybe someone else discovered his secret."

"But remember, Cy. Someone still had to get inside the library. How could someone get in there and kill the Colonel?"

"I'm just hoping that the camera holds a picture of our murderer. It would be devastating for us to find the camera, only to find that the murderer discovered it and removed the film."

We were almost to my house when we discovered this revelation. I was so happy I tooted Lightning's horn.

"What're you doing, Cy? Signaling to your next-door neighbor?"

I craned my neck and made like a periscope to see if I could spot the enemy. She was nowhere to be seen. I pulled into the driveway, sprang from the car, and dashed into the house. It was time to call Louie Palona, Saturday or not.

I called his house, a suspicious male voice answered.

"Good morning, Louie. Did I ever tell you that you're my favorite gadget man?"

"I am sorry but Louie has gone to Italy for the month. Please feel free to check back with him in June."

"Good try, Louie. But this is a matter of life or death."

"Your life and my death, Cy. What's so urgent that you're calling me on Saturday?"

"Remember the Colonel's house. Well, there's a camera there that might have a picture of the Colonel's murderer."

"Cy, I already checked that camera. Remember?"

"No, this is another camera. A hidden camera."

"And you want me to meet you there and give it a going over, too?"

"It shouldn't take long, Louie. After we find it."

"You mean you don't know where it is? Why don't you find it, then call me."

"No, no, Louie. It's in the closet. It shouldn't take long to find it."

"Okay, Cy. I'll meet you there in thirty minutes."

Lightning made tracks for the Colonel's house. Louie would really be put out with me if no one was home and we couldn't get in. I had a key to the library, but not the house.

Lou and I arrived at the house, and luck was with us. The front door was open with a robbery in progress. Just kidding. Trish was in the living room and ushered us inside. I asked her who was home, and she said that only she and her grandmother. Everyone else was out for at least the morning. As we were talking, Martha shuffled into the room.

"Oh, hi, Cy, Lou. What brings you here? Do you have some news for me?"

"We might have a breakthrough in the case. I've another man joining us in a few minutes, and I need to ask you and Trish to go to your rooms until we've checked something. I'll come and get you when we've finished."

Neither the young woman nor the older one gave us any trouble or spewed a barrage of questions. Both complied with our wishes and withdrew immediately to the stairs.

"I don't think it'll take long," I called out as the two women mounted the stairs.

I heard a car pull up outside and looked out the window. Louie didn't waste any time getting to us. I opened the door and waved to him. He waved back and then reached into the car to retrieve some equipment.

I knew Louie liked to spend his Saturdays with his family, as often as possible, so I didn't waste any time.

Quickly, I showed Louie the closet, then stepped aside so that he could see what he could find. Lou and I waited until Louie finished.

"Sorry, Cy, but I couldn't find anything. Could it be another closet?"

"It could be, but I'd like to try something else first. Let's step back into the closet."

"That's a small closet, Cy. I'm not sure I want to be in it with you."

"I promise not to tell anyone."

"Very funny, Cy. Okay, what do you know that I don't?"

I led the way, stepped into the closet, and twisted and pulled the bracket in the back. The wall slid away.

"Before you check anything else, let's take a look at the passageway. The Colonel's clue might have meant for us to go through the closet to the passageway. He just didn't have time and enough books of the Bible to spell it all out."

Louie looked at me as if my brain were in its sleep mode.

It took a few minutes. The camera was well concealed, but we found the panel that hid it. The wood fit so well together that Louie didn't notice a thing until he got within two or three inches of the panel. Once he discovered it, he slid his fingers around until he found the place where the panel unscrewed and lifted out. Behind the panel, Louie found a camera that made him slobber with envy. Louie called it state-of-the-art. I called it a small, well-concealed camera.

Within minutes, Louie had printed a series of pictures, all of which were of the Colonel, or a long-haired man I'd never seen. Not only had we discovered who killed the Colonel, but we had discovered how. By studying a series of pictures, we followed an unsuspecting long-haired man as he entered the passageway through the closet, took out a blowgun of some sort, slid a poisonous dart inside, created an opening in the library wall, inserted the blowgun into the opening, and blew the dart. The assassin continued to watch until he was sure his quarry was dead. Then he yanked a string until the dart slid back through the hole in the wall. He reached into his pocket, removed a plastic bag, and carefully slid the dart into the bag. Then he recovered the hole he had made in the wall, turned to face the camera he knew nothing about, checked to make sure the coast was still clear and left the passageway. Because I knew what had taken place on the other side of that wall, I shed a few tears. Louie withdrew to allow Lou and me a few more moments of mourning.

After a couple of minutes, Lou and I stepped out to join Louie. Louie reentered the passageway with us to see what else he could discover. While Louie searched the wall hunting for the wood that covered the hole that was large enough to admit a blowgun, Lou and I selected one picture and mounted the stairs to see if either of the two women could identify their loved one's murderer. I wasn't ready to let anyone know how the murder was committed, just in case someone who lived in the house knew about the passageway, had committed the murder, and would later give himself or herself away. See, even though we kept referring to the murderer as a "he," we knew that the murderer could have been either a man or a woman.

When we returned with no more answers than we came with, we discovered that Louie had found a well-concealed place where the murderer had used some type of saw to remove two round pieces of wood, and then after they had served his purpose, he returned them to their original places in the wall. Lou and I looked through the top hole into the library. The hole, cut just below a shelf that held books, looked right across the library in front of the desk, to the door on the other side. The hole below stood just above a series of books. Obviously, the murderer had cut one hole to see through, and another one to insert his blowgun or the similar instrument that he used. He or she had made two trips, one to cut the openings and leave the note, the second to commit the crime.

We thanked Louie for his help, allowed him to rejoin his family, something I wished I could have done for the Colonel. After taking a few more minutes to recompose ourselves, we remounted the stairs to let the women know that the house was once again theirs. Both thanked us for what we had done, even though we hadn't yet solved the murder.

Since no one else was home, we decided to wait until Monday to show our pictures around town and hopefully identify the Colonel's murderer. Lou and I told Martha we were beginning to get somewhere, hugged the two women goodbye, then left for my house to go over what clues we had and make plans for Monday. We had made progress. We had pictures of the murder being committed. But somehow I felt that we still had a ways to go. I had little confidence that anyone would be able to identify the person in the photograph.

19

We knew a little more as we drove to my house. The murderer was either the hippie from the woods, Daniel Terloff, or someone wearing a disguise. My guess was the disguise. The other would turn the case that had been difficult to solve into one that ends swiftly. Well, as swiftly as we could bring it to a conclusion, having no idea what woods Terloff was in.

When we arrived at my house, my next-door neighbor wasn't within strangling distance, so we hurried inside, eager to get to work. At least we had no more puzzles to solve. At last, it was down to business as usual.

I laid some candy on the table, Lou tossed down a couple of bags of M&Ms. The way we did it, it looked like the card game was about to begin, and both of us were about to ante up.

"Okay, Lou, let's look at what we have. We now know who was murdered and how. We have no idea why, because each suspect had a different why. Anything you care to say before we begin?"

"I'll let you lead, Cy."

"Okay, let's start with the easy part. Our murderer is either someone who looks like the man in the picture or someone in disguise. If it's the first, I'd cast a vote for

Daniel Terloff, the guy who's now living in the woods. We need to check with Sam on Monday, find the name of someone who knows Terloff, and see if Terloff looks like our unkempt man."

"Of course, Cy, there is the remote possibility that someone who knew the Colonel way back when could have grown long hair and a beard."

"That's true, Lou, but, if so, more than likely it is someone we don't have on our list. The Colonel mentioned only three people that he'd had a problem with, and one of those is dead. Besides, I doubt if Carla Bauerman could've grown a beard. The other suspect is still here in town, and I doubt if he's altered his appearance. I'm inclined to think that the murderer is someone in disguise. If that's true, then the most obvious person is Carl Bauerman, the bereaved father of Carla, who left his teaching job, hightailed it to New York City, started an acting career, stayed there a while until he uprooted himself and headed to California. The problem is that while he has moved around in California, we have no evidence that he's been in our area, or even left that state."

"Nor, Cy, do we have any evidence that Terloff has been here? And another thing, why would Bauerman need a disguise? No one here knows him, and I think we've done well to include him as a suspect. As far as we know, even the Colonel never met him. We never heard anything about him threatening the Colonel. Just that his daughter and wife died near the same time, and he became distraught and left the state to start a new life. Remember, we've gone back a ways to find these people. I doubt if any of them would think he'd be recognized if he showed up looking like himself. The people I think would need a disguise are the ones someone would recognize because they are in and out of that house on a regular basis or at least live somewhere in Hilldale."

"That's what I like about you, Lou. You're always complicating our job. Besides, if we wait a while, if things go like they usually do, we'll have a couple more suspects come Monday."

"So, what do we do now?"

"Well, Sam is looking into the suspects who don't live in Hilldale. We've got the ones who do. I want to leave the family alone for the time being and look elsewhere. While I plan to leave them alone, I want to stop by tomorrow after church and show this picture to everyone who lives in the Colonel's house and to the other people on the street. I want to see if the next-door neighbor, Downey, thinks this is the man he saw enter the Colonel's house. My guess is they are one and the same, but I want to know what he has to say. Also, I want to show the picture to the other neighbors, see if any of them have seen this guy on the street. If that doesn't do us any good, we'll check the street behind the Colonel's house. It could be that our murderer cut through the back yard and down the driveway to keep from being seen. It sounds logical. Remember, Mark Blakeman, the student who saw someone when he was delivering pizza, said that the guy came from around the side of the house. Besides, most murderers don't park in front of the house or in the driveway of the place where they plan to commit murder at least not on a street like this, and in the daytime. And not if the murder was premeditated, and I believe this one was. Let's see if anyone recognizes the guy, or at least if anyone has seen him before. To save time, I'll take one side of the street and give you the other. We'll each take a copy of the picture and have at it. It'll make for a long, tiring afternoon, but more people are home on Sunday than any other day."

"And after that?"

"Well, provided neither of us knocks on a door and the woman who answers says, 'Where did you get such a good picture of my son?' we'll sleep on it until Monday morning. Then, I'll call Sam to see if he has anything else on any of our out-of-town birds, then, after breakfast, we'll visit A-1 Plumbing and Dunleavy Pest Control, see if anyone recognizes the man in the picture. If Robert Collins is there when we visit A-1, we'll talk to him. I'll check with Sam to see where Tom Johnson, the pest control technician, lived. We'll talk to some of his neighbors, show them the picture, and see if they recognize it. I don't know how much we can get done in one day, so we'll play it by ear. We also have Michael Belding to see. I want to make him nervous, so we'll show up at the high school at the end of the school day. We know he had it in for the Colonel, so I won't spare him anything. I just won't do anything that'll get us in trouble. That leaves us Blakeman, Earl and Myra Hoskins, and the Colonel's friend, Joe Guilfoyle. We'll see Blakeman right after class, and save the Hoskins until they get off work for the day."

"It sounds like we've got a busy several days ahead of us, Cy. We'll need plenty of candy."

"I'd think so unless our murderer comes to us and confesses. Of course, we might pick up something when we start showing the picture to our suspects and might find someone who knows the murderer. Maybe someone will give himself or herself away when they see we have a picture of them committing the murder. Maybe someone will try to divert suspicion to someone else by saying that the picture looks like it could be so-and-so in disguise."

"So, what do you plan for us for the rest of today?"

"Rest and relaxation, my friend. How would you like to call up the girls, see if they want to accompany us to The Feed Bucket tonight?"

"Sounds good to me."

"The girls don't mind if we stack three plates high with food for every dainty one they half clean."

After I said that, I wondered if Lou would have one of the dainty, half-clean plates.

+++

137

Our dinner invitation, late in coming, was accepted, and I took Lou home to relax, to get his mind off the case for a while. I returned undetected by my neighbor, plopped down in my recliner, eager to finish reading *The Alpine Advocate*. After a brief nap, I picked up where I'd left off. The town of Alpine interested me, tucked away in the mountains of Washington state. Daheim's book, the first in a series that travels through most of the alphabet, much like Sue Grafton's do, introduced me to the characters of a small town, and a murder that takes place there. The protagonist is a woman who owns the small-town newspaper. If offered a choice, I'd choose Carolyn Hart's *Death On* Demand protagonist, who owns a bookstore devoted exclusively to mysteries. Still, if the book held up, as I figured it would, Alpine was a town I wanted to revisit. I just wouldn't want the rigors of putting out a newspaper.

+++

At 6:30, right on schedule, Lou pulled up in front of my house in his 1957 red Chevy. While he never admitted doing so, Lou either polished it or had someone do it, because the car shined anytime I cast my eyes upon it. Even the white interior gleamed in the light. By 7:00, we'd picked up the girls and were on our way to The Feed Bucket.

+++

Each time we double-date, we drop Betty off first afterward. Each time, I walk her to the door, we tell each other we enjoyed the evening, and then give each other a slight embrace. Lou, on the other hand, would get a peck on the lips before he returned to the car. While he did so, I'd slip out of the back seat of the car and open the passenger's side front door, while pretending I wasn't watching the romance on the front porch. While I felt good for Lou that he had someone, each time I saw him and Thelma Lou hug or kiss, I couldn't help but think what could've been if my Eunice had lived as long as I have.

+++

I was quiet that night as Lou drove me home. If he'd have asked, I would've lied and told him I was thinking about the case.

When I got home, I was grateful I had a few more pages to read in Daheim's book. It would keep my mind off Eunice.

20

I always sleep a little later on Sundays. I am able to do that and still get to church on time for an ample supply of donuts, and for Lou and me to deposit ourselves in our customary seats on the back row of the church. I'd found out a long time ago that our pastor was loud enough that he could be heard on the back row. And both Lou and I attend church to receive God's message through the sermon. We don't go to be seen or to drum up business. In our line of work, church isn't the best place to drum up new business, and Lou and I aren't eager to acquire any more business.

On that Sunday, six days after the Colonel was murdered, I listened as our pastor talked about Zacchaeus. The scripture that Sunday was short, just ten verses from Luke, but our pastor's message was powerful. I almost wished my next-door neighbor was there, on the other side of the church, to hear it, too. Almost. I still had some growing to do. It was hard for me to love my neighbor, and whoever it turned out murdered my friend.

+++

I wasn't used to working on Sunday. Lou and I did it when necessary, but we didn't make a habit of it. Because Sunday work was unusual for us, both Lou and I'd forgotten God's message for us that day. I mean the message that had to do with the case. Actually, Lou hadn't forgotten it. He'd merely failed to tell me, but then we never discuss business until after we leave church. We do our best to focus on the church service up until then.

We were about to step into The Rocking Horse Café when Lou remembered he hadn't shared that day's message with me. Even though no one else was around, he grabbed me by the sleeve and pulled me aside.

"What's the matter, Lou? See someone you know? Or did you suddenly decide you want to eat somewhere else?"

"Maybe I decided that only one of us knows today's message."

"Oh!" I exclaimed. "Shoot."

"It is impossible to see what you have not seen."

"Really? Care to explain? Does this mean that we are to forget about the long-haired man in the picture? Or that neither the next-door neighbor nor the pizza delivery guy actually saw anyone enter the house?"

I looked at Lou. He stood with his hands on his hips, and the look on his face wondered if I would ever learn that he never knows what the clue means. At least not at the time he receives it.

I stepped around my partner and opened the door to the Rocking Horse. I perused the menu then reflected on the clue of the day while I waited for my food. Suddenly, the clues were getting as difficult as the ones in the puzzle. Had God decided that Lou and I were ready for tougher problems? If so, I begged to differ.

+++

Neither Lou nor I saw any reason to canvass the entire street. We weren't running for election. Not every vote counted. I doubted if anyone at the far end of the street would've seen the long-haired man with the beard. In a way, I felt like Richard Kimble, but then I wasn't being accused of the Colonel's murder. I merely wanted to find our murderer, even if he or she was bald. We would check the few houses around the Colonel's house and do the same on the street behind, provided we hadn't solved the case by then.

We found everyone at home at the Colonel's house. Lou and I had already worked out a plan where I would show the picture and he would study the face of the person looking at it, to see if we got a reaction that wasn't verbalized. Also, as best we could, we would look from picture to person to see if we could see a resemblance. That would take some doing if the person who held the picture was a woman.

Each member of the household studied the picture. Some even covered the beard and the hair, hoping to come up with a suspect. Jennifer seemed startled when she looked at the picture, but I couldn't tell if she recognized the person or not. She handed the picture back to me, and I handed it to Scott. I wondered if she was startled because she thought it was her husband, but then they were supposed to have been together on the afternoon of the murder. I compared the eyes, but even eyes can be made to look different. I could see no resemblance between Scott and the long-haired man with the beard, but then I had problems figuring out all those "firsts" in the second word of our puzzle.

Ten minutes later we left the house no more informed than when we entered it. I hoped that our visit with the next-door neighbor would be better.

+++

We shuffled up the walk, hoping that Bob Downey was at home. As far as we knew, he was the only neighbor who

142

saw someone enter the Colonel's house. Not wanting to alert the entire neighborhood that we were on the prowl, I dispensed of slamming down the brass knocker and used a pudgy finger to ring the doorbell. Luck was with us.

Downey opened the door and looked at us like he was having trouble placing us.

"Oh, you're the one in charge of the investigation, aren't you?"

"Very perceptive, Mr. Downey. You have a mind for faces, which is why we are here."

"Would you like to come in?"

"No, this is fine."

I handed Downey one of the pictures.

"Is this the man you saw enter the house next door?"

"So, you caught him. Where did you find him?"

"Just answer the question please."

"Well, I can't say for sure. I got only a quick glimpse from a distance, but if I were in a court of law I'd say the preponderance of the evidence says 'yes.'"

"Wow! That's a big word, Mr. Downey. What kind of work did you say you do?"

"Nothing now. For most of my life, and I do mean most of my life, I was an over the road truck driver. My momma died when I was eleven. My daddy took me on the road with him and Uncle Jonas. They took turns driving and teaching me the things I missed by not being in school. Kind of like the reverse of homeschooling. Then, when I was sixteen, they taught me how to drive a rig. I continued to do that until I decided to settle down here a little over two years ago."

"And what caused you to choose Hilldale as a place to live?"

"I never had a place to call home. Daddy, Uncle Jonas, and me, we kept driving, traveling all over the country. Daddy taught me how to save my money, and I decided that whenever I got tired of trucking, I'd find me a place and settle down. I was just outside of Hilldale when I got tired. I always thought that one place was as good as another, so it didn't matter where I settled."

"So, you never married?"

"Nope. I've got me some lady friends around the country, but I never married. I was married to my truck. Well, at least until I decided to quit."

"So, where's your truck now?"

"Some guy offered to buy it right after I settled down. It was a new rig. Cost almost half as much as this house. Well, not quite half, but it cost a bundle."

"And what happened to your dad and uncle?"

"Both died. Three years apart. Cremated both of them, as per their wishes. Put them in a container, tied it on my rig, and let them blow off into the wind as I drove down the highway."

"Seems like there aren't a lot of people who know you."

"Oh, a lot has gotten to know me over the years. Just haven't seen many people for too long at a time."

"Well, we're gathering the background on everyone who knew the Colonel. Care to tell me some people we can check with?"

"The Colonel?"

"The man next door who died."

"Oh, I didn't realize he was a Colonel. I didn't really know him. Saw him a few times out in the yard and we waved back and forth. That's all. I was never in his house. He was never in mine. You know how it is with neighbors these days."

"Still, mind giving me a few names?"

"Not at all, but everyone I hauled for is dead except for Art Pickens, and he's retired. Lives in Billings. That's in Montana. Then there are those lady friends I told you about. I'd call when I was in the neighborhood. Had one in Santa Fe, one just outside New Orleans, and one in Omaha. Will that do?"

I indicated that those names would do fine. He wrote down the four names, addresses, and phone numbers. I planned to have Sam check them to see if everything checked out.

"You planning on being around, Mr. Downey?"

"I never did plan much of anything other than work. Now that I'm retired if I have a hankering to go somewhere, I just pick up and go, come back when I feel like it. As I said, my daddy taught me well. I never needed money for much of anything, so I'm pretty well set for my retirement years."

"No chance of you up and moving is there."

"No. Nothing like that. If I go anywhere, it'd just be for a week or two. I'm still enjoying this nice little town."

"So, you think this is the guy you saw going into the house next door?"

"Well, as I said, I can't say for sure, but as far as I can tell the hair is the right color and length, and the beard looks about the same. It wasn't like he stood there and posed for me."

"And have you ever seen anyone who looks like this anywhere here in town either before or after that day he went into the house?"

"Can't say that I have. For two reasons. I don't see a lot of people, and most of the people I've seen around here don't have long hair and beards. There are a lot more beards up north, particularly in the winter."

"And how long did you say you were a trucker?"

"I'm forty-four now. Forty-two when I quit. I was eleven when Momma died and Daddy took me on the road with him. Sixteen when he and Uncle Jonas taught me to drive a rig on weekends. Eighteen when they let me start sharing a little of the drive with them. See, truckers are only supposed to drive so much each week, and with three of us driving we could spend more time on the road."

"Well, thank you for your time, Mr. Downey. If you see this man again, be sure and let us know. Just call the department."

145

"I'll do that, but if he's done something bad, I'd say he's hightailed it out of town by now. Maybe all the way to Mexico."

"You could be right. Well, thanks for your time."

+++

Lou and I shuffled back to Lightning, got in, and discussed what we'd learned at the two houses, which wasn't much. We resumed our visit with the Colonel's neighbors. No one else on the Colonel's street had seen the long-haired man. We drove away to the street behind the Colonel's house and began again.

+++

"I'm Lt. Dekker with the Hilldale Police Department. I was wondering if you've seen this man."

The elderly gentleman took the picture, studied it for a minute, and then handed it back.

"I think so."

Having received a "no" at every other house, my brain, which was on auto-pilot, almost caused me to turn to leave. It was then that I realized the man's answer.

"And when was that?"

"Let me see. It was the day I went to the doctor. I was coming home, pulled in the drive, and almost hit this guy running through. He stopped, stunned that I was there, so I got a good look at him. I'm pretty sure it's the same guy."

"And can you tell me what day it was?"

"Yeah, let me check. I only went to the doctor once that week, so it was Tuesday, a couple of weeks ago."

"Are you sure it couldn't have been last Monday?"

"No, it wasn't then. My wife and I went to our daughter's for the weekend. Didn't get back until almost dark Monday night. No, I'm sure it was on a Tuesday."

"Do you remember what time of day it was?"

"I'd say a little before 11:00. Maybe closer to 10:30. I always schedule my doctor's appointments early in the day, so that I don't have a bunch of people ahead of me. I was Dr. Wheeler's second patient that day, so I'd say I got home somewhere around 10:30, give or take a few minutes."

"What did the man do when he saw you?"

"Well, he just stood there a minute, stunned, as I said. Then he took off running down the street. By the time I got out of the car and walked back to see where he went, he was gone.

"I never saw him before, and I've never seen him since. Sorry, I can't be of more help, Lieutenant."

I took down the man's name, phone number. Dick Morrissey. I doubted if I'd need him again unless we collared the long-haired man.

I thanked Mr. Morrissey for his time, turned and finished our canvass. Because one person on the street had seen the man, we continued our canvass down the street in the direction Morrissey had indicated. But no one else had seen our long-haired man.

+++

Now we had had three people who'd seen the long-haired man. Only one of them saw him on a different day. Did that mean that the long hair and beard wasn't a disguise? Or that our murderer did a trial run? Could it be the day he made the hole in the wall and left the note? Only time would tell. But with each new witness, I became more convinced that the long-haired man wasn't a figment of Downey's imagination. A pizza delivery driver offered some credibility, but a man who saw the long-haired man up close for a few seconds told me there was a long-haired man in the neighborhood and on at least two occasions. What that meant, I had no idea.

+++

It took all afternoon to complete our canvass. I wondered how local politicians, who do door-to-door canvassing, ever get to most of their constituents. It didn't matter. I had no plans to run for any office.

After a brief conversation, Lou and I opted for an early dinner at Burkman's. If you want a good steak in Hilldale, Burkman's is the place to go. And both Lou and I wanted a good steak that night to gather enough strength for the next day, and I wanted a couple of good desserts to replace the calories I'd burned going door-to-door.

Depending on the restaurant, both Lou and I like our steaks medium or medium-well. Don't bring me a steak that looks like something the dog will eat. And don't bring me one that resembles something that has been sacrificed to God. I want a juicy, but not bloody, steak, fit for human consumption. I didn't want to make a pig of myself, so I bypassed the sixteen-ounce Porterhouse and selected the fourteen-ounce New York strip, instead. Lou started to order the six-once sirloin, but one look at me told him he had to order one that was at least eight ounces. Both of us ordered baked potatoes. I passed on chives, whatever they are, and sour cream. I told our server to be liberal with bacon bits and cheese and throw in enough butter for them to swim in. Our server laughed, not because she was making fun of me, but because she admired a man who knew which food groups to eat, and how much of each was just enough. Lou too ordered a baked potato, but with a small amount of butter. I know our server wanted to shake her head but wanted a tip even more. For our other side item, both of us chose baked apples. I decided to wash mine down with sweet tea. Lou chose an orange cream soda.

One item on the menu caught my eye, and I suggested it to Lou. I felt it was calling our names, and he agreed. When it came time for dessert, we tried something called

Chocolate Pudding Cake Extreme. On the bottom was a yellow cake, filled, and I do mean filled, with chocolate pudding. A caramel sauce drenched the top and sides of the cake, and whipped cream engulfed the entire delicacy. Walnuts were liberally sprinkled on top, and a cherry looked on from above. It looked so good that I ordered a double helping. I was glad that I had no more walking to do that day. If I knew the new Lou, after eating a measly amount of his dessert, he would go home and do some of those Wii exercises. Poor thing. He was going to have to wash his clothes in hot water, just so they could fit him again.

As soon as the anesthetic wore off enough that Lou and I were able to take up our beds and walk, we left Burkman's, knowing that the Chocolate Pudding Cake Extreme would call us to return soon. As would the steaks. Well, at least one of us.

+++

With Lou deposited in his nest and the night still young, I picked up a copy of Parnell Hall's *A Clue For The Puzzle Lady*. Cora Felton and I had little in common. She smoked, she drank, she'd been married several times, and she didn't do puzzles. She did, however, solve a murder every now and then. So, we had one thing in common. I was about to get to know Cora a little better, and I suspected that she'd be good for a few laughs along the way.

+++

As is many times the case, a good meal soon leads to a bad nightmare, which means my next-door neighbor and I were about to come face to face, without actually doing so.

In my dream, Lou and I were walking from house to house, handing each person a picture. At each house, whoever answered the door returned the picture with the same comment, "No, I've never seen anyone uglier." Finally, I looked at the picture and realized why. I had in my fat little hand a picture of my next-door neighbor. At one house, I held the picture at an angle that caused the picture to reflect in the mirror inside the house, and the mirror broke. If I hadn't been a policeman, I would've been dead meat at that house. When I looked down, I discovered that I had a second picture of my neighbor. In this one, she looked much better. She had long hair and a beard, and the hair was combed so that it covered her face, and exposed her ears instead. I couldn't say much for her ears, but at least they looked better than her face. Just before I woke from my nightmare, I knocked on a door, and the woman who answered was accompanied by a dog that looked like the one next door to me. When I showed the woman the picture, the dog snatched it from her hand, chewed up the picture, and spit it out. I looked down at the picture pieces that lay on the carpet. Finally, my next-door neighbor looked better.

21

I awoke Monday and immediately groaned. It wasn't a day to read. It wasn't even a day to work on our puzzle. It was a day to drive all over everywhere and question anyone we saw. One look at our list told me it would take us more than one day to complete our agenda. I wondered where we would be at the end of our travels. Would we have any more idea who had murdered the Colonel?

+++

I was still savoring the previous night's delectable dessert and I wasn't ready for green eggs and ham, so as soon as I heard my friend pick up the phone, I said, "Sam, this is Cy. I just wanted to see where your travels on my behalf have taken you."

"Oh, I haven't been anywhere, Cy."

"But you'd better have let your fingers do the walking."

"Well, that, and other people. Okay, here's what I've learned since we've talked. Nothing. Well, not exactly nothing. I've found a lot of places in California where Carl Bauerman isn't. Some places where he's been, but he hasn't stayed in any of them any longer than six weeks, or however long a play lasts. He has spent time out there in recent years, but he keeps moving as if he doesn't want anyone to catch him. Still, everywhere he's been, he's been a consummate actor and a model citizen."

"When is the last time anyone saw him?"

"Well, none of the people I've talked to have seen him in over a year, and that was his friend who visited from New York. I've found places where he's lived, but every neighbor tells me the same thing. They never saw him. Yet he did live there, and he showed up when it came time to practice or star in a play."

"I assume you have police out there who are working for you?"

"I do, and in each case, they've shown a picture of Bauerman, and a picture of the long-haired man with the beard who was seen entering your friend's house. In each case, the person has identified Bauerman, and in no case has anyone seen that long-haired man out there. Bauerman has definitely been a lot of places, but that other guy is native to our area."

"What can you tell me about Bauerman?"

"Just what I've told you before."

"How old a man is he?"

"If he's still living, he's fifty-five."

"Are you saying he could've died?"

"Yes, but, if so, he died within the last year or so. He was seen up until then."

"How big of a man is he?"

"Well, the people we talked to say he is average height, and slender."

"Do you have any pictures of him?"

"Just distance shots. We've blown them up, but they're not that distinctive. I do have a picture of him the last year he taught at the high school. Will that do you?"

"It'll have to. Lou and I will stop by to pick it up later. Anything new on Terloff?"

"Not yet, only that we know he's still in the state because enough people see him from time to time, but always in a different place."

"So, he's here, but not here. Are any of these places close to Hilldale?"

"Not really, but close enough that he could get here within a couple of hours or so. I haven't talked to anyone who has seen him here lately."

"Can you get me a picture of him, too?"

"You can pick that up with the other one."

"Anything new on Tom Johnson, that pest control tech?"

"I thought you were checking up on him, Cy."

"Lou and I plan to check out the place where he worked. I want you to see if you can find out anything else about him before he went to work for that place in Indiana, and, if Lou and I don't come up with something, I want you to see if you can follow his trail out of town."

"So, is my work done?"

"You wish. I've got a guy here, Bob Downey, the next-door neighbor. He's been here a little over two years, but I'd like for you to see what you can find out about him before he came here."

"Do you know where he's from?"

"Here, there, and everywhere. But he did give me the name of one guy he worked for, and three women he has scattered across the country."

"Ex-wives?"

"Not according to him. Just women he knew that he stopped in to see whenever he was in their area. I don't know if I told you or not, but Bob Downey claims to be a retired trucker, only he retired early. He says he's forty-four and retired a little over two years ago."

"You've got a strange group, Cy. Guys from late twenties to mid-fifties, and all over the place. Some of them live near here, others way across the country, and all of them are hard to find."

"I found the next-door neighbor okay. It's just those guys you're looking for that can't be found. You're not losing your touch, are you, Sam?"

"Are you ready to have someone else do your dirty work?"

"Not on your life. Just giving you a hard time. Just like you do me."

"Well, you do have a picture of your murderer, Cy. You'd think you'd find him by now."

"We don't know for sure that this guy is our murderer. It just seems that way. I'll let you go. We'll stop by later and pick up those pictures."

+++

I was about to slip out the back door and drive away before my next-door neighbor could see me. About to. God must've been looking out for me because I did something that morning I seldom do unless the weather is bad. I lifted one of the blinds and looked out the door. As I looked down, I saw the toe of a shoe, a shoe that looked like it might belong to an ugly woman. Did the scourge of the earth plan to jump me as soon as I opened the door?

I sneaked away, headed to the front door. Surely, she couldn't be two places at once. She wasn't. Her fluffy companion was. I backed away from the door. Drastic times called for drastic measures. I opened the door slightly. The curious mutt eased its nose over to the door. I opened it a little wider, bent down, and lifted the trespasser, took it back to its own front porch, where I found its leash and hooked the leash over the front doorknob.

One down, and one to go. Then I sneaked back to my house, slipped inside as quietly as possible, washed dog smell off my hands, and slipped out the front door, again. I tiptoed across my yard and the yard of my neighbor on the other side, eased around the house, until I came to an opening in the backyard hedge, an opening that allowed me to open Lightning's passenger side door, without being seen from my back porch. I locked Lightning's doors, inserted the key, and started my vehicle. I managed to back most of the way out of the driveway before the evil one rounded the corner and rushed toward Lightning. It looked like I was going to have to start leaving bear traps in my yard, just to get in and out of my house each day.

I pulled down the street and stopped. That woman figured I was gone for the day, so she rushed to my front porch looking for her watchdog. I didn't pull away until I'd watched her until she finally found her coconspirator.

+++

"What kept you?" Lou asked me, as I pulled up in front of his building, and he opened Lightning's door.

"Enemy invasion."

"You mean your neighbor broke into your house?"

"Almost," I said, and then I proceeded to tell him about my early morning activity.

"You might want to stay away from your house for a while. The ASPCA might be paying you a visit."

"I didn't hurt the little dog. I just took it back to its house."

+++

I'd had such a harrowing experience I'd forgotten to ask Lou what God's message was. We were in the Blue Moon at the time. Lou took his finger, dipped it in his syrup, and wrote "Houdini," then made it disappear. It was a few minutes before I could follow up.

"So, Lou, does this mean that one of our locals is going to disappear?" I asked as soon as we left the restaurant and secured ourselves in my car.

He gave me his "you'll never learn" look.

"Well, it could be that we'll learn something about someone who's already disappeared."

Lou's look didn't change.

I remembered that the college student who delivered the pizza on the Colonel's street got out of class just before 11:00. I drove up to his building, just as someone abandoned a spot in front of the building next to his. Was it to be our lucky day?

A few minutes later, Lou and I returned to Lightning with a confession from the college student. I wish it were that easy, but of course, it wasn't. Like two others before him, he said he thought it was the guy he saw, but he couldn't testify to it. That was okay. So far we didn't have anyone for him to identify.

+++

We left the campus area and drove to Sam's house.

"It took you that long to eat breakfast?"

"No, Sam. Some of us have more suspects than others."

"Well, at least yours are easier to locate."

"You mean you haven't found anyone since this morning."

"No, they're all too busy playing hide and seek."

We cut the chitchat, and Sam handed me pictures of Terloff and Bauerman.

"This guy isn't some long-haired hippie," I said, as I looked at Terloff's picture."

"Both of these pictures are around ten years old. Evidently, Terloff wasn't at his campsite when Olan Mills called about a recent special."

"You mean Olan Mills is still around?"

"I have no idea, Cy. You might try Googling them."

Sam laughed, knowing that I'd never Googled anyone, nor did I have the means to do so. At least now I realize that Googling is something you do on the computer. That way I don't look too stupid. Okay, maybe I do to some people.

+++

I took the pictures and Lou and I headed to A-1 Plumbing. As expected, Robert Collins was out on calls. I showed the woman behind the counter my credentials and pulled out the pictures.

"Is either of these men Robert Collins?"

"He doesn't look anything like either one of them."

"And I assume you've never seen either of these two men?"

"Not as far as I know."

"Well, do you have a picture of Collins I can have?"

"Just a second. I've to check with Mrs. Abney."

The woman left, then returned with an older woman.

"May I help you, gentlemen?"

I went through the identification process again and asked for a picture of Collins. I told her that I didn't think he was the person I wanted, but I needed a picture of every person who had been in the Colonel's house. Reluctantly, she complied.

+++

Lou and I entered Dunleavy Pest Control. A young man in a uniform approached us. "May I help you?"

I identified myself.

"Is there something wrong, Officer?"

"There's something wrong, but I don't think that Dunleavy Pest Control has anything to do with it. I'm inquiring about a former employee, Tom Johnson."

"Yes, Tom worked here until a few weeks ago. Is he all right?"

"I don't know. I'm trying to find him, but I don't know what he looks like. Are either of these two men Tom?"

"The one guy's too young, and Tom would never have long hair or a beard. Tom had more of a Marine look."

"Do you have a picture of him?"

"We should have one somewhere. Let me check."

He returned with a picture and said something that was foreign to me.

"Ah, the miracle of computers. I found a picture of Tom and printed it for you. Here it is."

The man was right. Tom didn't look anything like our long-haired suspect. At least not as far as his hair was concerned. Tom's hair was short, and he had no facial hair. And his chest and arms were larger. Terloff was a skinny guy. So was Bauerman.

"I'm looking into something that happened at the Hardesty place on Cherry Hill Lane. Could you tell me how many visits you made there, what man made the call, and the dates of those calls?"

The man sat down, hit a few buttons on his computer, jotted something down for us, and returned to the counter.

"Here you go."

"So, there were two calls, and Tom Johnson made both of them. Are you sure?"

"That's what the computer says."

"Is it always right?"

"I've never known it to be wrong. Besides, if possible, we send the same man back for a second call unless there was a problem the first time."

"Do you have any idea where Tom might be now?"

"No, like I told the cop that called before, Tom left suddenly to take care of his ailing mother. He acted like he'd be back as soon as she got to feeling better."

"What kind of worker was Tom?"

"Really knew his stuff. Of course, he came with a good recommendation from another pest control company out of state. We checked him out before we hired him. Never had anyone complain about Tom. He always did his work right. Always on time."

I pocketed the new picture, and Lou and I left. It was past time for lunch.

22

It was a little after 2:00 when we slid down off our stools and exited the Blue Moon. I knew that school let out at 2:45, so we drove out to the county high school to get our first look at a man I hated before I ever met him. As soon as we arrived, Lou and I stopped in the office, let them know that we were investigating a murder and that we were there to question Michael Belding. We received puzzled looks from the student worker and the secretary. I wanted to smile but didn't. My request for a picture brought the principal into the proceedings.

"Is Michael a suspect?"

"A lot of people are suspects. We just need pictures of everyone on our list."

Reluctantly, the principal complied.

I asked for directions to Belding's classroom and was told that school was almost over and was asked to wait until after school let out before we questioned Belding. We agreed but told the principal we wanted to be outside Belding's room when school ended, so he couldn't slip away without us seeing him. This statement brought more curious looks.

+++

More than one student looked us up and down as the bell rang, school ended, and they flooded the hallway. We waited until the traffic flow lessened, and stepped into the classroom just as a man attempted to leave.

"Can I help you with something?"

"You can if you're Michael Belding."

"I am, and who might you be. I don't do consultations with parents without an appointment. I'd be glad to make an appointment for you for another time."

"Now's good, and we're not parents. We're police."

"Police? Has one of my students gotten in trouble?"

"No, we're here to talk to you."

"About what?"

"About James Buckham Hardesty."

"Oh, him."

"Yes, him. As I understand it, you didn't like him."

"That's right. He cost me my job at the university."

"And you threatened to get even."

"A lot of people make threats. Let's just say I didn't cry a lot when I found out he died."

It took all my self-control to keep from hitting him.

"When did you find out, Mr. Belding? When you watched him die?"

"I didn't kill him."

"You weren't at school when he died. Where were you?"

My statement was a bluff. Either Belding knew when the Colonel died, or he didn't, but I wasn't ready for his answer.

"I was sick that day. I was home in bed."

"Any witnesses?"

"Just the dog. Does he count?"

"Mr. Belding, I don't think you understand the serious nature of our visit. Would you feel better if we talked downtown?"

"No, it's just that I'm still mad. That man cost me my job. I could've amounted to something."

"I imagine you yourself cost you that job, and I doubt if you'd amount to more than you do now."

"I beg your pardon."

"Listen, Belding, we have a picture of you. We'll be showing it around, and if we find anyone who saw you in the area of the murder, we'll be hauling you downtown."

"I'll have your badge."

"I don't think you're man enough to wear it. Just watch your step. I assume you've heard those stories about what happens to men in prison."

"Get out of my room."

"I will, but if we find anyone who can place you in the vicinity of the murder, we'll be back to get you."

With that, I turned and Lou followed me out the door.

It took me a few minutes of sitting in the car before I calmed down. I didn't like that man, whether he murdered the Colonel, or not.

+++

We wanted to check out the house where Tom Johnson lived before he left town. I stopped by a payphone and called Sam. He gave me the address. It was a street I'd seldom driven down, but I knew where it was.

I pulled up, looked at the house. Actually, it was a duplex. According to the address Sam gave me, Johnson rented the right side. The windows were still bare, so evidently, no one had moved in yet.

I walked up to the unit on the left, rang the bell. A woman came to the door. I identified myself and asked her what she could tell me about Johnson.

"Evidently, he was quiet. Occasionally, I heard someone over there, but most of the time, nothing."

"How often did you see Mr. Johnson?"

"Come to think of it, I think I only saw him once. See I work and he worked, and I think we had different schedules."

"Miss Elliott, I'd like for you to look at these pictures and tell me if any of them is a picture of Mr. Johnson, and if you recognize any of the other men."

"Sorry, can't say that any of them is the guy I saw coming out one night."

"Are you sure?"

"Yes. You mean one of them is this Mr. Johnson, who was supposed to be renting the place?"

"That's right, but maybe the person you saw was someone visiting him."

"Could be. Sorry I can't help you more."

"That's okay. If you think of anything else, just call the department."

Lou and I turned away just as a man was coming out of the house next door, the house next to Johnson's side of the duplex. I caught his attention, and Lou and I hurried over to question him.

"Yeah, I seen somebody in there a few times. Actually a couple of guys, but not at the same time. But there was something funny about that place."

"Funny? How do you mean?"

"Well, it was like no one actually lived there. I remember one time this one guy came in, and a little while later, this other guy left. I never did see the one guy leave, even the next morning, but I saw him come in the next night, then I didn't see either one of them for a while."

"What did the two guys look like?"

"One of them was sort of thin, the other more muscular."

"Mr. Simons, I'd like for you to look at these pictures and tell me if you see either of the men you saw enter or leave the house, and if you recognize any of the men from anywhere else."

"This one. I saw him two or three times. Mainly going into the house at night. Never saw him leave, but once."

I took the picture from Simons, noted that he'd identified Johnson, the man the woman on the other side of the duplex had never seen.

"But none of these are the other man you saw leave?"

"Nope. This guy's the only one."

"Well, thank you for your help. Let us know if you think of anything else, or see any of these men again. Just call the department. They'll get in touch with me."

Lou and I checked with a few of the other neighbors, but like most neighborhoods these days, no one could tell me anything about anyone who lived in the right side of the duplex.

+++

It was getting close to supper time. We'd wait to see Joe Guilfoyle, the Colonel's friend, the next day. He was retired. We expected to catch him in the daytime. Same for the Hoskins, only we'd have to catch them after they got home from work. We also wanted to show the pictures to Martha and the rest of her household, but most of them would be gone during the day Tuesday. We'd wait until late afternoon to pay her another visit. It looked like Tuesday would be just as busy for us as Monday. With all the leg work we were doing, I hoped that we'd soon crack the case.

+++

As I drove Lou home, we discussed our plans for the next day. We agreed to do something we seldom did in a murder investigation. We planned to take the morning off and spend time with our new friends at Scene of the Crime. At 10:00, anyone who wanted could attend and take part in the roundtable discussion of books we'd read and authors we'd recommend. Lou and I were the new guys on the block. Most everyone else had been a part of the group for at least close to a year, but we were made to feel like one of the gang from the beginning. Still, as far as we knew, no one in the group knows what we did for a living. And just as well.

Because Lou and I felt like we were lagging behind the others, I wanted to get home and read as much of the Puzzle Lady book as I could. Lou felt the same way. If I didn't fall asleep, I thought I might stay up until I finished. That way I would have one more book I could talk about at the next day's roundtable discussion, although I expected I would listen rather than talk.

23

Tuesday morning dawned. I rolled over and tried to think of a reason to stay in bed. I thought of plenty. Then I thought of three reasons to get out of bed; breakfast, Scene of the Crime, and a desire to put an end to this investigation and bring the Colonel's killer to justice. Any of those was sufficient to make me stumble to my feet and get on with my day. Thankfully, winter had long since passed, and a quick look out my window revealed a sunny day and no nasty neighbor lurking on my property.

I decided to give Sam more time to track down some suspects. Besides, I knew that if Sam had something really vital to the case, he'd get in touch with me. He knew where I was, or where I would be. He could leave a message at the Blue Moon.

For some reason, I stepped from my shower and had a craving for eggs over easy. If only I could solve all my problems so easily. In only a matter of minutes, I'd tickle my insides with egg yolks and whites. And bacon. And sausage.

I picked Lou up and immediately got a math lesson.

"One plus one equals three, Cy."

"I think you need more math classes, Lou."

"No, I mean that's our clue for the day. 'One plus one equals three.'"

"You mean God needs more math classes?"

"Very funny, Cy."

"Since you're never able to interpret God's message for the day, let me give it a try. I believe God is telling us that we need to increase the number of desserts we eat each day."

"Cy, did you ever wonder why I get the message each day, and you don't?"

"No, I already know that."

"And the reason is?"

"Otherwise you wouldn't have anything to do."

"Are you saying I don't contribute to the case? Maybe I should interrogate the suspects."

"Maybe you should drive each day. Your car. Maybe I can ride in the back. Sounds good to me."

"Okay, and when I finish eating breakfast, I'll bring you out a doggie bag of the things I pick out for you."

+++

We pulled up in front of the Scene of the Crime, eager for a diversion. Murder is okay in my book, as long as it's in a book, and it's not a true-crime novel.

We opened the door of the bookstore, the last of the regulars to arrive. Everyone greeted the two of us like we were about to remember them in our wills, even Mrs. Evans, the owner, although it was like we remembered her in our wills each time we stopped by. Like many who salivate over a good mystery, Lou and I have a habit of buying more books than we can read before we return for more books. When we left the store that day, Agatha Christie, Erle Stanley Gardner, Ellery Queen, S. S. Van Dine, Rex Stout, Ngaio Marsh, John Dickson Carr, Mary Higgins Clark, Carolyn Hart, Rita Mae Brown, Mary Daheim, Lillian Jackson Braun, Sue Grafton, and Tim

Myers left with us. We like to read our authors' books in order, so most of the books that accompanied us as we left the store were either the first or second book that each author wrote. Exceptions were made for Christie and Gardner. We wanted to collect all of their books as soon as possible.

Before we left, Lou and I sat in on the roundtable discussion of the month, "What is the cleverest written mystery you've ever read?" Lou and I were new to the game, so we kept quiet and took notes. Both of us like clever. Who knows, maybe somewhere, somehow, if Lou and I read enough books we'll run into someone who is as clever as we are? Not in real life, but anything's possible in a book.

We'd gotten to know Mrs. Boddley on previous trips to the Scene of the Crime. I guessed Mrs. Boddley to be in her late seventies or early eighties, but that was only a guess. What wasn't a guess was who Mrs. Boddley's favorite author was. She told us more than once that she fell in love with Agatha Christie's books at an early age. She had several Christie favorites but felt *The Murder of Roger Ackroyd* was her best and most clever. Mrs. Edmundson disagreed. She felt Christie betrayed her readers when she wrote *Roger Ackroyd*, but loved *And Then There Were None* and *Murder on the Orient Express*. Mr. Morgan chimed in with his choice for most clever, John Dickson Carr's *The Three Coffins*. While all three of these people had quite a few years on me, Ellie Callahan was a newlywed, and like Lou and I, had come to know all of the masters of suspense recently. Ellie agreed that Christie was the best, but couldn't decide on which book she thought was the cleverest. Like Lou and I, Ellie purchased several mysteries at a time and followed each classic mystery with a modern-day whodunit. Lou and I merely wanted to solve our modern-day whodunit, so we could participate in the bookstore's discussions to come.

+++

We ate lunch and then it was time to work off some of those calories. In order for us to get in a good workout, I parked at the curb instead of in the driveway of each house we visited.

I began with Joe Guilfoyle, supposedly the Colonel's best friend. Actually, I had no evidence that he wasn't. It's just that our years on the force have taught us never to take anything for granted.

Mrs. Guilfoyle answered the door, seemed surprised that two men wanted to see her husband. She told us that he was in the garage and excused herself to get him. I interrupted and told her we needed only a minute of his time and would walk out and talk with him in the garage. Reluctantly, she agreed. I could tell she hoped she hadn't sent her husband unwanted visitors. She had.

"So, what brings you over here, Lieutenant? I thought I answered all your questions the other day."

"You did answer the ones I had the other day, but I stayed up late last night coming up with more questions. Actually, you never answered one to my satisfaction. Where were you on the afternoon of the murder?"

"Right where I am now until it came time to visit with my friend."

"And why did your wife think you'd left?"

"You'd have to ask her that."

"Wouldn't she have heard the car leave?"

"I never took it out of the garage. See, when the weather was warm enough I'd walk over to Buck's."

"I know it's just a few blocks, but wouldn't you get tired doing that?"

"It's only two blocks, and I always take the cut-through when I walk."

"The cut-through?"

"Yeah, there's a path halfway down the block that's used for walkers and bicyclers. It's not wide enough for a car, so elderly people like me feel comfortable using it. I particularly like to use it in the spring. After all the bad weather that winter brings, I'm glad to see warmer temperatures and gentle breezes."

"And I don't guess you saw anyone on your way over?"

"No, no one until I saw Martha when she returned."

"Tell me about that, Mr. Guilfoyle."

"I thought I already did. Anyway, I'd gone over like I always do on Monday to visit with Buck, only, as you know, no one answered the door. I rang and I knocked. I thought maybe he could have been in the backyard, so I walked around back to see. As you know, he wasn't there, either. So, I came back to the front, thinking that he might have been in the bathroom, or had fallen asleep. It was just after I rang again, and waited a bit, that Martha pulled into the driveway. I told her what I just told you, and she hurried to the house to find her husband. When she couldn't find him, she called you."

I decided to change the subject.

"Mr. Guilfoyle, I'd like for you to look at these pictures. Tell me if you recognize anyone."

Guilfoyle looked over the pictures carefully.

"I recognize Michael Belding, but none of the others. Are these your suspects?"

"Each of these men threatened the Colonel a long time ago. I was hoping to find someone who'd seen them near the Hardesty residence sometime shortly before or on the day of the murder."

"I haven't seen Belding in years, and I haven't seen any of the others, but then I'd say I probably just missed one of them on the day of the murder. Too bad I wasn't a few minutes earlier."

My words exactly. Too bad I wasn't a few minutes earlier. Then, maybe my friend would still be alive.

I asked Guilfoyle if he knew of anyone else who might have had it in for the Colonel, but he couldn't think of anyone. I thanked him and Lou and I left.

+++

I looked up Belding's address, and headed there, hoping to get there before Belding got home from school. I wanted to see if we could locate any neighbor who might have seen Belding at home the afternoon of the murder. We located only a couple of neighbors, but none of them could remember seeing Belding at home any weekday before school let out. We were getting into Lightning when Belding came home. He spotted us, gave us a disgusting look. I smiled and waved. I hoped he thought he was our only suspect.

24

As we left, I looked at my watch, wondered if Earl and Myra Hoskins would be home from cleaning and maintaining houses. I took a chance, drove by their house. We were just getting out of Lightning when the Hoskinses pulled into their driveway. Earl eyed me warily.

"Something else we can do for you, Lieutenant?"

"You mind if we step inside a minute?"

"We're tired. We've had a busy day today."

"This will just take a minute."

With his wife's prodding, Hoskins agreed to give us a few minutes of his time. He had nothing new to enlighten us with on his whereabouts on the afternoon of the murder, so I turned to something else.

"I'd like for both of you to look over these pictures and tell me if you've seen any of these people."

"This one," said Myra, pointing at Robert Collins. "But then we know Robert. Earl was the one who recommended A-1 Plumbing when the Hardestys needed a plumber. You don't mean to say he's a suspect."

"I don't think so. I'm just having people look over pictures of people who've been in the Hardesty house or have been seen in the neighborhood."

"Well, Robert's not the kind of man who'd do something like this."

"Who is the kind of person, Mrs. Hoskins?"

"That's just it. I don't know anyone who'd have done it, but someone did. Must've been a stranger."

I thanked the Hoskins for their time, and Lou and I turned to leave.

+++

It was a little after 4:30 when we pulled up in front of the Hardesty house. I hoped everyone was home, and that someone would recognize at least one of the people whose picture I had. Someone did, but I wasn't sure what it meant.

Martha was relieved when she learned that we were there only to show pictures of some possible suspects, to see if anyone in the household recognized any of them. No one recognized Bauerman or Terloff. Martha thought Belding looked vaguely familiar, and she said that Johnson was there to spray for ants. Both Trish and Jennifer said they saw him when he was leaving one afternoon.

I was about to turn and leave when Martha made a comment that surprised me.

"This guy was here the first time, but it was a different guy each of the other times."

I was pretty sure that the man at Dunleavy's had told me that there had been only two calls to the Colonel's house and they were made by the same man.

"Are you sure there were three calls made, and each by a different man?"

"Yes, and Buck made sure I was here each time to receive them since he couldn't hear the doorbell when he was in the library."

"Did each one follow the same routine?"

"As far as I know. I didn't watch any of them that closely, but I did make up some excuse to walk through the

173

house every few minutes. All three men concentrated on the first floor of the house, but they did go upstairs and spray, too. They said it was just in case someone had taken some food upstairs and attracted the ants. I don't know how we got them in the first place. We'd never had ants before. It's as if someone dumped an ant farm in the house."

I don't guess any of them was the long-haired guy I showed you a picture of?"

"If so, he might've scared me. No, it wasn't him. I haven't seen him before or since."

I made a mental note that Lou and I would make a second trip to Dunleavy's. I looked at my watch. Our second trip would have to wait until the next day. In the meantime, we'd check with Downey, next door. He'd been helpful the first time. Maybe he could identify one of these other guys.

+++

I rang Downey's doorbell. He opened the door, and I got the feeling that I was losing my welcome.

"Back so soon, Lieutenant."

"Yes, Mr. Downey. You've been our best help so far identifying visitors to the house next door, and I was wondering if you'd mind looking at a few more pictures to see if you recognize any of them."

"I can probably save you time, Lieutenant. The long-haired man is the only person I've seen going to or from the house next door, except for the people who live there, and that older man who visits on occasion."

"Well, maybe you've seen some of these other people around town."

He motioned for me to hand him the pictures. He wanted to get our discussion over with and get back to whatever he was doing. Downey looked through the pictures, seemed a little stunned by one. Maybe it was the long-haired man again. I'd forgotten to take that one out.

"Just the one I picked out before. Some of these others may be well-known members of the community, but I don't get out much, except when I leave town on a trip."

"Oh, do you travel much, Mr. Downey."

He laughed.

"Lieutenant, I traveled so much when my daddy and I were in the hauling business that I'm plum tuckered out. I take a short vacation once or twice a year, but I've had enough driving. Now, I fly when I go."

"Where have you been?"

"Oh, I went once to visit one of the women I told you about, and I took a vacation to the Keys once. Rented a car in Miami and went all the way to Key West. That was nice. I wanted to see it because it was one of the few places in the U.S. that I'd never seen."

I thought about all the places in the U.S. I'd never seen and wondered if I'd see any of them before I died. Maybe I was happier just lying around. I may never know.

+++

We'd accomplished more than I expected that day. Well, more in the way of people we talked to. I couldn't see where we were any closer to solving the murder, but then murders have a way of getting solved quickly after you've spent enough time.

+++

"So, Lou, any ideas?"

"Well, I was thinking about taking the books I've bought at Scene of the Crime and finding myself a big hammock tied to two palm trees on a deserted beach."

"Do you mean I have to solve this case by myself?"

"No, every now and then I'll take a break from reading, lie there and think of you, back here in Hilldale, stomping through the snow, showing these pictures to everyone."

"So, you think it will take me that long to solve this case by myself?"

"Well, it might. If I'm not here to give you your clue each day."

"Enough of this chitchat. Any ideas about the case?"

"Just that I think it was someone in disguise. Enough people saw this guy. We have a picture of him. And if we keep leaning on everyone, maybe the right guy will fall over."

"I just wish I knew how much of this stuff to pay attention to and what to discard. The fact that the guy probably had a key and wore a disguise makes me think it was someone who lives in the house, except that I can't see anyone who lives there murdering anyone. At least not Martha or any of the girls, but disguise or not, I think we are looking for some guy. The only other woman in the picture is the cleaning lady, and she is one of the few people who has an alibi for the day of the murder."

"It is definitely a curious case, Cy. I can't see where anyone had a motive that would make him or her murder the Colonel, even though some of our suspects did threaten the Colonel years ago. Of course, one of them is dead, and one's moved away. That belligerent Belding seems the most likely to have done it, but then the ones who seem most likely seldom are guilty."

"When you throw in those who are hard to find and those who were in the house but don't seem to have even known the Colonel, that makes it even tougher. Maybe a good night's sleep will open our eyes to new possibilities in the morning."

"I guess that's my cue to get out, Cy."

Lou reached into the back and grabbed his bag of books he'd bought at the Scene of the Crime oh so many hours ago that morning. I'd planned to go home and look over the books I'd bought. I knew Lou would exercise first.

+++

I eased Lightning into the driveway, tiptoed from the car much like Wile E. Coyote does as he sneaks up on the Road Runner to no avail. I turned the back door key and stepped into my sanctuary before the vulture or her bundle of fluff discovered I was home. I noticed that there was another car at her house. Maybe she'd given up on me and had found a deaf and blind man who coveted her advances. I could only hope.

+++

I was like a little kid at Christmas as I opened the shopping bag that held my new treasures. Carefully, I removed the books one at a time, separated them into stacks of current and classic authors, then, one at a time, flipped the books over to read the back cover or the inside flap. When time permitted, I planned to select one, and begin to read. Of course, I have a few other treasures ahead of them, ones I had purchased on an earlier trip to the bookstore.

Sometime before long, I'd have to go shopping for a bookcase. Lou didn't have that problem. Even though Lou's apartment was smaller than my house, it came with a built-in bookcase that could hold hundreds of books. I needed to upgrade. At least modern technology hadn't found a replacement for a bookcase. Well, some people say they have, and while I might try books on tape if I ever take a vacation, I am not about to buy a computer so I can read a book. I am perfectly happy holding a book in my hands while leaning back in my recliner. Some things are better left alone.

25

I awoke Wednesday morning and immediately knew that I wasn't paralyzed. The pains I gained from walking and standing on my feet were still with me. As I lay there, I decided to gamble. If I could make it out of bed, I'd lie in a tub of warm water for a while, and see if that helped any of my aches and pains. Maybe a bookcase wasn't all that I needed. Maybe I needed a hot tub, too. But the more I thought of it, the more I grew afraid that I'd come home someday and find my next-door neighbor in my hot tub, and that she was alive. I'd have to burn the hot tub in order to remove all the poisons from it. Maybe I could burn my next-door neighbor before I bought a hot tub. As I thought of that, I smiled, which caused the pains in my legs to increase. I think God was telling me I was breaking at least one of the Ten Commandments.

A day or so later, I emerged from the bathtub a man-sized prune. I used six towels to dry my body, then got dressed, asked God for forgiveness one more time, and set my day in motion.

Sam had gotten off the hook long enough. It was time to see if he'd circumnavigated the globe and captured all of our suspects.

"Well, Sam, do you have everyone ready for the lineup?"

"Oh, who's playing?"

"I don't mean some ballgame. I mean have you rounded up the usual suspects."

"Cy, do you know how many people there are in the world?"

"I don't want everybody. Right now I'd settle for Daniel Terloff, Carl Bauerman, and Tom Johnson."

"Well, Cy, it looks like I managed to round up all but three of them."

"You haven't found any of them?"

"Well, in a manner of speaking, I found one of them, but we aren't exactly hanging out together."

"What you're saying is you found someone who's seen one of them?"

"Bingo."

"Well, I've haven't got all day, Sam. Which one?"

"Terloff. I talked to some of the guys he hung out with when he was here at college, and a couple of them said he'd been back in town recently, although neither guy could give me the date they saw Terloff. Oh, and he doesn't have long hair and a beard. At least he didn't when he was here."

"And you have no idea if he was seen before or after the murder?"

"I tried to pin them down, but neither could be sure. At least it was around that time."

"If it was after, he still could've been our long-haired murderer who trimmed his locks after the murder to avoid suspicion."

"If so, it didn't work, Cy. You still suspect him."

"I suspect everyone."

"Well, I didn't do it, Cy. I have a corned beef sandwich on rye who'll testify as to my whereabouts."

"You mean you still have it."

"No, but I've pictures of us together."

"Go take your medication, Sam."

"Wait, Cy. I almost forgot. I do have something for you."

"Well, at least you're doing a little bit of work. What do you have?"

"I located that guy that Downey, the next-door neighbor, said he drove for. The reason I couldn't find him sooner is that he retired last year and he and his wife have started spending their winters in Arizona, and just got back. Anyway, he said that Downey made several trips for him over the last few years and was one of the best haulers he ever had. Said he was wondering if Downey managed to stay retired, or took to the road again. He was glad to know that Downey seemed to be enjoying retirement."

+++

I was about to step out of my back door when a woman lunged for me. I narrowly escaped and dashed for the front door. How could she be that fast? She was at the front door, too. I was about to slam the door and call for backup when I heard the words I never wanted to hear.

"You might as well come out, Cyrus. We've got you surrounded."

"We?"

"Yes, we. My sister Hortense has come to visit. I remembered that you have a friend and that you didn't want your friend to be without a woman, so I called Hortense and invited her to visit. Thanks for suggesting it, Cyrus."

"I didn't suggest any such thing. Why don't you and Horrible go to her place instead? What zoo does she live in, anyway?"

"Cyrus. Oh, how sweet. You're already kidding Hortense and you haven't even met her yet. Hortense! Come here! Come and meet my little huggy bunny."

I saw my chance, slammed the door, locked it, and stumbled toward the back door that I hoped Hortense had abandoned. She had. I managed to get out and lock the door, and Lightning got up a full head of steam before Ugly and Uglier rounded the corner and almost got clipped by a runaway Volkswagen.

+++

Lou saw the painful expression on my face.

"So, your next-door neighbor finally picked your lock."

"Not quite, but almost. And, in a way, it's worse."

"She made you sign some note that the three of you will live together?"

"Something like that, only it's the four of us. Or should I say five?"

"I didn't sign anything, Cy, so keep me out of it. And what do you mean by five? Did she find another animal?"

"In a way, but this one's yours."

"The way you're talking, Cy, she has a twin sister."

"Bingo."

"You mean she really has a twin sister?"

"Surely I told you that before."

"If so, I managed to forget. Are they identical?"

"Well, I didn't hang around long enough to find out, but to a guy running for his life, they looked equally ugly. Now, let's change the subject. I don't want to think about my next-door neighbor this close to breakfast."

"Okay. The Road Not Taken."

"I'm not much on poetry, Lou, but I know Frost wrote that one. Has to do with choosing one of two ways to go in life. Don't see what that has to do with our murder, but maybe time will enlighten us. Do you think it means that Tom Johnson hasn't left town? He quit his job before the murder, and if he's our murderer, you'd think he'd hightail it out of town, so I doubt if it has anything to do with him."

"If you're through rambling, Cy, I'd like some breakfast."

I couldn't argue with that. Lightning lurched into action and before Lou and I could think of everything we wanted for breakfast, Lightning had slid into a spot right in front of the door of the Blue Moon.

+++

Properly nourished, Lou and I listened to our food sloshing around in our stomachs as we slid off our stools at the Blue Moon and navigated the few steps to Lightning. The two of us hoped that loose ends might allow us to solve the case, and the only loose ends we could see were how many pest control men made how many calls to the Colonel's house, and did those calls have anything to do with the murder, or was it merely something else that was keeping us from solving the case.

I recognized the man behind the counter at Dunleavy's, and he recognized us.

"Something else, Lieutenant?"

"I want you to go through your records to make sure of the number of times you did work at the Hardesty home, the dates the calls were made, and who made the calls."

"I thought I gave that to you before, Lieutenant."

"You did, but what Mrs. Hardesty said doesn't match what I remembered you to say. I want to double-check to make sure."

A couple of minutes later, the man turned back from the computer to give me the information. His records showed two calls, not three, and one man, Tom Johnson, made both calls. He showed me where Johnson signed an electronic form after completing both calls. I wasn't about to challenge that, because I didn't know what he was talking about.

+++

"Lou, I think we need to take some time, sit down, and see if we can make sense of what we have."

"And we thought those word clues the Colonel left us were hard."

Lightning breathed hard as he dashed for my house. He slowed considerably when he saw an intruder in our yard. I saw no ugly women, but a small dog stood on my front porch, guarding the entrance. When she saw us, she perked up, jumped up and down, and began to bark. I feared for my safety, reached into my pocket, pulled out a pen and tossed it into the yard. The small white creature darted toward the pen just as two ugly women sprang from the front door of the house next door. As the dog dashed to see what I'd thrown, Lou and I lumbered toward the front door of my house.

"Cyrus, what did you throw to my dog?" I heard my neighbor screech as she lunged to what I'd tossed before the dog grabbed it.

I almost thought about my next-door neighbor too long, because she'd captured the pen from the dog's teeth and was looking to sink her fangs into my hide. If the two women hadn't tripped over each other, each trying to be the first one to my front porch, Lou and I would've been goners. One woman's shoulder collided with the other one's jaw. I was curious to see if the collision improved either woman's looks, but not curious enough to put myself on the endangered species list.

+++

"Okay, Lou. Let's take a look at what we have and see if we can make any sense out of all this. We have our friend, the Colonel, dead. We know that he was killed by a poisoned dart from a blowgun and that the person who killed him stood in the passageway and blew the deadly object through a hole in the bookcase, then retrieved it by a string that was attached to the dart. But why would someone retrieve the object?"

"Maybe because they can tell so much by DNA these days. Of course, it could've been that the murderer was hoping that Frank would diagnose that the Colonel's death was due to a heart attack. There are a lot of similarities between the two types of deaths, at least as far as they might be perceived."

"Still, whatever the case, I don't think any of that will lead us to one person over another. So, let's look at all our suspects, and whatever motives each one might have. We'll begin at home, and work our way to a distance. First, we have Martha. Martha could've wanted the Colonel's money, and she could've sneaked back home, murdered our friend, and left before his friend Joe was due to arrive. But I can't buy that. I think the Colonel would've given Martha anything she wanted. I think the same is true for each of his granddaughters, although either of them could've committed the murder because one of them had skipped her last class and the other one was out of class in time to come home, commit the murder, and leave. And if it was Jennifer, did that mean that she and her husband did it together? They both said they were together at the time of the murder. Yet neither has a witness that they actually saw that house that Scott wants them to move into. Was the Colonel so against that, and Scott so much in favor of that, that he was willing to murder the Colonel to get what he wanted? On the surface, I'd say 'no,' but stranger things have happened."

"I can't see the family doing it, either, Cy. Nor do I think the boarder, Tom Brockman, did it. What was his motive?"

"I can't see any motive for him, either, but he did say he was in his office, and others said he wasn't."

We continued to mull over the possibility that someone who lived in the house murdered the Colonel, but we could come up with no likely suspect. I doubted if we'd fare better when we got to the more likely suspects who lived somewhere else, but someone had to have done it.

We changed focus for a few minutes and tried to make sense of the day's clue. *"The Road Not Taken."* Did it mean that someone didn't go somewhere they were supposed to have gone, or that someone chose one thing instead of another? We focused on the first. Could it mean that Martha never left the house that day until after she murdered her husband? The autopsy did show that the Colonel hadn't eaten any lunch. Was it because he was too busy doing something else, or because someone kept him from eating. He wasn't tied up. And he had been out that day, even if his wife hadn't. He had been out, hadn't he? Wasn't the day he died, the day he set up his second camera? Or was it merely the day he provided the clues for us? Everything was becoming jumbled in my mind, but then those things happen sometimes when the case doesn't seem to be going anywhere. Too bad the Colonel hadn't installed cameras on the front and back doors. Come to think of it, that wouldn't have done us much good unless someone in the house did it and he or she donned the disguise while inside the house. But that doesn't make any sense, either, and three witnesses saw the long-haired, bearded character outside the house. I'd been on this case so long it was hard to keep each thing straight.

It was time to line up the M&Ms and break out a new bar of Hershey chocolate. Any excuse would've worked for Lou and me to turn to our candy, but to improve our thinking seemed like a worthy candidate.

I would like to say that the candy enlightened us enough that we solved the case before lunch, but if that were to be true, we would've solved it the first day. Things were almost so bad that Lou and I wished for another puzzle. Almost, but not quite.

26

Rosie chastised us for eating lunch somewhere else the day before, but wiped our shovels and handed them to us. We were back in her good graces. Of course, we knew that we had the upper hand. If we quit eating there, the Blue Moon would have to find forty men to replace us, or close to forty. Rosie didn't want either to happen.

By the time we'd left the Blue Moon and returned to my place, we'd reaffirmed that meringue sticks to lips and teeth, although neither of us knew the reason why. Nor were we determined to find out. We had enough to worry about. If we found out someday that some person died because meringue stuck to his or her teeth, we'd give the issue more time. Until then, we'd stick to solving murders.

+++

"Well, Lou, we really accomplished a lot this morning. What say we get back to the case at hand and pin this murder on someone?"

"Does it have to be the guilty person?"

"Either that or Belding. He committed murder in his heart. He would've done it if he thought he could get away with it, and it could've been him, but let's wait on him. Let's start closer to home. Bob Downey. Maybe Downey didn't see anyone, and sneaked over when no one was home and committed the murder."

"So, what's his motive, Cy?"

"There you go, Lou, trying to complicate things. What do we know about this guy, anyway?"

"Well, he was a trucker, and as far as we know, he had no ties to Hilldale until he moved here."

"So, do we eliminate him?"

"I don't think we eliminate anyone, Cy, but he doesn't seem as likely a suspect as some of these guys. And besides, we know that Downey was telling the truth. Two other guys saw the long-haired man with the beard, and he was telling the truth when he told us he was a trucker."

"Still, what's to keep him from donning a disguise, sneaking over here and murdering the Colonel?"

"Nothing, but what's his motive? A dispute over the property line?"

"Okay, let's move on. Next, we have Joe Guilfoyle. Supposedly, he was a friend of the Colonel for a long time. What could've made him snap and kill his friend? He could've been slipping out of the house, instead of trying to get in, when Martha returned home the day of the murder. But my gut feeling tells me he really was a friend of the Colonel, and that we need to look elsewhere to find our killer."

"I agree."

"What about the maid and handyman?"

"Supposedly, she has an alibi. Maybe she's the only one who does. Supposedly she was cleaning someone's house that day. Her husband left, but she didn't. And what's their motive?"

"Only one possibility that I can think of. Maybe the Colonel found out something about one of them, probably Earl, and confronted him, and threatened to tell everyone the Hoskinses worked for."

"It would've been hard for them to find other families to replace the ones they lost. No one lets just anyone into their homes these days, especially doesn't hire them, without references. People who fire you don't provide references."

"Next. Staying in town, let's tackle Michael Belding."

"I'd love to, Cy."

"He had a motive, and he has no alibi. Home sick, so he says. No witnesses. But if he is our guy, and he's never left town, why did he wait so long to kill the Colonel?"

"To keep himself from being suspected."

"But it didn't work."

"But he wouldn't know that."

"Okay, we'll keep him in the mix. Let's go on. How about Tom Johnson? He was in the house. We don't know if he was there once, twice, three times, or more, but we know he was there. That means he had a chance to steal a key or make an imprint of one. Now what reason would he have for murdering the Colonel, I have no idea. He seems unlikely, except for the fact that there is a discrepancy on how many times he was in the house, and he's disappeared."

"Cy, have you thought about why the pest control company says one thing, and Martha says another? Do you think Dunleavy's is trying to cover up something, is Martha trying to divert suspicion to someone else, or is it merely a fact of a faulty memory?"

"All are possible, but why would the company not admit to a third call, unless the third call was on the day of the murder, which it wasn't? And why does one person say there were two calls made by the same man, and another says there were three calls, each one made by someone different? Not only could Martha be trying to divert suspicion to the pest control company, but someone else, who actually murdered the Colonel, could be doing so, too. It could be that Tom Johnson is off somewhere, taking care of his mother and that that is all there is to it.

"Before we move on to someone else, there's something else to consider. Neither Bob Downey, Michael Belding, Carl Bauerman, or Michael Terloff could've had a key to the house. None of them have ever been in the house. And two people saw someone enter the house using a key. More than likely, that person was our murderer. Everyone who lives there has a key. Anyone else who has visited the house could've stolen one when they were there. According to Martha, no keys were ever kept downstairs, so whoever stole a key, provided a key was stolen, had to have been in the upstairs of the house at one time or another. More than likely, at some point during their acquaintanceship, Joe Guilfoyle has been upstairs. The maid and handyman have been upstairs. And one, two, or three men who worked for the pest control company have been upstairs, but some of our suspects have never been in the house. At least as far as we know, and Martha concurs."

"So, who are we up to now, Cy?"

I studied my sheet of suspects. Otherwise, I'd lose my place.

"I guess we're up to Terloff. You know, one of the guys who has a motive, but no key. He's been seen a couple of times. We know that he doesn't have long hair and a beard, but I'm pretty much convinced that the long hair and beard were a disguise. Still, Terloff had no key."

"So is Bauerman the only one we have left?"

"As far as I know."

"Well, let's pin it on him and get this over with."

Lou's remarks were enough to tell me it was time for another candy break. I picked up a package of Lou's M&Ms, ripped it open with my teeth, and plopped one into my mouth. I don't even remember what color. I know that somewhere someone has come up with a study that tells your personality based on which color of M&M is your favorite, but I couldn't care less about that.

I emptied the bag of M&Ms on the table and then one at a time flicked them over to Lou. Lou started flicking back. It wasn't long before we had a collision in mid-table. Lou and I began to imitate two drivers explaining to a police officer that it was the other guy's fault. After we cracked up a few times, I lifted myself from the table, went to the refrigerator, plucked a Hershey Almond bar from the cold storage, returned to the living room, and handed it to Lou. He imitated me as carefully he slid the bar from its wrapper, studied it, and pulled out his knife from his pants pocket. I couldn't understand why. There was a perfectly good piece of chocolate and almond I could extract if only Lou had handed me my candy. Instead, he opened his knife, cut a hole in the middle of my chocolate bar around the centermost almond. I keeled over as if Lou had cut out my heart. He bent over. I opened my mouth and accepted the piece of chocolate Lou had chosen for me. A day or so later, both of us regained whatever sanity we'd had before and returned to the case.

"As you said, Lou, all we have left is Bauerman. So, is he somewhere out in California, here in Hilldale, or somewhere else unrelated to our case?"

"More than likely."

"More than likely what?"

"More than likely one of those three."

"Lou, did your parents have any other kids?"

"You know they didn't, Cy. Remember, when I was born my mother was put in quarantine one place, my father another place, and me somewhere else."

"Come to think of it, you're right, Lou. I remember now. They put you in a bassinet with Heloise and Hortense Humphert."

We both enjoyed another laugh necessary to endure the case that wasn't going our way. Then our thoughts returned to Bauerman.

"Let's see what we know about Bauerman. His daughter died in an accident. His wife died of cancer. He left the state and moved to New York, took up acting. Stayed there a couple of years, moved to California, continued to act. He's been seen in California as late as a year or so ago, but moved around during his seven or so years in California. Sam secured dates of several plays he acted in, and people in California have confirmed that Bauerman did act in those plays. Some even saw pictures of the man who lived an hour from here and the man who acted in New York, and they say that all three Carl Bauermans are the same man. So, even though we don't have any good pictures of Bauerman in California, we know that he's acted there a lot. What we don't know is if he's donned a disguise of long hair and a beard and murdered in Hilldale."

"Any way Bauerman and Johnson are the same person?"

"It doesn't seem likely for two reasons. One, Bauerman, even last year, was described as a thin fellow. Johnson is burly. Also, Bauerman was seen in California last year. Johnson was in Indiana for two years and then here for a year; however, it is worth considering. Everyone seems to have been moving around. Jennifer and Trish were out of the country for years. Jennifer's husband Scott has been in the area only for a short time. Tom Brockman, who rents a room at the Hardesty house, isn't from here. Bob Downey was an over-the-road trucker until he moved here two years ago. And who knows where Daniel Terloff has been the last ten years? Only Martha, Joe Guilfoyle, and Michael Belding have been here the whole time. What that means, I don't know. I just know that someone murdered the Colonel, and the odds are it was a man. But even that isn't one hundred percent."

+++

Once again the day was getting away from us with no solution at hand. Was this case taking longer than usual, or did we merely think so because the victim was our friend? I remembered the Chief's and the Colonel's advice to us, and Lou and I agreed to put the case on hold until the next day. At that point, everything seemed at a standstill. I hoped there would be new evidence the next day. Otherwise, I didn't know what direction we'd pursue.

+++

For some strange reason I'll never understand, after we ate we decided to drive by the Colonel's house before I dropped Lou at his apartment. It wasn't one of my better decisions. Naturally, as we neared the Colonel's house Lightning slowed and two well-fed men turned to look at the house where their friend and mentor used to live. It was dark and cloudy, but that was no excuse for what was to happen.

"Look, Lou! See that?"

Someone was running up the Colonel's driveway, but it was too dark to distinguish who it might be. As quickly as I could, I stopped the car and forgot that I could no longer run, or that I had never been able to overtake anyone in a race. Evidently, Lou too forgot that I couldn't run, for as I stumbled around to his side of the car, he was on my heels. My wheezing should have alerted anyone within two miles, and probably did, but I couldn't help myself.

Trying to save ground, I rounded the house, just missing the enclosed patio; however, I failed to miss the planter of flowers that loomed in front of my feet. The corner dug into my shins, and I became airborne. Well, not for long. The ground failed to give way as my stomach plowed into it. I envisioned meatballs spewing from my mouth and flying in every direction, but I was able to keep everything down. I was even able to do so a second or so later when a defensive tackle landed on my posterior. Actually, it was his knee that landed nearby, causing me to forget all about the pain in my stomach, and the grass I had eaten against my will. My partner overshot the runway, sliding over me and landing just beyond. His shoe clipped my ear as it went by. More than likely this happened within a millisecond of when my good friend started grazing, as well.

We both lay there until an angel of the Lord hovered above us. The light was intense, but no one said, "Fear not."

I was having trouble turning my body, so I waited until the angel came down to a more acceptable position.

"Why, Cy, Lou, what are you doing here?"

The angel sounded vaguely like Trish, her light a flashlight.

"Just getting our yearly exercise," I sputtered, as soon as I could talk.

Within days, Trish summoned Scott, who came and helped us to our feet.

Sometime late the next afternoon, or as soon as I could breathe again, I brushed the grass from my body, and gave them my explanation.

"Maybe you saw me," Scott said. "I just took out the trash a few minutes ago."

"Maybe so, but if you did, the trash took off around the back of the garage and through the yard behind just before Lou and I fell."

I couldn't recognize anyone, and there was the possibility that our marathoner wasn't our murderer, but someone had run up the drive and taken a shortcut through to the next street.

Lou and I thanked them for their trouble, then limped back to see if Lightning had waited for us.

When we were firmly ensconced in the car, Lou turned to me and said, "Cy, next time you see someone and forget that everyone in the world is faster than you, let me know. I'll drive around to the next street and cut them off."

"And what if they don't cut through to the next street?"

"Then I'll drive around and take a nap until someone helps you up and lets you resume your meanderings."

"Lou, I didn't realize that you were so close to me. How come you weren't wheezing?"

Lou waited until I made eye contact with him. As he started to open his mouth, I held up my hand to silence him. Lou was going to credit his Wii for that, too.

+++

I was ready to lean back in my recliner and read a good book. One good thing about a mystery novel, as opposed to a real murder, is that within two or three days, I'd know who committed the crime. I liked it better that way. The people we'd met at Scene of the Crime enlightened us about cozy mysteries. Many authors wrote two series, and most of the time the reader prefers one series to the other. I'd already read the first book in Carolyn Hart's *Death On Demand* series, aptly titled *Death On Demand,* and I was about to tackle the first book in her Henrie O. series, *Dead Man's Island.*

+++

Sometime before I awoke, I began to dream. I dreamed of my next-door neighbor, but it was a dream, not a nightmare. As I left to pick Lou up one morning, I jangled my keys, wanting to make all the noise I could. It worked. My next-door neighbor opened her door and dashed outside. She found herself wrapped in barbed wire from head to toe. My good friend Wile E. Coyote had sneaked over to her place the night before and wrapped the front of the house in barbed wire, prohibiting my neighbor from catching me as I left for work or returned home.

Impatient, and wanting to catch me before I left, she ripped her rags away from the wire, darted back into the house, and cut through to the back door. She was halfway down the slide before she realized that her back porch and steps had been replaced by a long slide that led down a hill.

My neighbor didn't stop until the slide ended at the muck and mire at the bottom. From muck and mire my neighbor came, and to muck and mire she returned.

The next nightmare I had about her, I ran around the back of my house, tripped over her dog, and landed on her. She reached up and grabbed me, began CPR. I think that is the worst nightmare I've ever had.

27

I awoke Thursday morning, turned and looked at the clock. I figured that if I slept another three hours, I'd be okay. Well, okay in the sense that I'd once again be Cy Dekker at his best. That wouldn't have worked. If I'd done so, my good friend the sergeant would've driven over to my house, hopped out of his classic Chevy, rang my next-door neighbor's doorbell, and presented her with the spare key he had to my front door. I didn't want to wake up with someone licking my face and realize that my face was being licked by the lesser of two evils, Muffy, my next-door neighbor's dog. I wasn't sure if I started calling the old vulture's dog Muffy because I forgot her name, because it aggravated my neighbor, or because I refused to call any dog Twinkle Toes.

It had been an unusual April, more sunny days than rainy ones. Maybe that means the rain is waiting for May. I glanced out the window, saw the new day was another sunny one, then dashed off to the shower and hopped in. Okay, stumbled in while holding on to something was closer to the truth, but hopped in sounds better. It takes longer to clean a beached whale that a submerged one, but eventually the water temperature began to cool, and, once again, I repeated the pattern that allowed me to step over the side of the tub a few hours before.

I brushed my teeth, combed my hair, dressed, learned God's message to me for the day by reading my daily devotional book and saying a quick prayer, and then threw a bear trap out the door to make sure the coast was clear. Evidently, my neighbor was too busy visiting with her sister to molest me. That suited me fine. I wasn't going to press my luck. I was leaving that joint.

+++

Lou opened the door, leaned in.

"The fatted calf."

"Really, I've always thought of you as more mature than a calf."

"I've always thought of you as some kind of bull, Cy."

"Watch yourself. So, have you just enlightened me with God's words for us today?"

"To use your terminology, yes."

"I hope this means that someone is going to prepare a grandiose meal for us today."

"You mean like usual."

I grinned.

"Yes," I said, spraying saliva everywhere.

+++

As Lou and I devoured our breakfasts, the payphone in the Blue Moon rang. Rosie turned from what she was doing and rushed over to answer it. She came back to where Lou and I were eating, leaned over, and said to me, "Someone asked for His Excellency. I assume that's you."

I laughed and ambled over to the phone.

"Dekker."

"You on course number five yet?"

"Sam, you know I chew my food."

"Oh, I forgot you bought a set of teeth to replace the ones you lost."

"Very funny. Listen, I know you didn't call me here just to see how much Lou and I are enjoying our breakfasts. Give."

"I just thought I'd bring you up to date on what I've learned about some of your new friends."

"And how are the Hilton sisters?"

"You're familiar with the Hiltons?"

"Well, I stayed in their hotel once."

"Cy, you've never been out of town. How did you learn about the Hiltons?"

"Okay. Lou and I were in the barbershop the other day. There was something on the TV about them, and one of the younger guys got to talking."

"Well, I hate to disappoint you, but my information is about some men you've been trying to locate."

"You've found them?"

"Yes and no. I can tell you this much. I located someone in California who saw Bauerman five months ago, but he appeared to be traveling through that particular town, not residing there. I've checked all the playhouses I could find, and believe me, there are a lot of them in California. Anyway, I can't find a play he's acted in in over three years, other than a couple of weekends where he stood in for someone. In New York, he was in a play every chance he got. Not true of his time in California. He's been there for seven years, and each year he seems to disappear for longer periods of time than the year before. And I've found no record of him anywhere else. There is definitely no evidence that he's been back in our area."

"Okay, what else do you have for me?"

"Well, I was just talking to someone at the department, and they've been trying to get ahold of you. Tom Johnson's next-door neighbor called, the guy in the house next door, not the woman who lives on the other side of the duplex. Anyway, Johnson came back. The neighbor saw him last night and called the department this morning. However, from what I can ascertain, Johnson left again."

"Don't you have anything better for me?"

"Ask and ye shall receive. Guess who's taken an apartment in our little burg. Daniel Terloff. Moved in a week or so ago."

"So one of our prodigal sons has returned."

"That's right. Let me give you the address"

I jotted Terloff's address down in my notebook, thanked Sam for getting in touch, then hung up and returned to Lou. I saw that Rosie was in the back, and there was no one else around.

"Well, Lou, I have bad news."

"What's that, Your Majesty?"

"You weren't listening. It's Your Excellency. Anyway, it looks like someone is about to kill the fatted calf for us."

"One of our prodigal sons returned?"

"How did you know?"

"Oh, didn't I tell you, Cy? I read the Bible now. I know the story of the prodigal son and the fatted calf."

"Yes, Your Arrogance. Do you mind if I finish my breakfast?"

"Oh were you still eating that? I didn't know. I dumped an ashtray on it."

"This place doesn't have ashtrays. Just finish your food. And don't play in it like you usually do."

There had been some debate among the mentally gifted, of which Lou and I were two, whether or not pancakes for breakfast count as a dessert. Both Lou and I are from the old school. We believe that pancakes are a part of the main course, and thus shouldn't be considered a dessert. However, both of us believe that a man should limit his fruit intake, so we ordered two slices of cream pie each. I ordered coconut cream and chocolate pie. Lou selected banana cream and butterscotch. Between us, we'd ordered most of the cream pie food groups, of which someone should have at least four servings a day.

+++

Lou and I opened Lightning's doors, climbed inside, fluffed our pillows, and buckled up. It appeared that the seatbelts had shrunk while we were having breakfast. After we had secured ourselves and were ready for wherever our mission would take us, I gave Lou the details Sam had told me. We dismissed the idea of traveling the entire state of California looking for Bauerman, and decided on which of the other two to tackle first. If our information was correct, Johnson had returned but skedaddled again, so Johnson's neighbor could wait. I wanted to get a look at the elusive Daniel Terloff. Nothing in Hilldale is too far from anything else, so in a matter of minutes, I turned on to Terloff's street.

28

I eased Lightning over to the curb. Before us stood a moderately priced apartment building of eight apartments, each with its own outside entrance. Each apartment was marked with a number, so it wasn't hard to find number three. We got out, walked up to the door, and knocked. A man of around thirty years of age answered our knock.

"Daniel Terloff?"

"Let me see. You have no religious tracts, so I doubt if you're affiliated with any of those religious groups people have a tendency to avoid. Although I am new to the neighborhood, you're not my idea of the Welcome Wagon, so I'll rule them out. You could be here to let me take advantage of one of those monstrous pizza deals, but I see nothing in your hands. From the looks of the two of you, you're not here to entice me into joining a health club. But when I look at the two of you, I cannot help but think of Frank Cannon or Nero Wolfe. So, I assume the two of you are cops, city or private."

"So, you're familiar with William Conrad. I am impressed that one so young is familiar with him. But did you know that he was the voice of Matt Dillon of *Gunsmoke* on the radio?"

"I imagine that every horse in captivity breathed a sigh of relief when James Arness was chosen for the Dillon role on TV."

"I don't know. He was a big man. But the young man knows his stuff. However, I'm disappointed that you don't think we are affiliated with a health club. I'll have you know that the two of us recently began an exercise program. We began with one trip up and down an escalator a day and are working our way up to ten."

The young man laughed.

"No matter who you are, you have provided free entertainment for me today. Yes, I'm Daniel Terloff. After a bad experience in college, I recently returned to this fair city after spending ten years finding myself."

"Then you should be impressed with us. It took us only a little over a week to find you."

"Then you must be police officers. If not, the department could use a couple of men like you. From the silence of your friend, I assume you go by the names Penn and Teller."

"And may I assume that you're starring nightly as a stand-up comedian in some fine establishment?"

"Touché."

"Let me introduce ourselves. I'm Lt. Dekker and my silent friend is Sgt. Murdock. As you so aptly guessed, we're with the Hilldale Police Department."

"And what brings you fine gentlemen to see me today?"

"Professor James Buckham Hardesty."

"Don't tell me that he's still sore about that can of paint?"

"So you admit you threw the can of paint at his house?"

"Has the statute of limitations run out on that yet?"

"I have no idea. We're here on a larger matter. Murder."

"Are you saying that the professor or some member of his family has been murdered?"

"Are you saying that you don't know?"

"I am. I've been back in Hilldale for only a few days. I'm currently looking for work, and have consulted an employment agency to assist me in that process. I'm also toying with the idea of going back to school."

"Col. Buck Hardesty was murdered a week ago Monday. Where were you on that day?"

"You're serious, aren't you?"

"Dead serious."

"You don't think I still had it in for Prof. Hardesty, do you?"

"Are you saying you didn't?"

"No, that was part of the reason I got away. I wanted to be able to control my anger."

"And you have?"

"Yes. I spent several years alone. Much of the good weather I spent in the woods, nature, spending time with God. It took a while, but I got over my vindictiveness. I stayed on in the woods because I liked the peace and tranquility that that lifestyle provided. I only came back because I know that eventually, I'll need to earn a living."

"And how did you provide for yourself during these last ten years?"

"I made friends. I did odd jobs. I accepted handouts. I had and needed nothing except a tent, a backpack, a sleeping bag for camping out in the winter, a few clothes, and enough food to get by."

"And you no longer resent Prof. Hardesty for not giving you the grade you thought you deserved?"

"No. I mean I still think I deserved that grade, but I came to think of it merely as a difference of opinion."

"And do you have an alibi for that day?"

"When did you say it was?"

"Monday of last week."

"I rented this apartment on Saturday, was here over the weekend. I was at an employment agency up until lunch on Monday, came back to my apartment after that."

"Mr. Terloff, I'd like for you to look at these pictures and see if you recognize anyone."

"Oh, I see you have an old picture of me. And I remember this guy, but I can't think of his name. He taught at the college. As I can remember, he was someone who didn't like Prof. Hardesty. He tried to get me to join him in some lawsuit. And this last guy looks like someone who might've lived in the woods as I did."

"Have you actually seen this person?"

"No, I saw a couple of guys with long hair and beards, but not this particular guy."

"I assume by what you said that you plan to stick around a while."

"Absolutely, unless the big city life becomes too much for me."

"Well, I wouldn't exactly call Hilldale a big city."

"No, but I've already encountered a few more humans than I did in the ten years I was away."

I thanked Terloff for his time, and Lou and I left.

I opened the driver's side door, got in, and turned to Lou.

"Well, Lou, what do you think?"

"About Terloff?"

"Right."

"He seemed like he was telling us the truth, but who knows. Except for Belding, no one we've met seemed to have it in for the Colonel. Yet most of the time it isn't the most likely suspect, at least not this far into the case. Those types you pick up in a day or two, or as soon as you can gather enough evidence to arrest them. There's no evidence leading toward anyone, except some guy who, more than likely, doesn't exist."

"You mean the long-haired, bearded guy?"

"That's right."

"Oh, he exists, all right, but more than likely not as a long-haired, bearded guy."

"Isn't that what I said?"

+++

We had time to cruise by Johnson's duplex before lunch. We did and found the neighbor in his yard.

"You the one who called?" I asked as we pulled ourselves from the car and approached him.

"That's right. You said to let you know, and I thought you might want to know that the guy next door returned. Only I didn't see him when he came back. I saw him when he was leaving again. I made some comment about not having seen him in a while, and he said he'd been away to take care of his sick mother, and his sister came for a few days to take care of her, so he came back to get a few of his things. He said he hoped to be back in a few weeks."

"Anything else that might interest us? Have you seen anyone else in the duplex?"

"No to both. No lights. No people. Just last night for a while."

"Did he seem nervous in any way?"

"Not nervous exactly. He seemed like he always seemed. In a hurry. The way a lot of guys are. But then it wasn't like I was around him a lot and got to know him."

"Well, thank you for your time, Mr. Simons."

Again, Lou and I returned to the car. Because Simons was still in the front yard, I waited until after we pulled away before pumping Lou.

"Any feeling on this one, Lou?"

"For some reason, I feel that this guy Johnson is either our most likely or least likely suspect. He could be someone who's telling the truth and has no idea we're looking for him, or he could be our murderer. The only thing that bothers me about him is what reason he would have for wanting to murder the Colonel. He could have gotten the key, but why would he want it? We can find no connection between Johnson and the Colonel. The guy's only been in town for a year, and it checks out that he was in Indiana for two years before that. And he does look too short and too stout to be the long-haired guy in the picture."

Lou was right. We could almost make a case for any of our suspects, but we could just as easily eliminate them. There didn't seem to be one person who seemed guiltier than any of the others. At least not to Lou and me.

29

We'd been gone from Johnson's duplex for only a few minutes when I had an epiphany. I felt so strongly about the feeling I had, it could've come only from God. I think I scared Lou when I yanked the wheel to one side and pulled over to the curb.

"Are you having a chocolate attack, Cy?"

"No, Lou, I'm having an inspiration so strong I feel we're about to end this case."

"You serious?"

"No, I just wanted to see if you were paying attention to what I'm saying. Of course, I'm serious. Hear me out. I have an idea, an idea where I think we can bring our murderer to justice in a matter of days. All we need is the cooperation of the Chief."

"Well, he's usually gone along with what we've wanted to do."

"I know, but this time I'll have to yank so many chains, there'll be some angry people out there. Plus, more than likely, I'll need Judge Heller's help."

"You've gotten that before, too. Cy, why don't you just tell me what you have in mind?"

"Okay, Tonto. We have a murderer, probably in disguise, since we haven't run into anyone who looks like the man in the picture. But what's the one thing that no one is able to disguise?"

"You've got me."

"Come on, Lou. How long have you been a cop? What is the one way where we can identify someone?"

"Well, I can think of three. There's fingerprints, dental records, and DNA. How'd I do?"

"You did well, my friend. I just needed to jiggle your brain. Here's what we have right now. We have all of our suspects in house, so to speak, except for two. I think we can locate fingerprints for both of those two. I want to set the ball in motion. A man spends time in a duplex. True, he might not have spent a lot of time there, but I think he spent enough time there to leave some prints behind. I want to get a crew to that duplex and see what we can find. I want to be there too, in case we find something other than prints. Also, I want to call Sam. I want Sam to get on the phone to Olive Grove, where that Bauerman girl lived, and see if he can locate any of Carl Bauerman's prints at that high school. Some schools require prints. Some don't. I also want Sam to see if he can find any of Bauerman's prints in New York, and do the same in California. I'm hoping that somewhere he can find some of Bauerman's prints. If he can find prints in each place, that's even better. At least we'll know if Bauerman was everywhere we think he was. So, when Sam and our local print crew are finished, we should have prints for our two missing men and live bodies of everyone else. Then, and here's where everyone will raise a stink, I want to round up all of our suspects, corral our three witnesses, and yank everyone downtown and have a lineup. To make things easier, I want a crew to make up each of our suspects and dress them in an outfit like our long-haired guy wore when he murdered the Colonel. So, now you have it? What do you think?"

"I think you've come up with a fine way for us to be permanently retired. I just hope we don't lose our pensions, but if we do, I've first dibs on Terloff's camping gear."

"Now that we've heard from the attorney for the defense, what does my friend Lou Murdock the cop think? Oh, and if you should someday go camping, I want to find someone to teach me how to use the Colonel's camera equipment. Now, once again, what do you think?"

"Oh, I think that some of our suspects will raise a ruckus when they have to go downtown and be part of a lineup."

"Suspects? I don't think our witnesses will want to participate, either."

"You mean because they're lying?"

"I mean because they'll say what they've said so far. Well, I didn't get that good of a look, and I wouldn't want to cause any harm to an innocent person. Nobody's gonna like this, Lou. But something tells me that when all is said and done, you and I will be on our way back to Scene of the Crime, and I don't mean the Colonel's house. I mean the bookstore."

"What about a trial, Cy? Won't we have to testify?"

"I don't think so, Lou. I think we'll be able to come up with strong enough evidence that our murderer will confess."

"So, do you think you know who it is?"

"I don't have a clue, Lou. That's the reason why I'm trying to bring this off. I think if we have a cattle call and make everyone play a part, then we'll get our murderer."

"Who do you mean by 'everyone?'"

"Everyone. Men and women. I mean the widow, the granddaughters, the grandson-in-law, the boarder, the maid, the handyman, the best friend, the man who threatened him who seems to have gotten over it, the man who threatened him who doesn't seem to have gotten over it. I even mean the plumber, whom we haven't even considered. And I plan to have all three witnesses there; the next-door neighbor, the college student who delivered pizza, and the old man on the next street who almost ran over him. And if I could find them, I'd bring in the pest control tech and the actor whose daughter died. Some of these people are going to be hot. Some of them are going to fits. But one of them is going to confess if we do this thing right. So, are you with me on this?"

"Right beside you."

"Mind eating a late lunch? I want to nibble on the Chief's ear."

"Remember, Cy, you got some candy in your pocket."

"Very funny. But since you mentioned it, we might as well gather enough strength to bend the Chief's ear."

"I thought you were going to nibble on it."

I ignored my friend and partner and grabbed the Hershey bar in my pocket. I was so worked up I ate three bites before we got to the station.

+++

"Okay, Cy, what's so important that you're willing to miss lunch to tell me about it?"

"I don't plan to miss lunch, Chief. Just postpone it a little."

"Just go ahead. I'm missing my lunch, too."

"So, it's okay if I go ahead?"

"How does Patrolman Dekker sound?"

"Okay, Chief. I forgot. I have a better sense of humor than you do. Here's where we are. We have a photo identifying the murderer, only no one we've met looks like the man in the photo. So, we figure that someone donned a disguise."

"I know all that, Cy."

"There's more. All of our suspects are in town except for two. One of them, an actor, hasn't been seen in this area in over ten years, but he's one of our strongest suspects. The other one, a pest control tech, has skipped town, said he's gone to be with his ailing mother. The second guy has rented a duplex. Since I've never seen him I want to get a warrant to search the duplex, see what we can find. I suspect we'll find prints if nothing else. In the end, I think those prints will help us. I don't want to go into detail, yet. Things need to fall into place first. I want Sam to locate prints for our missing suspect, something I think Sam will be able to do without too much trouble. Now, that's the first part."

"I don't see any problem so far, only you might be able to save yourself time spent getting a warrant if the landlord agrees to let us search the place. Now, what else do you have?"

"I want to bring everyone in and put them in a lineup. We've got three witnesses who've seen our murderer in his or her costume. I want our experts to make up and dress each of our suspects in an outfit similar to what our murderer wore. I want to get everyone's prints, and if we get a match of the prints we already have, I want Judge Heller to give us a warrant, while we hold our murderer to see if we can come up with any evidence he or she might have hidden somewhere at home."

"Are any of these people liable to throw a fit?"

"I'd say most of them, Chief. But I think if we do this the way I've mapped out, we'll get a confession that day."

"And if we don't?"

"Then, I'm willing to let things play out."

"Are you sure about that, Cy? Remember, we're talking about your friend here."

"Oh, don't get me wrong. It'll be hard. But I think it's going to work. Just give me a chance, Chief."

"Are we talking about bringing in any important people?"

I ran down the list of everyone I planned to bring in. The Chief seemed satisfied with it.

"Do you know how many people it will take to make this happen, Cy?"

"A lot, but a solved murder will make it worth it."

"You really think you have a shot at pulling this off, don't you?"

"I do, Chief, but it won't work unless we involve everyone."

"Okay, I'll stick my neck out. You've never failed us yet. Take whoever you want. There doesn't seem to be too much going on right now. How do you feel about talking to the owner of that duplex first?"

"That's fine, as long as it's a go if he or she says 'no.'"

"I think I can handle Judge Heller. It doesn't seem like anything too outlandish."

Lou and I shook hands with the Chief, left to go to an abandoned phone to call Sam. Sam, like the two of us, worked from his home, and he could usually be found.

"Sam, old buddy."

"Oh-oh, I don't like your tone, Cy."

"Guess where I am? At the station."

"Don't tell me they've finally arrested you?"

"No, I think we're about to break our murder case, but I need your help."

"What do you need this time?"

I told Sam about the prints we needed and the three places I wanted him to look to find them. He seemed relieved that it wasn't something worse.

"I'll see what I can do, Cy. I might have them this afternoon. I might not have them until tomorrow. Either way, I'll do what I can to get them for you.

"So, you think you've about cracked this thing. Does that mean you won't need my help any more?"

"I don't know about anymore, and I'm not making any promises, but I'm feeling good about this, even though all I'm holding right now is a pair of deuces.

"There is one other thing I need right now. Look up in your records and give me the name and phone number of whoever owns that duplex Tom Johnson lives in."

I wasn't going to ask Sam where he kept his information. Then we'd get into a discussion about how

Lou and I should step out of the dark ages and get a computer. A few seconds later, he gave me the information I needed, including an address, if I needed to go there.

"Well, good luck, Cy. I'll get busy on this. Where will you be?"

"I'll probably have to get back to you, Sam. I've got to grab some lunch and then get to a house here in town to see what we can find."

"Never too busy to eat, huh, Cy?"

"A man has to live. Later, Sam."

I called Margie Burton, the woman who owned the duplex, found her at home, explained who I was, and what I needed. I arranged to meet her there at 2:30. She was willing to let us in, as long as I could prove that I worked for the police department.

I hung up with only one thing left to do. I ran downstairs to get a print crew lined up for the afternoon. Things were in place. Our operation had begun. It was time to grab something to eat and try to end the investigation.

30

We pulled Lightning behind a large, dark-colored sedan, the kind of car old people drive. I rechecked my shirt for stains, cut the ignition, and stepped from the car. As we did so, a short, stout, elderly woman stepped from the car in front of us.

"I'm sorry, but I can't show the duplex today. It's not for rent, anyway."

"I assume you're Mrs. Burton."

"That's right."

"I'm Lt. Dekker with the Hilldale Police Department. I talked to you earlier."

"What's the matter, Lieutenant? Your real car break down?"

"I beg your pardon. This is my real car."

I was about to whip out my credentials when the lab boys pulled up.

I waved at them, then waved my credentials at a woman who thought I should drive a tank, just like the rest of the department. She seemed satisfied, but I wondered how much of her satisfaction had to do with my credentials, and how much had to do with the other men who joined us, none of whom were in uniform.

"If you don't mind, Lieutenant, I'm going to let you in, then leave. I have another appointment. I'll show you how to lock up."

I was surprised. I'd already suspected Mrs. Burton as a woman who would stand with her nose as close to our work as possible. I'd misjudged her, just as she'd misjudged me.

"That'll be fine, Mrs. Burton. I'm not sure how long this will take. I won't know until we get inside."

Once inside, I wondered why we were there. Johnson had removed just about everything from the duplex. I could tell Mrs. Burton was surprised.

"Has Mr. Johnson given his notice, Mrs. Burton?"

"No, as a matter of fact, he's paid through next month."

She shook her head and left. I waited until she did and then told the lab crew what we wanted. What we wanted was anything that would help us learn more about Johnson, but we wanted prints more than anything.

Lou and I wandered around, touching nothing. As if there was anything to touch.

"Kept an immaculate house, wouldn't you say, Lou?"

"Impeccable."

A quick sweep through the four-room duplex told me there wasn't enough stuff to have a garage sale. I doubted if we could sweep up enough dust to make someone sneeze. Even an empty house gathers dust. At least that's what I had always heard.

Lou and I decided to wait in the car until the lab boys finished. There were two slices of pie left.

If either neighbor was home he, next door, and she, on the other side of the duplex, was keeping out of sight. I remembered that the woman said she worked long hours, but Mr. Simons, in the house next door, always seemed to be home. I checked the driveway. His car was gone. At least we'd been able to find him when we needed him.

Sometime later, after a thorough going over inside, three men emerged. One motioned to me. Lou and I stepped from the car. We'd already removed any evidence of pie from the premises, including our premises.

"Find anything?"

"Not much. It seems like this joker didn't want us to. We found two prints and three partials that he missed. That's all. Still, that should be enough to identify your bird."

"Thanks. We'll check in later."

+++

We were closer to Lou's place than mine. We went inside. I called Sam.

"Just got off the phone, Cy. I should have what you want by in the morning. How'd it go where you were?"

"Ran into a cleaning freak. Even did his best to clean his own prints."

"Rather thoughtful of him."

"Yeah, but not thoughtful enough. He missed a couple of places."

"Well, that's best for all of us. Leaves the place clean, yet leaves us what we need."

"Yeah, everything except who he really is. I hope we're able to know real soon. Say, Sam, would you happen to know if we have any prints on file for Tom Johnson?"

"We have something on file for a couple of Tom Johnsons, but I'm not sure if either is your Tom Johnson. Is that the guy whose prints you lifted?"

"It is. Maybe we'll have prints on file for three Tom Johnsons."

I hung up from talking to Sam, wondered what to do next. It was a little early to eat supper, yet there wasn't enough time for a nap.

+++

Lou and I went over the case, discussed our suspects, and tried to see if we'd forgotten anything we needed to do before bringing the case to a close. Of course, much of that depended upon things falling into place the way I thought they would. I wondered if I was losing my mind. Many said I already had. If so, this was another move that would add to the evidence.

On the surface it seemed ridiculous to proceed in the manner I proposed, without any idea who our murderer was. But in another way, under the circumstances, it seemed like the best way to proceed. Maybe we'd know more when we found out something about the fingerprints, but I doubted if that alone would lead us to our murderer. My guess was that the prints in the duplex, and those in Olive Grove, New York City, and California wouldn't be prints we'd have on file, prints of a convicted felon, or a fugitive from justice. Still, in my way of thinking, the more we knew, the less we still had to find out.

We hadn't set a time yet to round up the unusual suspects. We didn't want to rush things. Our mass roundup might seem like overkill, but something told me it was the best way to proceed.

Lou knew me like a book, and he knew never to interrupt me when I was deep in thought. I mulled over the case and the steps I planned to take. When I'd convinced myself that more thought would add nothing, I turned to Lou.

"Well, did you have time to read a book while I was gathering my thoughts?"

"Is that what you were doing, Cy? Why did it take you so long? Word around the department is that you don't have to travel far to gather your thoughts."

"I know, Lou. Jealousy is a terrible thing. One of these days, I'll retire for sure, and four people can replace me."

"What about me?"

"Oh, we can find someone to replace you, too."

"Very funny. Haven't you heard about us strong silent types?"

"Funny, I've never known you to be strong or silent. You hide both well."

+++

I deposited Lou in front of his apartment building, watched him waddle up to his front door and headed for home. I thought of hanging around and watching him do his exercises, but I was in too much of a hurry to get home. There were no dogs waiting for me when I arrived. No witches, vultures, or vermin anywhere in sight. Maybe I was about to embark on a weekend I'd remember for some time.

I put on my slippers, leaned back in my recliner, and cuddled up with Henrie O. Well, not in the physical sense. As far as I could tell, Henrie O. had a few years on me. If I were going to step out, I'd do so with a woman so young and beautiful that it'd make the other guys in the department jealous. If only I could find someone young, beautiful, and stupid. I smiled as I remembered things some friends had told me, but refrained from looking up Blondes Dating Service in the phone book, nor did I check any local sorority.

31

I woke Friday morning a new man. Okay, so I awoke, and upon further examination, I found out I was the same middle-aged man I'd been for the past couple of months or so. Still, it sounds good to say I awoke a new man. The middle-aged man I'd become stumbled from the bed, arrived at the bathroom without stubbing any toes and turned to face the mirror. I looked at the man I saw in the mirror. Not the fairest of them all, but at least the fairest for two houses, even when one of the houses contained an out-of-town guest. As I stood there, I considered plastic surgery. Not for myself, but for my next-door neighbor. Considering that plastic surgery does nothing to hide a personality, I decided to hook her up with the Witness Relocation Program instead. I kicked myself for not owning a computer. People have told me that you can find anything on a computer. My choices for my neighbor were a leper colony and an island inhabited by cannibals. I felt the second was a better choice. I had nothing against lepers, and once the cannibals recovered from indigestion my next-door neighbor might cause them, they'd either move on and look for their next meal or become vegetarians. When Heloise Humphert was a child, I imagine that her parents had dreams for her, dreams that would land her picture on the side of a milk carton. I, on the other hand, would proudly display a picture of my neighbor in a large boiling pot with nearly naked men wearing make-up and carrying bones as they danced around.

I shook my head to rid it of thoughts about my neighbor. I didn't want God to punish me by letting all my suspects leave town.

It was a big day for me. It was time to get on with it. I took off my clothes, stepped into the shower, and did the best imitation I could of Niagara Falls running over a barrel. Okay, you can only do so much on a small budget. Still, I thought I was remarkable as the barrel. As for the part my shower played of Niagara Falls, I decided to cut back on production costs, in case there is a drought later this year.

I refrained from drying myself doggie style, and used a towel, instead of shaking myself into traction. I brushed my teeth, dressed, studied what God wanted me to know that day that Lou was not going to share with me, and ambled over to the phone. Just before I got to the heavy black instrument, it rang.

"So, which one of you riffraff is calling me so early? Oh, hi, Chief. I thought it was someone else."

The chief and I spent a couple of minutes with our heads together, so to speak, and arrived at a time of 3:00, when we'd assemble the troops at the station and make plans for Operation Shakedown, or Dekker Prevails. Since time was limited, I didn't share the possible names of my project with the Chief. Otherwise, I might've been a part of Operation Shakeup, as in the Chief throwing a party to introduce everyone to the new head of homicide. Before we hung up, the Chief informed me that he was already on the job at the station. I told him I was going over my plans for the day. I refrained from sharing with him that so far my plans were breakfast, lunch, and supper.

I hung up the phone, breathed a sigh of relief, and was about to pick up the obtrusive instrument when it rang again.

"Yes, Chief. Forget something?"

"Cy, that Chief thing is okay in public, but when it's just the two of us it's okay to call me Sam."

I knew it was never too early in the day for Sam to enjoy a good laugh, so I let him know how I answered the phone on the previous call. I was right. It wasn't too early.

"So, Cy, who should I call instead?"

"Instead of what?"

"I mean, who's your replacement. I've got the info on those fingerprints."

"Very funny. I merely lost the use of the Chief's condo in the Azores."

"The who?"

"The Azores. It's a group of islands."

"I know that, but do you have any idea where they are?"

"Of course. They're like any other group of islands. They're out in the middle of the water. But enough of this diatribe, what did you call to tell me?"

"I just wanted to let you know that Bauerman is Bauerman is Bauerman."

"Is that another way of saying that the fingerprints in all three locales match?"

"It is."

"Thank you, my servant. I was sure that they would."

"Then why did you have me go to all that trouble of making sure?"

"One, you needed something to do. Two, it always helps if you know rather than perceive."

"Well, I wouldn't want you to perceive, Cy. It might be dangerous."

My stomach growled and I put an end to such an enlightening conversation.

+++

I was getting cocky, but I didn't want Lou to know, so I asked him the clue of the day.

"Kind Hearts and Coronets."

"Do what?"

"Kind Hearts and Coronets."

I lost my cockiness. I had no idea what my partner was talking about. Maybe we'd solve the case anyway.

+++

Lou and I figured that time would pass more quickly if we occupied our minds. So, after breakfast, I dropped Lou at his place, returned to mine, and finished reading my first Henrie O. mystery. Unlike some of the other authors where I liked one series much better than the other, I enjoyed both of Carolyn Hart's series. Well, at least I enjoyed the first book in each series and hoped to get to the second book in each series soon.

It was almost lunchtime by the time I finished reading. I called Lou, and he too had finished reading *Dead Man's Island*. Over lunch, the two of us would discuss the book we just completed and contemplate what book to read next. Why hadn't we discovered reading mysteries earlier in life? Both of us found it so much fun to solve a case without working up a sweat. We found that solving murders in print is much easier on the constitution than solving them in real life, although Lou and I had stumbled from a perfect record in print.

+++

Since our minds were on food, I called Antonio's to order food for everyone in the department who would be working that night. Lou and I would pick it up and distribute it to each officer at his or her post. After taking care of that, I called the Blue Moon to see if they would provide breakfast for everyone the next day. After Rosie realized I was serious, she checked with the cook and both agreed to come in early to prepare a feast for our suspects, witnesses, and officers. Lou and I didn't want to go without food, and we didn't expect others to do so either. With all of that taken care of, I drove the two of us to the station to prepare for bringing the case to a conclusion.

32

Word had filtered throughout the department that Lou and I were working to solve a murder case where a friend of ours was the victim. Few of the men knew the Colonel, even remotely, but most of them knew us and wanted to help in any way they could. It wasn't mandatory that everyone participates, but our good friend Lt. George Michaelson had rounded up a good number of men to help us. Even Frank Harris, the medical examiner, agreed to help unless he had an autopsy to perform.

We allowed a few minutes for late arrivals, and then at 3:05, I stood up to deliver the state of the union address.

"First of all, let me say that Lou and I appreciate your help. With the Chief's blessing, we're proceeding with this case in a way I think will help bring it to a conclusion. I'll be honest with you. I've no idea who our murderer is, but I believe it's one of the people you'll be rounding up."

"So, you've been working on this case for a while, and you don't have any idea who did it. I thought you said there's something different about this case."

The group roared and tension was relieved.

"Ladies and gentlemen, we have now heard from our friend George Michaelson, the perfect example that if you hang around long enough, you will be promoted to

Lieutenant. And finally, at age eighty-two George received his promotion."

Again the group laughed. While laughter was necessary, the men and women who joined us that day didn't come to be entertained. So, I returned to the business at hand.

"Let me share with you what we need for you to do. We are gathering all the suspects, no matter how unlikely the possibility that they murdered Col. Hardesty. Altogether, there are eleven of them. This will not be the highlight of some of these people's day. Some of them may even get ugly about coming and being a part of a lineup. A lineup. We all know that there's no reason to have a lineup without someone to point out the guilty party and that a lot of police departments have dispensed lineups altogether. But I feel that a lineup is the best way to bring this case to its conclusion. So, in addition to our suspects, we are inviting three witnesses to join our party. Believe it or not, I think our witnesses will be as reluctant to attend as some of our suspects. The reluctance of these individuals is where you come in. I believe that some of these people will want to stay away so much that they might try to flee. We plan to deliver our invitations this evening, but we will not require their attendance until tomorrow morning. Therefore, we need two to three officers to watch each house overnight. One residence houses five of our suspects, and one of our witnesses lives next door to that house, so we will not need two or three officers for each witness or suspect. Five officers should be sufficient for those two adjacent houses. One other residence houses two suspects. If you're posted at a residence, under no circumstances are you to allow anyone to leave that residence. We believe that our murderer is a master of disguises. Man or woman, young or old, all are required to remain inside. That might create a handicap at one residence because all who live there are college students, and this is Friday night. You will not be required to keep everyone in the building at home, just

225

everyone who lives in that apartment. We will post one officer at the front door of the apartment, and another under the window. Under no circumstances are you to leave your post at any time before another officer replaces you.

"Each person will be informed that he or she is to be ready to come to headquarters at 8:00 tomorrow morning. We will provide food and beverages for all who need them. Each team will drive one or more people. None of these people are to be allowed to come on their own, no matter what reason they might give for doing so. After we have finished all we plan to do here tomorrow, some or all of these people will be allowed to leave without an officer going with them. We will let you know who the people are when the time comes.

"Some of you will be going with Lou and me to the home of your assignment, where you will remain until midnight, and then return shortly before 8:00 tomorrow morning. Others of you are free to leave after learning your assignment. You know to report to your designated residence at midnight. Now, are there any questions?"

The silence and lack of hands allowed me to conclude.

"Let us hope and pray that there's no major disaster of any type prior to gathering these people here tomorrow morning. Good luck. Sergeant Murdock and I will take each of you to your location, and then check back with each of you from time to time until 1:00 a.m., after we're sure that all replacements are in place."

+++

We gave each officer the name and address of whomever he or she was to watch that evening. In no case was there only one officer per suspect or witness. In most cases there were three; one to watch the front, one to watch the back, and one to relieve whoever needed to take a break. I informed everyone to detain anyone who tried to leave the premises and that Lou and I would arrive at each location as soon as possible to explain to each resident what was happening.

By the time all of us left headquarters, it was almost 5:00 on a Friday evening. I remembered when I was young, so Lou and I made tracks to the apartment of Mark Blakeman, college student, pizza delivery man, and witness. Luckily, we found him at home.

I knocked on his door and realized I'd made an impression.

"You're that cop that was here before."

"And now I'm that cop who's back again. I'm here to inform you that we request your assistance tomorrow morning. We have captured someone who may or may not have been the man with the long hair and beard that you saw leaving the house on Cherry Hill Lane. We'll have you look at several people in a lineup to see if you can make an identification."

"Hey, man, I told you, I didn't get a good look at him."

"That's okay. After you look over all the people in the lineup, if you feel that you cannot make a positive identification, then tell us. In the meantime, I'm leaving a couple of officers for your protection. You're to remain home this evening."

"You can't do that. I've got a date tonight."

"I'm sorry, but you'll have to cancel it. Call her and change it to tomorrow night."

"I can't do that. Come on, man."

"Sorry, but you'll have to stay home."

"Come on. This girl's a babe. Weren't you ever young?"

"I'm sorry to inconvenience you, but you'll have to stay home. And don't try to sneak out. My men will be watching, and if they catch you trying to leave, they'll cart you downtown and you'll end up spending the night in a cell.

"Someone will bring you downtown tomorrow morning. I don't know how long the identification will take, but I want you to know that someone will knock on your door at 8:00 a.m. Be ready to go. And don't worry about breakfast. Breakfast will be supplied by the department."

"Eight o'clock? On a Saturday? What's wrong with you guys?"

"We're just trying to bring a murderer to justice."

"But I already told you I can't identify the guy."

"That's okay. We have another witness."

"Why didn't you say so? Fine. Call me if he cannot identify the guy."

"Eight o'clock. Be ready. And remember, don't try to leave. Otherwise, you'll be the first one there."

We left to a groan and a slammed door. We didn't want to take any chances. We posted one officer outside the only door to the apartment, and a second officer by the only window the apartment had, in the back. A third officer patrolled the area and was available to relieve or assist either of the other officers.

+++

Our next stop was at the Hardesty house. Luckily, everyone was home for the night, and no one had plans for the evening. I gathered everyone and informed them of our plans. I told everyone that we had three witnesses who'd seen someone leave the house and that each person who knew the Colonel would take part in the lineup. There were no groans, except when I announced the time everyone would be required to leave, but the groans were quickly replaced with cheers when I announced that breakfast was being provided by the department and that there was nothing continental about it. Martha smiled. She remembered how much Lou and I liked to eat.

+++

Lou and I had only a short walk to Bob Downey's house. I didn't care who knew we were there. I raised the knocker and lowered it with enough resolve to raise anyone inside. Thirty seconds or so later, Downey answered the door.

"Well, Lieutenant. It seems as if we are quickly becoming friends. What can I do for you this time?"

"Mr. Downey, I have good news. We have apprehended someone who matches the description you gave us of the man you saw entering the Hardesty house on the day of the murder. We want you to come downtown tomorrow morning and look at several people in a lineup, to see if you can identify anyone as the man you saw on that afternoon."

"I'd rather not do that, Lieutenant. As I told you before, I don't think I got a good enough look at the individual to pick him out of a lineup."

"Experience has taught us that sometimes people think they cannot identify someone, but when they get a second look, they realize that one of the people is the one they saw before. You don't have to worry, Mr. Downey. You will be on one side of a glass partition, and none of the people in the lineup will be able to see you. Also, we have a second witness. I want to see if the two of you agree on who you saw."

"A second witness?"

"Yeah, there was a college student delivering pizza on the street that day, and he saw someone, and his description of the individual was similar to yours, so I think the two of you saw the same person. This will give us a good opportunity to see if the two of you agree on who you saw."

"But what if I get down there and can't identify your suspect?"

"That's okay. That happens sometimes. Also, sometimes we have someone who says it might be number three or number five, but there's no way that it's one, two, or four. That helps us, too. While we cannot make a positive identification, we can at least eliminate some of our suspects and devote more time to the ones who might be the one we are looking for."

"So, what time do you want me?"

"We're making it easy for both of you. I doubt if our suspect gets wind of this, but just in case, we have some officers watching your house, protecting you this evening. One of those officers will knock on your door at 8:00 in the morning and give you a ride to headquarters. Also, don't worry about breakfast. The department is providing a full-scale breakfast for you."

"Do you think tomorrow will put an end to this? I'm beginning to wonder if I should've spoken up, or not."

"We think we have the right guy. We're hoping that we can get a positive ID tomorrow, and put this guy behind bars where he belongs, but I can't promise you anything. And don't worry about your identification. Just let us know if you see anyone who you positively think is the guy who entered the house next door on the day in question."

"Okay, Lieutenant. You guys better come up with a good breakfast. And remember, I know a good breakfast. Over the years I found some of the best truck stops in the business."

I thanked Downey for his time, then placed the men and told them Lou and I would return later with food. That got us plenty of smiles. Everyone knew that if anyone would let them down on food, it wouldn't be Lou or me.

"Say, Cy, how come you didn't let either of these witnesses know that there's a third witness?"

"Well, Lou, I didn't want anyone to think there are so many witnesses that their appearance isn't important."

"Well, even one other witness seemed enough that Blakeman wanted to back out."

"Both of these guys would want to back out whether we had no other witnesses or one hundred other witnesses. We need everyone because no one knows who might really be the person who can help us."

+++

Since Dick Morrissey was nearby, we chose his house to visit next. The old man who saw a long-haired man with a beard run down his driveway a few days before the murder was at home and answered the door quickly. Unlike the other two witnesses, he was eager to assist us and told me that he might be able to identify the perpetrator if he could see his eyes. Unlike each of the other two witnesses, he saw the suspect up close. On that day, the man in question didn't stop running until he braced himself against Morrissey's car, and, stunned by the situation, he didn't move for a few seconds afterward. In my mind, Morrissey had the best chance of giving us a positive ID, but I wasn't going to discount what the others had to say.

33

"Say, Cy, you got your Taser ready for this next guy?"

"Oh, I'd love to use it, Lou. After I disable him, you shoot him with some pepper spray, and then throw some poison ivy on him for good measure."

We had no idea if Michael Belding was our murderer or not, but we knew that he'd showed no remorse when he learned the Colonel had been murdered.

I pulled up in front of the house, and the two of us got out of the car. We walked up to the door and knocked. A woman answered. I felt sorry for her already.

"Is Mr. Belding here please?"

"Whom shall I say is calling?"

"Tell him it's Lt. Dekker with the Hilldale Police Department, about that matter we discussed the other day."

"You've already talked to him? Michael didn't say anything to me about it."

"I guess it slipped his mind. With some people, I make an impression. Others I don't. I guess he's one of the others. Just tell him that I'd like a minute of his time."

"Just a minute, we were just sitting down to eat."

I wondered who ate that early, then realized it was getting close to 6:00. I was glad that we caught him just before he ate. If I could do anything to make his meal a little more unpalatable, I'd be happy to oblige. A few seconds later, my new best friend came to the door.

"What do you want? I told you to quit bothering me. You want me to sue?"

"No, I want you to come to breakfast. Tomorrow morning we wish for you to be a guest of the city for our annual suspects day breakfast."

"Is this some kind of joke I'm supposed to understand?"

"Well, we do plan to feed you breakfast, and we'd like for you to stand up with some other people to see if anyone recognizes you. Never know where you might run into friends."

"Not interested."

Belding started to shut the door, but I stopped him.

"Mr. Belding, attendance isn't optional. You're one of our most prized guests. Not only are we inviting you to our breakfast and costume party, but we'll be providing a ride for you. Just think, your own chauffeur."

"Still not interested. You're not making any sense."

"Let me make it simple. We have three witnesses who saw a man enter or leave the victim's residence on the day of the murder. You will be one of many who will participate in a lineup so that our witnesses can tell us if you are or aren't the man we're looking for."

"I already told you, I was home in bed that day."

"So, you say. If at some point, we find any witnesses who say you were home in bed that day, we will allow them to identify you in a lineup, but since we have not yet been able to find any, and we want your participation in our current event, we'll see you in the morning."

"Listen, lay off me and find somebody else."

Again, Belding tried to shut the door.

"Mr. Belding, I don't think I'm getting across to you how much your attendance means to us. Let me put it another way, tomorrow morning we'll have an officer here at 8:00 to drive you to headquarters where we'll feed you, then require your assistance in our lineup. If you would rather go tonight, that is fine, too. We have a nice, small, one-room suite that you can share with some of our fair city's other misguided inhabitants.

"Now I'm sorry we cannot afford something better for you, but you must understand that is all that we can provide on such short notice. Humble us this one time, Mr. Belding. If for some reason you choose not to open your front door at 8:00 in the morning, the officer standing over there has been trained in opening even hard to open doors. Just in case you're one of those people who have a habit of walking or driving in your sleep, we are leaving three officers outside your home tonight to wake you should that happen. See how much we care, Mr. Belding?"

"You'll see how much I care when I get through slapping you with a lawsuit, cop."

+++

"Mr. Terloff."

"Lt. Dekker, isn't it?"

"Oh, it's so good of you to remember my name."

"I do my best. Of course, it helps when you're one of the few people I've met since I've been back."

"That's one of the reasons why I came back today. I want to give you more opportunities to meet people. Tomorrow, we're having breakfast in your honor, and we're going to give you a chance to stand up and see if anyone recognizes you."

"Huh?"

We have three witnesses who saw someone enter or leave the victim's house on the day he was murdered. We want them to see everyone who might have had even the slightest reason for murdering Professor Hardesty, so we can eliminate those who had nothing to do with his murder."

"Sounds cool. I'll be there."

"We're even going to provide a ride for you. Eight o'clock tomorrow morning that officer over there will knock on your door and expect you to be ready to go downtown with him.

"Remember, we're providing breakfast. Also, protection. We'll have some officers guard your house overnight."

"Cool. That'll give me something to tell the grandkids, provided I ever have any."

+++

Lou and I merely shook our heads as we pulled away. What kind of night were we having?

"What do you think about all of this, Lou?"

"I don't know what to think, Cy. We've got a suspect who's excited about taking part in tomorrow's festivities, and two witnesses who are reluctant. Shouldn't it be the other way around?"

"Yeah, and who are we supposed to believe is our murderer, the guy who's going in kicking and dragging, or the one who might step outside in the morning and ask the officers if they'd like to leave early, so he can be the first one there."

"I know I don't know what to make of it, Cy."

+++

We had three more houses to visit before we dropped by Antonio's to pick up the food. We expected Earl Hoskins to be our biggest problem, and we were right. Well, right except for Belding.

"Lieutenant, I don't understand why you're bothering Myra and me. We liked the old guy. We didn't have anything to do with his murder. You should know that."

"Mr. Hoskins, we are hoping that the lineup tomorrow will help us solve Col. Hardesty's murder and bring the murderer to justice, but even if it only helps us eliminate some people from suspicion, that will be a big help and will allow us to zero in on fewer suspects. We're having everyone downtown, even Mrs. Hardesty."

"I know she didn't do it. And why do you have to have us go downtown on our day off? I had things to do tomorrow."

"So did I, Mr. Hoskins, but because someone murdered Col. Hardesty, I have to work. I'm sure the inconvenience will not be that great if we can bring the murderer to justice."

"Do you really think you'll get the murderer tomorrow, Lieutenant?" Mrs. Hoskins asked.

"I don't know. I just know we have three witnesses who saw someone. Whether or not any of those witnesses will make a positive identification, I don't know. We can only hope."

+++

We left the Hoskins house with only two more houses on our schedule. So far things were going well. Everyone had been at home. A few minutes later, we had one hundred percent attendance. Joe Guilfoyle said he was willing to do anything to bring his friend's murderer to justice, and Robert Collins, the plumber, couldn't understand why we wanted him but was willing to comply.

34

I was tired after visiting eleven suspects and three witnesses and speaking with all the officers after each visit to let them know how great I felt the danger was that someone inside might flee. I didn't want to lose anyone, even those who seemed unconcerned, so each time I made out like there was some chance the suspect or witness might try to leave because there was. We knew only how each person reacted to us, not what was in his or her mind. If we knew that, we wouldn't be doing what we had planned. We'd have already read our murderer's mind and arrested him or her.

Tired, hungry, ready to collapse, that pretty much described Lou and me. But our work wasn't over. We arrived at Antonio's to pick up the food. I'd never seen so many sandwiches before; Strombolis, hoagies, ham and cheese, turkey and bacon. It was almost enough to cause Lou and me to flee. Well, not really, but if some of the officers declined our offer of food, I wouldn't press them.

I was curious to see how our college student was behaving, so Lou and I started our run near campus. Someone had opened the door twice, sighed, and reluctantly closed the apartment door. Someone had even looked out the back window. I hated to nix Blakeman's date, but sometimes love has to take a back seat to justice. All was proceeding well until we arrived at Belding's house. Lou pointed and I looked at a scuffle taking place on the front lawn. Neighbors stood in their doorways, looking on in awe. As I pulled Lightning up to the curb of the house next door three officers pulled Belding to his feet.

"Well, Mr. Belding, how nice of you to take us up on our offer of accommodations for the evening."

Belding mumbled something I couldn't understand.

Mrs. Belding stood in the door, downcast.

Two officers escorted Belding over to a squad car and into the back seat. He yelped as they bent his head to allow him to get in. After Belding was firmly ensconced in the car, a couple of the officers came over to fill us in. Despite his wife's protestations, Belding came stomping out of the house ordering the officers to leave. They stood there and took his spew of expletives, but when he took a swing at one of them, they drew the line. He was so irrational that it took two of them to hold him down so the third one could put the cuffs on him. I would've loved to have forgotten about Belding for a couple of weeks, but we needed him for the lineup, just in case he had been coherent enough to have committed the murder. I'd begun to doubt his guilt, but sometimes the most likely and most irrational acting one committed the murder.

I encouraged the officers to eat before they left, giving Belding an opportunity to calm down, and to allow as many of his neighbors as possible to see what his temper had brought upon him.

+++

We saved the Hardesty and Downey houses for last, knowing that two of the men who volunteered for duty were our good friends Lt. George Michaelson, and Frank Harris, the medical examiner.

"Well, Frank, so you finally are willing to admit that you have little work to do."

"No, Cy, I just know that wherever you are a body is soon to wind up there, so I wanted to save you a phone call."

"Well, Frank, I'm sorry to disappoint you. The only dead meat I've got for you at present is in the form of Strombolis, hoagies, ham and cheese, and turkey with bacon."

"Are you serious? You actually showed up with food. And to think that George had offered me ten-to-one odds that you wouldn't. I could've made a bundle. What happened, guys? Go on a diet?"

Evidently Frank hadn't noticed Lou's diminishing waistline. I wasn't about to point it out. The way things were going Frank had already suggested getting a Wii to everyone he met who wasn't on a slab.

"How dare you use the "d" word in our presence? I'll have you know that I always take care of my friends."

"And what would you have done if you looked in the back seat and realized that there weren't enough sandwiches for everyone?"

"I told you that I always take care of my friends. I would've gone home and called and ordered you a couple of pizzas as soon as I'd finished eating."

Frank laughed.

"I'm sure you would've, Cy."

Just as Frank finished his comment, George waved and walked up.

"Everything's secure here, Cy. So, what brings you here? Don't tell me you're making good on your promise of dinner. Late," he said, looking at his watch, "but at least you're here. What happened, they give you some fancy food that you don't know what it is? You know that Frank offered me five-to-one that you wouldn't bring us any food, don't you? I should've taken him up on it."

"The way Frank tells it, it was ten-to-one, and you offered it to him."

"Yeah, but that was after he offered me five-to-one."

"Well, at least both of you were able to hold on to your money. Now, do you want something to eat, or not?"

"Yeah, but we've got some young guys with us, not as tough as Frank and I. We'll let them go first. You did bring enough for everyone, didn't you?"

"It depends on how much everyone eats. We've got only twelve sandwiches left."

"See, Frank, we were right. They only brought enough for themselves."

I looked at my watch. It was a little after 8:00. I was hungry and tired, but we didn't get a lot of opportunities to spend time with our friends, so we plopped down on the hood of George's car and ate with them. We could see two sides of both houses from where we were. The younger guys took their food to the back of the houses and watched what we couldn't see.

+++

It was after 9:00 when Lightning coasted to a stop in front of Lou's place. Everywhere we went the officers told us they were okay and encouraged us to go home, get some sleep, that the next day would be a busy one for us. All three of the officers assigned to Belding's house agreed to split up after they delivered him to jail, and each one went to reinforce another team of officers.

"Well, Lou, this is almost it. At least I hope it is. With what we have and the possibilities we have for tomorrow, I think we can bring the perp to justice."

"I sure hope so, Cy. I'm ready to get this one behind us. So, do you have any more of an idea than you did?"

"Not really, Lou. I mean I have a couple of ideas, but, as you know, sometimes it turns out to be someone you don't suspect. I know I'm going to be very disappointed if tomorrow comes and we don't have someone behind bars."

"Well, then quit being disappointed, Cy. We already have someone behind bars. Remember Belding?"

"Yeah, and I hope that some of those drunks in with him throw up all over him, maybe even knock him around a few times. I hope he starts something with one of the violent types."

"Cy, correct me if I'm wrong, but you seem to be taking a liking to Belding just like you have your next-door neighbor."

"I think you're right, Lou. Maybe we can send them away together. Don't know where we can find a leaky raft, do you?"

"We won't need a leaky raft. Both of them would try to throw the other one overboard before they were out of sight of land."

"You really think Heloise would throw a man overboard?"

"You've got me there, Cy."

"Okay, we'll see what we can do about a leaky raft."

The two of us shared a laugh.

"Or, I could identify my neighbor and you can name Belding as her accomplice."

Lou got out, walked up to his apartment door and waved. I nodded and patted Lightning on the backside to let him know it was time to go home.

All the way home I thought of all of our possibilities. Did our witnesses actually see someone enter the Colonel's home, or did one of our witnesses commit murder? Did everyone in the house love the Colonel as much as he or she pretended? Actually, I didn't think that Tom Brockman loved the old man, and I didn't know if the Colonel's grandson-in-law did or not, but they acted like they were on good terms with him. Was it possible that our murderer was closer to home than we suspected? Was there really a stolen key? Or was an outside suspect created to take our suspicions away from those who lived there? And was his good friend Joe really his good friend Joe? Was he unable to raise the Colonel that day as he said, or did he get caught just after leaving, and have to make up an excuse that the Colonel didn't answer the door? I remembered that his wife thought he left the house early.

So where does that leave us? What about Earl and Myra Hoskins, the handyman and the maid? I thought she was okay, and her alibi checked out, but what about his? He could've sneaked over and murdered the Colonel, but did he? And what reason would he have had?

That brought me to Michael Belding. On the surface, he seemed too crazy to be our murderer, but was his craziness an act? Did he force us to arrest him tonight, hoping that he'd be in jail tomorrow and wouldn't have to take part in the lineup? Supposedly, he was sane enough to teach a high school class. Did that mean he was sane enough to plan a murder in advance because I was pretty sure that the Colonel's murder was premeditated? Everything pointed to that. The threat. Everything.

So, where did that leave us? Well, it left us a plumber we'd never considered, Robert Collins. He seemed the most unlikely of all our suspects. Did that mean that he is our murderer? I didn't think so, but then, over the years I've seen murderers who were just as unlikely.

All who were left were Daniel Terloff and two guys who were hard to find. What about Terloff? The guy seemed like he's having the time of his life. Is this all a ruse? Did he really change how he felt about the Colonel after spending several years in the wilderness or was he trying to make us think that he had changed?

Who else did we have? A guy who drives around and sprays for bugs who wouldn't have seemed like a suspect at all, if he hadn't disappeared. Or did he? He had been back to the duplex he rented. How many times I didn't know, but he did return.

And then there was our most likely suspect who was the hardest to find, Carl Bauerman, actor extraordinaire. All we had of these last two were pictures and fingerprints, but was that enough to find them?

I arrived at my house, hoping that the next day revealed more than that night had done. I was hopeful. I was confident.

+++

Nights where I have a particularly satisfying meal are not the only nights I have nightmares. It is also true on nights when I go to bed extremely tired. That night was one of those nights.

I went to sleep, found myself dreaming. There were officers outside my next-door neighbor's house. She went outside to make sure none of them got away. One at a time she invited them in but got nowhere. She was hoping that either she or one of the cops would try on the handcuffs. Reluctantly, she went inside, smiling, saying "Cyrus is the one for me." A first nightmare led to a second. The second one was worse. I sat in my car in the pouring down rain. Lightning flashed. No, I don't mean my car opened its doors. I mean the kind of lightning that goes with thunder. It, the lightning, and a screen a distance in front of me revealed that I was in a drive-in movie theater. I felt steam on my neck, a burning in my flesh. I turned to my right and screamed. There, braced against my body, I found my next-door neighbor, the ugly one herself. Her breath had burnt a hole in my shirt collar. Her drool had caused my skin to blister. I screamed again. It was worse than I thought. Muffy was eating all the popcorn. I lunged for the door but found that someone had removed the knob. I reached out for the keys, to lower the window, and hoped it was wider than my girth, but the keys were not there. I heard a jingling and pushed my neighbor away long enough to see her dog carrying a tub of popcorn and a ring of keys jump over the seat into the back seat.

I was about to give up hope when I awakened. Even awake, I found something against me and something in my mouth. Not something as terrifying as my neighbor, but something. I spat out my keys and they fell to the floor. Once again I reached for a knob, only this time I found one. I turned it and lunged from my enclosure. Simultaneously, I heard and felt a thud. It was almost as painful as the sight of my next-door neighbor. In a matter of days, I regained my senses and found myself on my bedroom floor. I looked up from whence I had come. I had never walked in my sleep before, nor did I've any idea that my bedroom closet was larger than my girth. I reached out and up for the top of my mattress. In more attempts than I could count, I was able to reach up, grasp my mattress, and pull myself to my knees. Sometime before dawn, I lifted myself to my bed, and, once again, drifted off to sleep. My nightmares were over. Well, at least I didn't have any more nightmares that night. I still had an unsolved case, and I didn't see a "For Sale" sign in my next-door neighbor's yard. Someday I would have to check into what it takes to have a house condemned.

35

I awoke Saturday morning to a strange noise. It sounded like my next-door neighbor might sound on her best day. I don't know how I could say that. My next-door neighbor has never had a best day. I slapped the alarm clock a few times, and finally, it shut up. When you set one as little as I do, you forget what allows them to make that awful racket and what makes them stop it. I contemplated lying there for a fortnight but realized that it would defeat my purpose of setting the alarm. It was time to get up and get things in motion.

It seemed like months since the Colonel called and invited us to his house.

Over the twenty-plus years I'd spent in homicide only a few cases had taken longer to solve than this one. I hoped that this one would come to a rapid conclusion in a matter of hours, and my choices on what to do on Monday would include coming home to read after breakfast, or giving Scene of the Crime some more of my money.

I initiated the twelve-step method to remove myself from my bed and stood looking at my clock, my old-fashioned clock. The hands pointed to 6:03. Yes, it has hands. I did say it was old-fashioned. I made it a point to consult the Guinness Book of World's Records to see if someone of my girth rising from a bed in only three minutes was a record. If not, I wasn't going to set the alarm again the next day in order to achieve that status. I tried my best to wipe the sleep from my eyes as I stumbled to the bathroom. If I hadn't tried both at once, I wouldn't have banged my elbow on the door casing. Naturally, it would have to be my right arm, my shaving arm. But I'd tough it out. Cops are known for toughing it out. Otherwise, I would've moved a long time ago. I remembered the time I dreamed that Lou and I showed up late enough for church that someone snatched the last donut just before we arrived. To miss out on a donut at the only place where my candy doesn't accompany me is toughing it to the nth degree. However, I'm not sure if toughing it out in dreams is quite the same.

Somewhere around 7:00, I surprised my next-door neighbor with my early departure and left tread marks in the street as she opened her front door. She sicced the dog on me, but that wimp was no match for Lightning.

+++

Lou opened Lightning's door, sat down, shut the door. He buckled and looked at me.

"Lou, do you think God's message for the day will help us solve the case?"

"I don't know."

"I don't know. God's message is 'I don't know.' Well if God doesn't know, who does? What you do mean, 'I don't know.' Doesn't the Bible tell us that God knows everything? There's even a word for it. What's that word, Lou?"

"Omniscient."

"That's it, Lou. Omni...whatever you said. All those words for God start with 'Omni." All this. All that. God's all everything. There's even a building in Atlanta named the Omni. Is it still there, Lou?"

"I don't know."

"Right, and who's on first. Anyway, I'll ask someone who has a computer. They'll know where to look to see if the building has been razed. If God doesn't know anything anymore, the building's probably gone."

"You could ask someone who's been to Atlanta."

"And I could call up the Omni in Atlanta, and if anyone answers, the building's still there."

"Cy, I think you're too charged up. Take a bite of candy."

"Good idea, Lou."

I reached into my pocket, yanked my candy out, took a bite.

"How's that, Lou?"

"I'd say you're still too charged up."

"Why's that, Lou? Because I didn't check to see if I'd eaten more than one almond?"

"Partly."

"And what's the other partly?"

"Well, in all the years I've watched you eat your candy, Cy, this is the first time I saw you take a bite, paper and all."

"I thought it tasted funny."

I pulled over and practiced some Lamaze breathing. It didn't work. My stomach was still there. And God still didn't know.

"Lou, why do you think God told you to say 'I don't know,' and don't say 'I don't know?'"

"God didn't say, 'I don't know.'"

"I know you say you don't say that God gives you the idea each day, but why did your thoughts tell you that?"

"They didn't, Cy. You asked me, 'Lou, do you think God's message for the day will help us solve the case?' and I said, 'I don't know.'"

"Right. So why did you say that?"

"Cy, get a grip. I said I don't know if you will use the clue to solve the case, not that 'I don't know' was the message."

"So, God still knows. Of course, He does. But what I don't know is today's clue. Enlighten me."

"Joanne Woodward."

"The actress?"

"No, the rugby player. What other Joanne Woodward is there?"

"Well, there's the rugby player."

Only the fact that Lou and I had pulled up in front of the Blue Moon kept Lou from choking me. We stepped out of the car, opened the door. I couldn't move.

"Now, Cy. Get ahold of yourself. We're not eating here today."

Somewhere far away I heard Lou's words, but up close I saw some old guy sitting on my stool. My stool. I thought surely our stools were like retired jerseys from sports teams. No one other than Lou or me would use them.

"Cy, stay calm."

"That's easy enough for you to say, Lou. No one's sitting on your stool."

"Would you like for me to ask the elderly gentleman if he'd be just as comfortable on my stool. Remember, Cy, we're not using our stools today. We're eating at the station with the others. You don't want this old man and Rosie to pick you out of a lineup, do you?"

"You mean Rosie would do that?"

"I don't know, Cy, but an old man's declaration carries a lot of weight."

"I carry a lot of weight, too, Lou."

"Just don't end up in the slammer with Belding."

"That's a thought, Lou. I'll throw this old man off my stool. They'll throw me in the slammer, and while I'm waiting for the lineup, I can beat Belding to a pulp. I wouldn't be acting as a police officer then, would I?"

"No, Cy, I'd say you wouldn't be acting as a police officer ever again. Now, what's that smell, Cy?"

"The old man smells, too."

"I'm talking about breakfast. You do still like to eat breakfast, don't you, Cy?"

"Of course, Lou. I guess it's that I'm nervous about today. Plus, I had two, not one, but two nightmares about my next-door neighbor last night. That's enough to drive anyone crazy."

+++

Lightning had never smelled so good. The smell of bacon, sausage, eggs, hash browns, biscuits, and gravy wafted from the back seat and stirred the air around us. Just like the night before, I was tempted to dash for home and serve a humongous breakfast for two. I envisioned the small bundle of fluff from next door gnawing on my ankle and food flying everywhere.

Lou and I arrived at the station five minutes before the first of our witnesses. We'd decided the night before that we'd whisk the witnesses in before we deposited any of the suspects. All of our witnesses arrived within a couple of minutes of each other, so each got a brief look at the others. None were told that those other guys were witnesses too. We didn't want talking among the witnesses, so we placed them in adjacent rooms, rather than put them together. The younger two seemed terrified to be there. And they were the witnesses. Lou or I asked each of them what he wanted to eat or drink, got it for them, and left them alone with their breakfasts. We told them we'd return after breakfast with details about the proceedings. We brought out our finest dinnerware and glassware for the occasion.

All of our suspects made it in unscathed. None tried to escape on the way to the station. We didn't care if suspects talked to other suspects, but we did separate them into groups of Colonel friendly and Colonel hostile, based on what we knew about them. We didn't want someone to recognize someone else and murder them on the spot.

I breathed a sigh of relief after each person had received his or her food. There was enough left for Lou and me to enjoy as much as we usually did. Unbeknownst to us, there was a box with our names on it. I opened it and smiled. There were four pieces of pecan pie for the two of us, with a note that said, "Sorry, but I couldn't figure out a way to add the ice cream." If I ever get married again, Rosie's the woman for me.

In a matter of minutes, George joined us, and there was still enough food for all of us. We refrained from bringing out the pie until after George excused himself to take care of some police business. While he was there, we went over the agenda for the morning.

36

I entered the first of the rooms that housed our witnesses just as a young woman was removing the tray and dishes.

"So, how was breakfast, Mr. Downey?"

"Better than anything I could fix myself, and I'd put it on par with those truck stops I frequented. But could you leave the glass and bring me some water?"

"No problem. We'll bring you a clean glass and a pitcher of water."

"Now, Mr. Downey, let me fill you in on what we're going to be doing here today. We have several people who will be taking part in a lineup. We'll take you into a room with a glass window that will allow you to see them, but they cannot see you. One at a time, we'll ask them to step forward and stand until we ask them to step back. I want you to concentrate on each suspect to see if he could be the person we're looking for. All of these people will look something alike, so look carefully. You will have a piece of paper that will allow you to jot down any notes you want to take because we don't want you to identify anyone or eliminate anyone until you've seen all the suspects. Because there are so many of them, we'll have more than one lineup. Any questions?"

"No, it sounds straightforward."

"Okay, each of the witnesses will go in one at a time, so you will return to this room after each set of people. I don't know how long all of this will take. We are still rounding up people for the later lineup. We'll let you know when we're through. And thanks again for your willingness to help."

"I don't think I had any choice."

"Well, we still appreciate your help."

+++

I stepped out into the hallway. An officer informed me that Lou had just left one of the witness rooms and entered the other. I waited for him to return.

A couple of minutes later, Lou returned and we compared notes. Only Dick Morrissey, the seasoned veteran with the best look at the long-haired man, seemed to be at ease with what was going to take place.

+++

Lou and I walked down a corridor to where the suspects were waiting. I took one room. Lou walked into the other. We decided to let the family and close friends of the Colonel be in the first lineup. That meant that we'd leave Belding in lockup a little longer.

I walked in, looked at Martha, and addressed the group.

"Good morning, everyone. I hope all of you had a good breakfast. I stopped in to let you know what we're doing here today. We believe that the person the witnesses saw enter your house was the same person we captured on film. This person had long hair and a beard. Since no one we know resembles this person, we believe that whoever it was wore a disguise. We've had a team of experts design a disguise that closely resembles that of the perpetrator. We want each of you to don this disguise, walk out to your assigned number, and take your place. When your number is called, you're to step forward and remain there until you're asked to step back. Any questions?"

"What if someone thinks the beard and long hair make me look like the murderer?" Scott asked.

"I don't see that happening unless you're the murderer, and you're not at the top of our list. When it's over, I think you'll feel much better than you do now."

"But how reliable are these witnesses?"

"Well, one of them told me he could definitely identify the man if he saw him. From talking to him, I'd say he can. At least, we'll know what he thinks after he has seen everyone we've brought in. And we have two other witnesses besides. Since all three will not see people at the same time and feed off each other, it would seem awfully convincing if all three identified the same person."

When I received no protests or other questions, I left them to themselves.

+++

Nervously, Lou and I stood in the hall waiting for our signal to summon the first witness. We arranged a schedule of from youngest to oldest, so Mark Blakeman would be first. In a matter of minutes that seemed like hours, George came and gave us the signal. I waited a few seconds, took a deep breath, and then opened the door to give Blakeman his cue.

Lou and I accompanied Blakeman to his observation post. He tensed as, one by one, six persons, who looked remarkably alike in long hair and beards, shuffled in and went to his or her spot.

The sergeant in charge had done enough lineups to know that things go better if the witness is given a few moments to study all the suspects before parading them forward one at a time. Lou and I studied them, too. We knew who the six were. I wanted to see if I could identify all of them in their getups. I guessed, but I wasn't sure. I wondered if the lineup was a good idea after all.

A minute or so later, Sgt. Watkins spoke, and number one stepped forward and held his or her station. I looked again. My guess is that it was Trish, but I wasn't one hundred percent sure that number one was a female. How were any of our witnesses going to identify someone he saw only briefly?

A few minutes later, the suspects were instructed to leave, and Blakeman turned around. As he turned, he appeared to be about ready to say something. I stopped him before he could, and told him that any comments about any of the suspects would have to wait. He acquiesced.

The suspects didn't actually leave, but since we wanted all our witnesses to have the suspects make the same dramatic entrance, we had them step out of the room.

Downey went second, and again things went off without a hitch. Well, I guess they did. I was off to inform Dick Morrissey that it was his fifteen minutes of fame.

+++

Each of the people we brought in was fingerprinted before taking part in the lineup. While Lou and I were busy handling the lineup, George headed off to see what results the fingerprints would give us. He returned with a smile on his face, just as we closed Morrissey's door after the second lineup. I knew from the smile on George's face, we had a match.

"So, George, my good friend, what do you have for us?"

"We have prints that match those we found in the house."

"I expected we might. And we have a positive ID from one of our witnesses. I wasn't sure we'd get that."

Lou, George, and I compared notes and found out that George's fingerprints and our witness identified the same person. All we had left to do was gather enough evidence to force our murderer into a confession.

"As you two know, the person who murdered the Colonel looked nothing like the long-haired man in the picture. Since we don't have the disguise actually worn by the murderer, I'd say that that evidence is hidden in a safe spot. George, I assume that Judge Heller is available to sign a search warrant for you."

"Right down the hall as a matter of fact."

"Then get a team over there and find something to help us nail our murderer."

I had no idea what evidence we would find, but I had an idea where we could find it. I instructed George and sent him on his way. Lou and I didn't want to give anything away, so we prepared a message for each group. We told the suspects that it would be a while longer, that we were about to consult our witnesses, plus there was word that another witness had stepped forward. That message was received with a collective groan, but let them groan for a while. We returned to tell our witnesses that there might be a couple of more suspects, and we were waiting a while longer to see if they materialized. We promised both groups lunch if the proceedings kept us past the noon hour.

I looked at my watch when George left, and again when he returned. Once again a smile creased his face.

"We have everything we need, and more. Look at all this stuff, Cy. And I found it just where you said I would."

"That's all a relief, George. Actually, I didn't know for sure that it would work, but then, I was telling the truth when I said I didn't know for sure who our murderer was. Well, let's get this over with."

37

We let all but two people leave, to go back to their homes, to go back to their lives, much as they were. One of those who remained would be charged with murder. Lou and I sat behind a desk as another officer led our murderer into the room.

"Please be seated."

The murderer complied, ready to listen to what I had to say, so I began.

"When this murder occurred, Sgt. Murdock and I looked over our list of suspects. Most of them fit into three groups; family members and close friends, workmen who'd been in the Hardesty house sometime within the last few months, and people who'd threatened the deceased at some point in time. We looked carefully at each of the suspects, no matter which group he or she fits. Common sense told us that more than likely the murderer was someone who had threatened Col. Hardesty at some point in time.

"Every murderer makes a mistake at some point. This time the murderer made a mistake of sending the deceased a threatening note. The note was meant to scare the old man, to make him feel unsafe in his own home, in his sacred library. Instead, it allowed Col. Hardesty to call his two friends he mentored since their childhood, Cy Dekker and Lou Murdock, now of the Hilldale Police Department homicide division. Without that phone call, Sgt. Murdock and I might never have learned the names of the three men who had reasons why they wanted to end Col. Hardesty's life. Even at well past seventy, the old man had a great memory and shared with us the only three people he could think of who wished him ill will.

"We found the first man quite easily. He'd never left town, and he'd never ceased to wish ill will on our friend. The other two took a lot more effort and involved a lot more people before we found them. One of them recently returned to Hilldale, after ten years away. When we confronted him, he seemed as carefree as anyone we'd ever met. He said he no longer wished harm on the old man, and, as it turned out, he spoke the truth. This young man proved that you can give up old grievances if you're willing to do what must be done.

"As we learned early on in our investigation, the third person, Carla Bauerman, died in a tragic accident some time back. We learned that her mother had also died, but her father was still living. We traced him to New York, and later to California, but in recent years, while he appeared in California from time to time, he seemed to disappear for long periods of time. Through the cooperation of other police departments and other organizations, we were able to secure sets of Carl Bauerman's fingerprints. The ones here in the state matched those we received from New York, and the ones we received from California, so we deduced that Bauerman was Bauerman, no matter where he lived.

"Around a year ago, a man named Tom Johnson moved to Hilldale, came from Indiana. He worked in pest control in Indiana and continued the work he'd learned so well when he moved here. A few weeks ago, Johnson left Hilldale, but he left behind something when he left. Oh, he didn't mean to leave anything behind, but there were a couple of places Johnson forgot to scrub, and, in a short time, we were able to learn that Bauerman and Johnson were one and the same.

"But there's more. This morning we lifted the prints of all those whom we invited to join us today, and so we learned that Bauerman and Johnson had a third identity. So, what do you propose we call you? Should we call you Bauerman, because that's the name you've gone by the longest?"

"That's fine, but just because I'm Bauerman doesn't mean I killed the old man."

"I'd agree with that. But there's more. One of our witnesses identified you as the man with the long hair and beard."

"Again, it's just his opinion against mine."

"Maybe. That would be for a jury to decide, but then I don't think we'll need a jury. A couple of hours ago, a judge granted us a search warrant, and what do you think we found? Not only did we find three drivers licenses and three passports, one in the name of each man whose identity you assumed, but we found all kinds of disguises, including the one you wore when you murdered our friend, the Colonel. So, what do you have to say about that, Mr. Bauerman?"

With that, Bauerman broke down and began to cry. In a minute or so, he composed himself and began to speak.

"You don't understand. Have you ever lost someone you love, Lieutenant?"

I covered my face so Bauerman wouldn't see my reaction, the tears I almost shed.

I could tell that Bauerman was about to confess. We read him his rights before he began.

"My daughter had her whole life ahead of her, and then this professor yanked it from her, denying her her goal. It was the only thing my daughter ever wanted to do. She couldn't handle her life being jerked from her. She went to the professor and pleaded, but it did no good. She tried other channels but had no success. My wife and I tried to reach her, but my wife was battling cancer and could do only so much. Carla turned to drink, something so many immature young people do, and, as you know, one night she missed a curve and wrapped her car around a tree. In a matter of months, I had no wife. I had no daughter. I had no life. Nothing else mattered to me, and it was then that I vowed that someday, somehow, I would get even with the man who took my daughter away.

"So, I went away for a few days and put a plan in motion, a meticulous plan that would take years to implement. I taught drama in school, so I decided to use my knowledge of acting to pull this off. I went to New York, learned how to act. I'd already decided to muddy the waters, become as many people as I could. I knew that ultimately fingerprints might do me in, but I figured if I became enough people in enough distant places I might be able to see it through. I learned how to act. I learned all about makeup and costume design. I learned how to look like one person, but make myself into three.

"All this time, I was still Carl Bauerman, but it came time to move on, time to become someone new, and so I did. I decided that Carl Bauerman needed to move as far away as possible, which turned out to be California. But as I left the east, I accepted a ride from a trucker, and experienced firsthand the life of a trucker, albeit briefly. But it was time for a new beginning. I contacted a friend, got a new identity. I became Bob Downey, trucker. Over time, I learned how to handle a rig. I split time between Bob Downey, long distance trucker, and Carl Bauerman, actor, grieving husband and father. I met people in the trucking industry, but not too many. I'd act in a play, then leave for a while to drive a truck.

"A few years later, I picked up another identity, that of Tom Johnson, bug man. I worked for a pest control company full-time, occasionally asking off to visit my sick mother. Who is going to deny a man's right to visit his sick mother? And so, on a limited basis, I juggled three identities, three professions. I didn't want someone to think that I was moving from identity to identity, but to think that Carl Bauerman, Bob Downey, and Tom Johnson were three different men.

"All this time, I lived on a shoestring, slept wherever I could, saved my money. I planned ahead. Slowly, I was moving toward a confrontation with the man who was responsible for my daughter's death. I moved to Indiana, to be close enough to find out whatever I could about the professor. I followed the sale of real estate in the area, waiting for a house to become available, a house close enough where I could plan the old man's murder.

"It was probably a stupid move on my part, but when a house came on the market right next door to the professor, I jumped at the chance to buy it. Not wanting to move too quickly, I waited for the right chance to move Tom Johnson with me. I was playing with fire. I knew it, but I didn't want Johnson to go away, and I was tired of spending so much time in Indiana.

"As time permitted, I studied the Hardesty household to learn each person's movements. I wanted to learn their patterns, without getting to know them too well, even though none of them had ever met Carl Bauerman. I learned who went where, and when. One day, when no one was home and the neighborhood seemed deserted; I sneaked across the back yard, removed a pane from the back patio, and deposited the inhabitants of an ant farm onto the Hardesty enclosed porch. My trick worked. The next day, Tom Johnson received a work order to go to the Hardesty house and spray for ants. In all, I made five trips to the Hardesty house. The first time I went dressed as Tom Johnson, and when I found myself alone on the second floor, I spotted a set of keys, and made wax impressions. I almost got caught, because Mrs. Hardesty sneaked down the hall just after I'd returned the keys to the purse.

"I might have gotten too cute and taken my acting experience too far, because on the second trip I donned a different disguise, yet signed the name Tom Johnson to the work order. I pressed my luck even further when I made a third trip. It was on that third trip that I discovered that my house and the Hardesty house had one convenience in common, a hook in the back of the living room closet that, if turned correctly, caused the back wall to slide away. In my house, as you now know, it slides away into a secret room. In the Hardesty house, it gives way to a passageway, a passageway I hoped to navigate, but soon found out that the old man was smarter than I. I couldn't figure out a way to enter the library from the passageway, or to enter the library without being photographed by that surveillance camera. I must say I was surprised when I found out there was a camera in the passageway, the day you showed me my picture.

"My only hope was to drill a hole in one of the library's walls, and so, one day, when I checked off that all of the house's residents had gone away, I entered the house, drilled a hole, and blew the note into the room. I see now how stupid that was, but at the time I only wanted to make the old man sweat for a while.

"Most of the house's residents were predictable in their coming and going, but Prof. and Mrs. Hardesty were not. I took a chance that day and practiced blowing a dart into the room to see how far it would travel. I attached a string to the dart, the same string I used to retrieve the dart on the day I murdered the old man.

"I'm not sorry I did it, although I'm sure the old man didn't deserve such a fate. But ever since my wife and daughter died, my life has been a living nightmare. I had to do it, and now I've to suffer the consequences.

"Well, there you have it, unless you have any questions."

"None of your three characters look anything alike. How were you able to do it?"

"Lieutenant, it's amazing what a person can do to make himself or herself look much different from his or her normal self. Take that lineup, for example. I think one or two of those people you paraded across were women, but I can't be sure. Is it true that that old man was able to identify me today?"

"How did you know it was the old man?"

"Well, he's the only one who came close enough to see me. How did he do it?"

"He said it was the eyes."

"Well, I'll admit the eyes are harder to disguise. We can change the color with contacts, but nothing else, other than change the skin around the eyes."

"But back to your disguises. You're a slender man. Tom Johnson isn't. How did you do that?"

"Simple, Lieutenant. I used an inflatable vest. And Tom always wore long sleeves, no matter how warm the weather."

There wasn't much more we could do. Bauerman confessed. We had it on tape, and on paper. Lou stepped out into the hall and motioned for an officer to take Bauerman away.

38

Lou closed the door and the two of us silently gathered our thoughts. I don't know how I'd have acted if I was in Bauerman's place. Belding, whose wife refused to call his attorney before Monday, would be a resident of the city-county jail until Monday. If it had turned out that Belding was our murderer, it would've been hard for me to control myself. Belding has lost only a job. Jobs are replaceable. Bauerman lost a daughter and a wife, and while sometimes some people learn to deal with the loss of a loved one before his or her time, people are much harder to live without than jobs are.

After a few minutes, Lou's eyes met mine, and we began to talk. I don't know how long we talked, but it was as long as it took. We'd lost a friend, and now it was time to give him up. After a few more minutes, we opened the door, but our day wasn't done. We had another stop to make. In a way two stops.

+++

Martha must have looked out the window, because she opened the door before we scuffed our shoes on the porch. She knew that it was over, and that's what we'd come to tell her. Before words were exchanged, Lou and I embraced Martha, and a few moments later, Jennifer and Trish, as they entered the room.

After sharing hugs with my friend's family, I began a difficult explanation of what had happened. I tried my best to show them Bauerman's point of view, without minimizing the Colonel's life and the grave results of what had happened because of Bauerman's actions.

When we'd finished, Martha looked at me and said, "Cy, what are you going to do now?"

"You mean right this minute?"

"I mean right this minute."

"I think you know what we have to do."

"Stay as long as you like."

With those words, Lou and I turned before others saw that our eyes were beginning to water.

"We've got to get something out of the car," I mumbled.

Lou and I walked out the door, and to the car. God had smiled upon us. There were leftovers from our version of feed the entire police force the night before.

On the way to Martha's house, we stopped by my place, snatched two Strombolis and two hoagies from the refrigerator, and warmed them in the oven. We weren't being pigs by taking two sandwiches each. There was no way we were warming up leftover fries, and it would take strength to do what we planned to do.

Lou and I walked up the driveway, around the house. We looked up as we rounded the corner and had our first glimpse of our treehouse. We continued to walk, but looked down from time to time to keep from falling. When the tree house was almost upon us, we stopped.

"You first, Cy. You're the oldest."

"And the heaviest."

"You said that. I didn't. Okay, quit stalling."

Lou and I knew what we had to do, for ourselves, for the Colonel. The Colonel told us the lift would hold up to five hundred pounds. The time had come to test that.

I set the meter, put our food in the lift basket, stepped on board, and prayed. I pushed the button to set things in motion, and in a matter of a couple of seconds, a surprised overweight lieutenant found himself up in the tree, and able to step into the tree house. I heard cheers from below. I sent the apparatus down and was soon joined by my friend and colleague.

"I just thought of something, Lou. The Colonel didn't say how much weight the tree house would hold, did he?"

"Don't worry about it, Cy. Earthquakes aren't common around here. If we fall, someone in the house will come running."

Somehow, my friend's words didn't reassure me all that much. I braced myself against the tree trunk and lowered myself to the wooden flooring of our tree house. Lou did the same. Neither of us wondered how we'd get up, until we were seated. Oh, well! We had just traveled back to our childhood.

I reached into our cooler and lifted out a couple of glasses, filled them with ice, then lifted out a couple of Diet Pepsis. We poured our drinks, prayed, and began to wolf down two sandwiches. We scarfed down the food in record time, and returned to the boys we once were. We sat there reminiscing for quite some time, until the sound of footsteps warned us we were no longer alone.

"Hey, Cy, Lou! Are you two still up there?"

"Why? Is the tree sinking?"

I heard the laughter from below, and then a reply.

"No, it's just that Jennifer and I think the two of you got to know a side of Gramps that we never knew. Would you mind if we came up and you shared some stories?"

"Do you think the lift will hold you?"

"Very funny, Nero Wolfe."

"So, you know him, too. Hurry up and get your carcasses up here, but be careful."

I did a double-take when they showed up at the same time, but then I realized that one of me weighed more than two of them. We were thankful that the Colonel constructed for us the largest tree house in existence, for there was plenty of room for everyone. I smiled as Trish reached back and lifted a pie from the basket.

I don't know how long it was when we finished our therapy session and four people descended from the tree house feeling better than they had. Lou and I hugged the girls, refused an invitation to stay for supper, and ambled off toward Lightning, who had been patient long enough.

"Hey, Lou, do you realize what we just did? We allowed girls in our tree house."

+++

Lou and I left Martha's house feeling better about things. We were on our way back to retirement, but it wouldn't be long before we were once again back at work

As I drove down the street, Lou turned to me and said, "Cy, now that things are over I need to tell you something I've kept to myself the last couple of days. I didn't want to tell you until we'd solved the case. Cy, this past week I've gained over two pounds."

I was about to congratulate him when he continued.

"I've eaten what you've eaten these past few days, because solving the Colonel's murder meant so much to both of us, but now that things are over, you're on your own again. Once again, I will cut back on what I'm eating. It's not that I don't like to do my Wii workout. I love it, but once a day is enough. If I eat right, I can cut back to once a day and lose weight. These past couple of days I was too tired to get in my second workout. And another thing, Cy, I want to invite you over to try out my Wii. After all, best friends should Wii together."

I knew he'd backed me into a corner. And I knew he was right. Friends Wii with friends. But I had no intention of hula hooping or doing any exercise that required me to try to stand on one leg. I had enough trouble standing on two. And there was no way I was cutting back from two pieces of pecan pie, friend or no friend.

Author's Note: Later on in the series, the doctor convinces Cy that he too needs to lose weight. And both Cy and Lou come into the modern era and buy computers, which help them in solving some of the murders. Plus, Cy gets a girlfriend, gets a different next-door neighbor, and gets a second home. And not only does Cy eventually get a dog, but the dog helps Cy and Lou solve some of their cases. Each of these things happens in a different book in the series as Cy and Lou's characters evolve.

Printed in Great Britain
by Amazon

43712620R00152